DATE DUE

JUN 27 '00			

DEMCO 38-296

AMERICAN INDIAN LITERATURE
AND
CRITICAL STUDIES SERIES

Gerald Vizenor, General Editor

The
Sharpest
Sight

The
Sharpest
Sight

by
Louis Owens

University of
Oklahoma Press
Norman and London

Excerpts from *The Sharpest Sight* first appeared in Mary Bartlett, ed., *The New Native American Novel: Works in Progress* (Albuquerque: University of New Mexico Press, 1986), 65–77; *Albuquerque Living* (January 1988): 42–44; and *Wicazo Sa Review* (Fall 1990): 7–14.

Text and jacket design by Patsy Willcox

Library of Congress Cataloging-in-Publication Data

Owens, Louis.
    The sharpest sight / by Louis Owens.—1st ed.
      p. cm.—(American Indian literature and critical studies
series : v.1)
    ISBN 0-8061-2404-0 (alk. paper)
    1. Choctaw Indians—Fiction. I. Title. II. Series
PS3565.W567S52   1991
813'.54—dc20   91-33072
                                                         CIP

The Sharpest Sight is Volume 1 in the AMERICAN INDIAN LITERATURE AND CRITICAL STUDIES SERIES.

The paper in this book meets the guidelines for permanence and durability of the Committee on Production Guidelines for Book Longevity of the Council on Library Resources, Inc. ∞

2   3   4   5   6   7   8   9   10   11   12   13   14   15   16

For my parents, Ida and Hoey

I am grateful to the National Endowment for the Arts, and to the University of California at Santa Cruz, for the time and support that allowed me to complete this novel.

The
Sharpest
Sight

The arrows of death fly unseen at noon-day;
the sharpest sight can't discern them.

One

The rain came toward the headlights in long, curving lines. Mundo flipped the switch on the spotlight to let the beam sweep across the edge of the road. Metal fence posts danced in and out of the light, the thick brush reaching between strands of wire toward the car and then leaping away. Rain caught the light in racing lines along the barbed wire.

He turned the spotlight off and let the car pick up speed down the side canyon. Now, without the big white oaks over the road, the rain sliced toward him as if it would come through the windshield. To his right, the hillside rose like a wall, oak darkened and heavy, while on his left the road fell away to the river a hundred feet below. In the darkness down there he could sense the river, swollen at flood-stage, nervous and out of control. Except for the muted sounds of the car and rain, the night was absolutely quiet.

The road leveled off and the brush retreated. He slowed and stopped where the gravel met a thin asphalt strip, the blacktop a glimmering line in the lights. To his left now the river was a weight that pulled at him so that he kept one foot on the brake and both hands clenched on the steering wheel. He let the engine idle and, feeling the muscles of his shoulders bunch with the effort, he glanced to his right at the lighted windows of the Nemi ranch house where it hunkered under a cluster of four- and five-hundred-year-old oaks close to the road. From the light of the porch and windows he could see the flaky pattern of the bark on the trees. Viejos, he thought, damned near as old as the old man. He shifted his eyes to the big, light-framed barn door, thinking that ranchers didn't keep hours like other people. Then he looked at the large-caliber holes dotting the stop sign in front of the patrol car, and he remembered the time that even he, Mundo Morales, whose family had owned it all once, had celebrated a dark night by putting a couple of holes in the sign. Beer and a buddy and a lever-action thirty-thirty and a night without moon or stars. Before Vietnam and the job at the high school, before becoming Amarga's deputy sheriff.

As he eased the car onto the pitted blacktop, he saw a woman's silhouette glide across the big front window of the house, the outline flowing like water. That would be Diana, he thought, seeing the slim arch of back and breasts and the shadow of long hair, thinking then of the dead sister and then, inevitably, of Attis McCurtain.

He swung the car left and accelerated toward the bridge, watching the rain curve in more sudden threads now as if he had entered the luminous web of a spider. When he pushed the gas pedal, the tires spun and the car fishtailed onto the bridge, and he stared with amazement at the silver rain woven about the car. And then he stabbed his boot down on the brake, and the tires locked, and the car slid toward the great cat that was there, in the middle of the bridge, crouched as if it would spring. The black coat gleamed in the rain, and the eyes shot yellow sparks back at him.

He waited for the jolt and the flat impact, but none came. For a few seconds he sat behind the wheel, feeling the shivering begin down at the base of his spine and creep upward. He shook his head hard and unclenched his jaws and, one at a time, lifted his fingers from the steering wheel. He opened his eyes. Then, feeling as if he moved in slow motion—a feeling he had come to know so well in Nam—he reached with one hand to shift the riot gun from its rest while with the other hand he levered the car door open. When he stepped out, the rain hit him in the face and he bent toward it, welcoming the shock and staring at the empty bridge in front of the car. He walked around the car, seeing only the wet concrete, and then he opened the door again and brought out the big, head-cracking flashlight, clicking it on and shining it beneath the car and into the darkened periphery of the lights. Finding nothing, he opened the door once more and switched the teardrop spotlight on, illuminating the width of the bridge for fifty feet.

There was no sign of the cat. He opened the car door and slid onto the seat, settling the gun in its rack and setting the flashlight beside him. What did it signify? The shivering began again and he tried the old trick of switching the path of his mind, thinking of something else, or of nothing. Outside, he sensed the flooding river, felt the vibration of the current against the bridge and heard the almost imperceptible sound of objects moving in the dark with irresistible force. He concentrated on that sound, feeling the power of the river as it swept down from the mountains and slid away in the night toward the sea. He looked out again at the curving rain, and then he shifted the spotlight so that it angled over the railing and onto the water.

It was an underground river, the largest one in California, the largest in the country, maybe the world. Most of the year it was nothing, like the people who had come to live along its banks, just a half-mile-wide stretch of sand and brush and scattered trees. But in the winter and early spring, when the rains came pounding down out of the coastal mountains, the river rose out of its bed and became huge, taking everything in its path. Growing up on the

5

edge of the river, he'd come to wait each year for the rising waters, grown to love with a kind of ache the seasonal violence when the river tried to destroy everything within reach. It was a strange, violent, backwards, upside-down river.

He got out of the car and went to lean over the wooden railing and watch the water slide through the circle of light. From the low hills on both sides came the sweet smell of drowned grasses and damp oak, mingled here close to the ranch with the reassuring odor of cattle and cut hay. The river was high, and he realized with surprise that he could almost lean down and touch the water. Where the spotlight angled out to form a large circle six feet from the bridge, he watched debris spin in and out of sight, chunks of dark wood and root, branches and bits of plank, the round and twisted shapes caught up in and measuring the speed of the current. In the powerful spotlight, he could see the bark patterns on the logs, the snakelike tangle of roots, even the darker swirling lines on the water.

And then, sliding slowly from beneath the bridge, was a face. The long black hair washed away from the forehead, and the eyes were open and fixed. He saw the dark eyes and broad nose and the mouth drawn back over white teeth and the body like one of the drowned logs swinging slowly so that now the feet aimed north. A hand rose in the choppy water as if in casual farewell. And then only the river.

Two

In the cabin, the old man rose to consciousness slowly, becoming aware of the sputtering of the kerosene lamp and the crackling of wood in the stove. He looked around the single room from his rigid chair, his dark eyes unfocused and straining for something in the shadowed corners. His long, silvered hair hung straight, dividing over his shoulders to touch the bare, sagging breasts of his thin chest. His hands and forearms, fragile and hollow looking as the bones of a bird, rested on his lap, and only his head turned as the eyes searched for something in the margins of the room. And then he heard the low, muted cry of the *koi* outside the cabin, and he knew the story was forming to the pattern he had dreamed. After a few minutes the panther cried again, this time from somewhere deeper in the woods, and when the sound faded he heard the horned owl—*ishkitini*—and he nodded his head. He reached to touch the small pouch hanging from his neck, and then he lowered his face into his bony hands. His body and mind ached. To follow the soul-eater so far across a single night had been difficult, more so than he could have imagined. To bring about the convergence of the nephew, the dark-skinned one, and *nalusachito* had required almost more strength than he had. And then to will the *shilombish* back here where it belonged and could be dealt with. That was hard for an old man. And dangerous, risking still more accusations of witchcraft, should anyone find out. He grinned wryly, thinking that if the people feared him now out here in the swamp, they would piss their pants if they knew the truth.

But the new story was begun. The old man rose stiffly and reached for a flannel shirt on a nail in the wall behind the stove. Pulling the red shirt over his bones, he thought of Hoey's other son, knowing that now he would have to try to bring that one home. Then he turned to the dark form that stood in a dim corner of the cabin. "It is time." The old man spoke with his eyes downcast, in a voice of sadness and dignity. "You must go now. Be brave, grandson. The other has gone before, and he has not found the bright path. It will be difficult for you." He seated himself again and folded his hands in his lap. "Don't worry. We will find them." He looked up again, and this time there was a note of irritation in his voice when he said, "It is time, grandson." The shadow stood unmoving in the corner. "Shit," the old man said, "Goddamnit." It wasn't supposed to happen that way.

Three

Attis McCurtain spun in the river, riding the black flood, aware of the branches that trailed over his face and touched his body, spinning in the current of the night toward something he could feel coming closer, rising up to meet him. He knew he was dead, and in death an ancient memory had awakened, a stirring in his stilled blood, moving with him and around him on the flood. Above him the streaking rain that was the last thing he remembered from life had disappeared, and now the river swept him beneath a ceiling of heavy trees, and odors of decay began to fill the thickening air. The sweet smell of rot was strangely familiar, and then the weighted air began to thin and the dark to grow less dense. There was a shore to the river, and along that shore stood thin old men and women with deep eyes and long, stringy hair. They grasped at him with hands gnarled and twisted as tree roots, the nails of the thumb, middle, and index fingers long and sharp as knife blades, slicing the damp air. Overhead the trees had become a tangle of branches, leafless and dead, and around him the water had begun to boil. The river was a froth of snakes, tumbling and tangling with him in the current. And then he began to turn, slowly, swinging in a wide circle, around and around in a great whirlpool, the dead trees etched now against a black vault of sky. *"Chahta yakni."* The words echoed as if he had spoken them. *"Chahta isht ia,"* a voice answered back.

Four

It was still gray, with the sycamore branches black against Pine Mountain, when Cole McCurtain came out that morning, past the shed and empty chicken coop, past the fifty-seven Chevy up on blocks and the row of black walnut trees. At the riverbank he stopped and turned toward the mountain three miles away, where a hidden sun was sending splinters of light down through the digger pines and oaks and probably the stones of the old graveyard. On the other side of the little, isolated mountain was the hospital, built into a curve of the river.

He heard the screen door of the house slam, and then a spaniel-mix dog went scuttering past him toward the river, the dog's orange back just a flash as it vanished into the thick brush of the bank downstream from the house. Cole watched the dog disappear and shook his head. He was a good dog, but too fast for a rabbit dog. A good rabbit dog shouldn't get too close to the rabbit, but Zeke damned near caught them every time, so that often as not they would light out for the next county instead of making a circle like they were supposed to. You can't train a dog not to be too fast, he thought, remembering his brother's words. You can't train a brother not to be too—whatever—he added, watching the red brush of Zeke's tail vanish.

"Yea, though I walk through the valley of the shadow of

death." In magic marker on the back of the jacket, blocky letters the way a kid would write it. Attis had sent the jacket back early along with the only letter he'd written over there, talking about coming home and about walking shadows and jungles that had three levels. "Don't let the bastards get you," Attis had written. "Don't let these motherfuckers get you, too."

He stood on the bank and watched the thick, brown water move past, clots of yellow foam and trash in the troughs of waves. After a couple of weeks the river would go down, sinking into the sand so that only scattered pools were left, with a little clear stream at the heart of the sand. And when the pools dried up you would see coon tracks pressed into the sand around the tails and bones of big fish. And then even the little stream would disappear and the river would exist only beneath the surface once again.

He followed the line of cottonwoods and brush that marked the riverbank, stretching a barbed-wire fence to step through into a barren alfalfa field that fronted the river. "I shall fear no evil, for I am. . . ." That was on the back of the jacket, too. "I am a half-breed, like my father," he thought as he looked down the bank for signs of Zeke. "Actually," he said aloud to the river, pronouncing his words precisely, "I am a three-eighths breed, since my mother is a quarter Cherokee like just about everybody who ever lived in Oklahoma." He gestured toward a cottonwood with the rifle. "Well, you see, the fact is she's really three-eighths Cherokee, since her mother was three-quarters and born in the Nation and had my mother when she was thirteen and not even five feet tall. So I guess that makes me a seven-sixteenths-breed—almost a half-breed like my father. Let's say I'm nearly a half-breed, whatever that means. Hoey McCurtain knows, but what I know from books in school and those old TV movies is that a half-breed can't be trusted, is a killer, a betrayer, a breed." He smiled as he finished the speech; it had become a litany, something he told himself frequently almost like a ceremony, always the same words and rhythm. ". . . the meanest motherfucker in the valley." He wore the jacket when he hunted the river, and he recited his identity when he wore the jacket. "I shall fear no evil," he thought, "for I am."

His father knew who he was—Hoey McCurtain, Choctaw from Mississippi, with chiefs in his family, or so he often said after a few beers. Cole had read about Choctaws, and sometimes he thought that it was just as likely his ancestors had been bone-pickers, growing their fingernails long for their task down there in Mississippi where he remembered air like water and water like earth. Boxing the bones and putting them away, as Attis had been put away in the state hospital. His father was dark, with broad shoulders and burnt-rust skin, black hair, and brown eyes except for the milky one where the carburetor had exploded in his face. Attis, too, was dark, but he, Cole McCurtain, was taller, thinner, lighter than they—from the Cherokee and Irish blood, he thought—an almost half-breed with green eyes made "slanty" from the epicanthic fold Indians often had. "It's hard to tell who you are in this family," Attis had once said. "Only thing for sure, there's some nuts blood somewhere in the ancestry." That even before he'd gone to Vietnam and come back.

In the fall, the rabbits stirred the leaves when they ran, breaking from one bright clump of brush to thrash across the leaves and disappear into an identical clump unless he used the twenty-two. The sky climbed high on fall mornings, and the crunch of leaves and small limbs was sharp on the air then, like breaking bird wings. Now, however, the winter leaves were a dead weight upon the earth, and the brush along the bank was sodden and still. The broken sky lay near to the ground.

When Zeke flushed the first rabbit, Cole was thinking about the Mekong Delta, trying to imagine a place he'd never seen, and when the dog yapped after the cottontail he watched the two of them until they vanished into another island of cottonwoods and brush along the bank. Then he 11 waited, listening to a flicker knocking against a dead tree close by, sounding as if it would take the whole tree down, the hammering nailing him to the cold morning. The patch of ground he stood on was hard with frost beneath the alfalfa stubble, and he could feel now the vibration of the river coming through his legs. He shifted the cold gun to his left hand and wedged the fingers of his right hand under his left armpit. In a few seconds the feeling came back and so did the rabbit.

A cottontail, its big white ass held high, the rabbit crawled like a cat out of a pile of brush twenty feet away. Then it sat back on its haunches and sniffed the cold air. The brown fur was sleek, and the ears twitched a little while the nose worked, but Cole was upbreeze so the rabbit couldn't smell anything except Zeke, wherever Zeke was.

Watching the rabbit, he remembered his mother's Cherokee stories about rabbits. Cherokee rabbits were smart. They lived by tricks in a world of words and had a good time doing it. He raised the rifle and aimed the notched sight at a spot just below the rabbit's ear. "Time for a trick," he whispered to the rabbit. He pulled back the hammer and shouted.

At the shout, the cottontail leaped and spun and disappeared into the brush it had appeared from, and then he saw Zeke sitting fifty feet further up the riverbank, watching.

"That'll ruin a good dog."

He turned to see his father standing a few feet away, his hands in the pockets of his old, red-plaid wool coat, the collar turned up around his thick neck so that the face was framed between black collar and black John Deere baseball cap.

"You go letting a dog down that way too often, you're going to break his spirit, even a old turdeater like that." He spat a stream of tobacco juice and shook his head.

"How come you didn't shoot? You practicing for big game, bear maybe?"

As he started to answer, Cole felt Zeke's nose against his hand where the rifle dangled at his side. He swung the long barrel of the gun away, uncocked it, and pushed the safety on. When he looked again at his father, Hoey McCurtain had shifted his head a little to one side to take advantage of the good eye. His father was the only person Cole knew who would pour gasoline in a carburetor to get a motor started and then look to see if the carburetor was flooded so that it would blow up right in his face. Not that he could think of his father as stupid. Hoey McCurtain was one of the smartest men Cole had ever met, in some ways.

A red-tailed hawk settled on a tall tree a few hundred yards dowstream. Cole saw that his father's hair had grown down past his ears and over the edges of his collar. Surprised that he hadn't noticed that before, he wondered if maybe Hoey McCurtain was going to start braiding his hair, though he didn't think that Choctaws braided their hair. He could ask his father. And then he thought about his father's question. He didn't know how to explain because it was the first time that he'd realized he didn't shoot anymore, that he hadn't shot for a long time. He tried to think back to a time when he had hunted for something more real than whatever it was he'd come to be hunting for now, and his memory ran up against the fact of Attis.

"Time flies when you're having a good time," their mother used to say when he and Attis were kids and thought it was too early to come in from whatever it was they were doing—playing stretch with pocketknives or knocking little birds out of trees with beebee guns.

"What's the matter, your tongue froze up?" Hoey McCurtain shifted the lump in his cheek and spat again.

Cole looked again at his father's longer hair. Hoey seemed to be more and more Indian every day, and the more Indian he became the stranger he seemed, as if he were trying to make himself into something Cole couldn't even imagine, something as impossible as the Mekong Delta, or the Mississippi swamp he had disappeared into every night when Cole was five and six. Lately, Hoey had been doing more reading, and he had begun complaining about what a bastard Thomas Jefferson had been. For a long time he had always been after Andrew Jackson, a rednecked sonofabitch, but recently he'd taken to throwing in Jefferson, claiming Jefferson had thought up trading posts as a way to get Indian land without shooting Indians, just get them in debt and take the land in payment. Now Jefferson was a phony blue-blood sonofabitch. "The father of our country, hah!" he'd snort, maybe confusing Jefferson with Washington, Cole thought.

Since he'd taken up reading about it, his father seemed to be getting angrier and angrier about what a raw deal the Choctaws had gotten in Mississippi. Before it had turned too cold, Mundo Morales—his brother's friend—had been in the habit of coming over, and the two of them would sit behind the house drinking Pabst Blue-Ribbon and complaining about what a raw deal their ancestors had gotten, Mundo pointing out how Moraleses had once owned the whole county, and Hoey McCurtain topping that with how the Choctaws had once owned all of Mississippi and Louisiana and more. "But I thought Indians never really *owned* land," Mundo would counter. With their black hair and skin the color of old blood, Mundo Morales and Hoey McCurtain looked quite a bit alike. The difference, Cole had thought when he watched them together, was that Mundo was the law and Hoey McCurtain the outlaw. Attis, out there in the hospital, was so far beyond both law and outlaw that he couldn't be defined.

"Indians don't yell 'bang' when they go after meat," Hoey said, hunching his shoulders deeper into the coat and looking off down the river.

Cole shrugged. "Which Indians? You told us there were more than three hundred tribes. Maybe some of them yell bang. Besides, maybe it was the Irish," he said, thinking that after all he was more Irish than anything else, one-sixteenth more, and Irish were supposed to talk a lot. Then he thought again of Mundo Morales and his father, wishing that he could feel like something the way they did, Indian or Irish or something. "You are what you think you are," Hoey McCurtain had once told him. Hoey McCurtain thought he was Choctaw, not just Indian but Choctaw.

"Irish my ass," he said. "Come on, let's get some breakfast before we go to work."

Cole reached down to scratch Zeke's spaniel ear, feeling that he'd let the dog down—Attis's dog—and surprised to realize that he had been hunting without shooting for a long time without knowing it, or without thinking about it, which amounted to the same thing. He could feel the river at his back as he followed his father toward the house.

In the kitchen Hoey fried venison and eggs, splashing grease up over the eggs to make the edges lacy and brown. Cole poured coffee for both of them and then stood nursing his cup and looking at a framed photograph on the dining-room wall. It was a picture of his mother, before he or Attis was born, when she'd been young and beautiful in Oklahoma. Her hair fell in thick, black waves, and her Cherokee blood was obvious in the fine edges of her cheekbones and the black pupils in her narrow eyes. He contrasted the photograph with the picture he carried in his mind. In that picture, she looked tired, more tired than it seemed a person could be, and Cole wondered how a woman with only one husband and two kids could get that way. Maybe from the disease that had finally consumed her while her oldest son was at war. Maybe from being married for twenty years to Hoey McCurtain, a California Choctaw living in a made-up world who was busy creating himself out of books and made-up memories so that it was plain he was leaving the rest of them behind. As if, Cole thought, you could really choose what you were going to be instead of just being what it was you had to be. The woman in the photograph had been what she could not avoid being.

15

"Put some coffee in the thermos," his father said as he slid two of the creamy brown eggs onto a plate and forked a piece of meat next to them and then repeated the action. He'd taken off the heavy coat and now stood in the kitchen doorway, holding a plate toward Cole with one hand while scratching his belly with the other.

Cole picked up his plate and said, "Thank you," and he remembered his mother's smile at such times. She would reach out to put a hand on his shoulder, a gesture it seemed one of them was always making back then, as if practicing for a day when they'd all be affectionate or something. Then she would turn back toward the stove, one of those old stoves that had gas burners but looked like a wood-burner. It was probably an antique, he thought.

"That old stove's probably an antique," he said as his father carried his own plate toward the dining-room table. "It's probably worth some money." His father looked at him like he was crazy.

After breakfast they drove through town out toward the fence they were building in the hills near Morro Bay. The town of Amarga was awake, with the ranchers and grain farmers coming in early to get first crack at the hardware store and feed-supply. They'd buy their supplies, and then they'd sit around coffee for two hours at Hong's Cafe talking about hard lives. The town wasn't much, with a bowling alley, a supermarket, half-a-dozen bare-ass stores of one kind or another and the same number of bars. Even after ten years it wasn't a town Cole could feel much about one way or another.

They drove by the county sheriff's substation, and through the dirty front window Cole could see Mundo Morales fooling around with his coffeepot.

"Mundo's in early," Hoey said. "He don't have to be there till later." They were silent for a moment and then Hoey added, "I guess he don't want to go back to being a janitor at the high school. I heard Bill Martin say that now

Mundo's not cleaning toilets he's going to clean up this shitty town. Bill Martin thought that was funny."

In front of Hong's, Louise Vogler, the high-school coach's wife, was getting out of her station wagon. Cole looked at her short skirt and long legs as she rose from the seat and shut the car door, realizing for the first time that the coach's wife wasn't much older than he was. How old was she, he wondered, twenty-five or six? With her husband sleeping and eating football during the fall, she sort of rattled around the town at loose ends, often getting up early to sit alone in the cafe in the middle of all those ranchers, as if just feeling men nearby was better than nothing. Her straight hair, turned up at the shoulders, and the skirt that rode up past her thigh gave Cole a terrible feeling of loneliness.

They drove the rest of the way in silence. The narrow road snaking over the coast range was empty except for the pickup they rattled along in, and Cole looked down at the live-oak and brush-choked creek a hundred feet below the road and remembered the black trout they had caught there. Squirming through the tunnel of creekbrush to drift a worm into the dark ripples below the little falls, he and Attis taking turns at each hole. The four-pound monofilament would drift unweighted from their cut-down fiberglass poles over the falls into the gently boiling pools, and then there would be a faint tug and a shiver on the line that tingled all the way up your arm, and you would pull a small dark tumult of shadow six or seven inches long out of the black water. It had always been cool and hidden down there, and they'd crawl and fish for miles down the creek where it fell toward the coast and feel that they were the only ones to ever fish the blackest pools.

It was still cold when Hoey parked the truck. They got out and walked up to the last post they'd driven, pulling on leather gloves as they walked. From the post a gold string ran up the hill. Cole went to an oak that dragged its branches close to the ground and pulled out the two-handled pipe they used as a post-pounder, and wordlessly they began again, driving the red metal poles into the shaley ground.

As his father drove the first post, Cole glanced at two clouds that hovered over the coast range a couple of miles to the west. Below them he could hear a car whining up the grade from Amarga. When he looked back, his father was pulling on the top of the post to see if it was firmly in the ground. He heard his father's satisfied grunt and was once again struck with how much pleasure such little things gave Hoey McCurtain, while the bigger things, like history, seemed to torment him.

For two hours they pounded the posts in a line up the ridge, and then Hoey tossed the driver into the tall grass. "Let's take a break," he said, "before hitting those corner posts."

Cole nodded and followed his father's eyes to the cirrus building up over the mountains. Then they went to sit near the thermos. While his father poured the coffee, Cole hunched into the fatigue jacket and looked around the hillside. Under the trees, the leaves and dead oats were still gray with frost.

"Sleepy?" With the question, his father reached a chipped mug toward him.

He took the cup with both hands and shook his head. "I was thinking about when we used to go deer hunting out near Creston," he said.

"I went out there in August. I asked you to come."

Again, Cole shook his head. "I was thinking about before."

Hoey McCurtain glanced at the sun finally rising through jagged clouds over the eastern ridge, pale and distant the way the sun was in winter. "You want to go see him?" As he spoke his eyes remained focused on the oak-covered ridge. "It's about time."

"Yeah." Cole held the coffee to his lips, testing the hot

edge of the cup with his tongue.

They sipped the coffee in silence for a few minutes until Hoey stripped the husks from an oat head and let them drop from his hand and then said, "This all used to be Chumash country, you know." He looked from east to west, seeing the thickening clouds lying along the coastal ridge. "Everything you see. And now there ain't no Chumash here at all, and we're here." He swirled the dregs of coffee in the thermos cap and tossed the grounds into the grass. "It's funny. Back there in Mississippi there ain't hardly any Choctaws left, compared to the ones in Oklahoma. Except Uncle Luther and a few others, mostly all them over on that new reservation near Philadelphia. And out there in Oklahoma are all them tribes that used to be somewhere else. Us Indians are a mixed-up bunch. It's like somebody took a big stick and stirred us all up." He stripped another head from a dead oat stalk and let the husks drop from his hand. "You know, I read about some tribes, like the Navajo and them others in Arizona and New Mexico, the Hopi and some others, that's still living where they always lived. Some of them people live in houses a thousand years old, maybe ten thousand. You imagine how that must feel?"

When Cole didn't reply, Hoey was silent for a few minutes, sipping the coffee. Finally he said, still looking toward the distance, "What you plan to do about the draft?"

Cole shrugged and looked more deeply into the mug of coffee.

"They'll come and get you the way they did that Jorgenson kid," his father said. "You don't owe this sonofabitchin government nothing."

Cole stood up and pulled on one of his gloves and then took it off again and shook bits of gravel out of the fingers. "I remember what you told Attis," he said. Then he walked to the pile of railroad ties they'd brought up for corner posts and started to move them around as though he were looking for something.

"No snakes this time of year," Hoey McCurtain said loudly as he, too, rose and pulled his gloves on. As he walked toward the ties, he added, "You don't owe the bastards nothing. They made Pushmataha a brigadier general, a goddamned general, him thinking that now it would be okay, now they'd all get to stay in Mississippi. They give him a gold medal in Washington after the Choctaws won the Battle of New Orleans for them. And then that red-necked sonofabitch Jackson sent in the troops to steal the land and cattle and slaves and everything else and move them all to Oklahoma, except it wasn't Oklahoma yet and he didn't now nothing about oil. My folks—your folks—didn't go. Hid out in the woods and starved and didn't end up with diddlysquat. Jackson said fuck the supreme court and marched all them Indian war heroes straight to Oklahoma. And Pushmataha, one of the greatest leaders the world ever saw, didn't end up with a pot to piss in. That's what you owe those bastards."

Cole had stopped with the post-hole digger on his shoulder and was looking back, wondering how much his father said was true. Had he read all those things, or did he just make up the facts he needed? "You were a paratrooper in the war," he said, thinking about the induction notice that had lain in his drawer for a week already. At first he had planned to enlist, to follow Attis, but then he got his brother's letter from Da Nang. "Do anything you have to," Attis had written. "Shoot your big toe off, cut your nuts off, but don't let them bring you here. You know what they do with Indians? They put us on point. The stupid bastards think Indians can see at night, that we don't make any noise, that kind of shit. It doesn't matter if you're a half-breed or full or whatever. They call you chief and put you out in the fucking jungle at night. We're killing kids here, Cole, little kids and old women and anything that fucking moves."

"That's because I was stupid," Hoey said. "I thought I had to be a warrior, just like all the other Indians that died in white men's wars. I didn't know a goddamned thing."

20

He pulled off the black cap and ran a hand through his thick, graying hair. "You know, Indians've had the highest enlistment rates in every war, way higher than whites or colored people. They been making Indians do their fighting ever since they first got here. The French and English did it in Mississippi, making Choctaws fight Chickasaws and Creeks and then finally making Choctaws fight each other. Did I ever tell you about Red Shoe?"

Cole turned away, stabbing the post-hole digger into the ground and levering up the loose dirt. Over his shoulder, he said, "I'm not an Indian. I'm mostly white."

Hoey McCurtain set the thermos back under the tree and carried a long steel bar to where his son was working.

"That don't matter. You're a mixed-blood and that's Indian. It's what you think you are that matters. You can't tell me you'd rather be white than Indian? Hell, a hundred years ago you couldn'tve testified in a court in this state because you got Indian blood. D'you know that? Indian people lost everything, even those rich Cherokees back in Georgia, because all some white trash drifter had to do was have a phony bill of sale. The Indian couldn't testify in court, so the white just got everything automatically. You know they tried to give the Choctaws part of Mexico when they drew up that Indian Territory?" he said. "They didn't even goddamned well know where the rivers ran. Pushmataha had to set them straight—and called Jackson a liar right to his face. You want to be white?"

Cole lifted the digger out of the ground, and his father stabbed the bar down hard several times to break up the shale, and then Cole lifted the broken rock out with the digger.

"What do you call that soul-catcher thing you told me about?"

Hoey McCurtain looked hard at his son for a moment. Finally he said, "Soul-eater, you mean. Some Choctaws call it *nalusachito*. Why?"

"Just curious." He jabbed the post-hole digger into the   21 hole and came up with nothing, so Hoey McCurtain started in again with the bar, breaking the rock and trying to remember what he'd told his son about the soul-eater, what some called soul-catcher.

On the warming hillside above them a ground squirrel whistled at the shadow of a hawk, and they both turned to watch the bird settle into the canopy of an oak.

"Ask Attis what he thinks about the draft," Hoey McCurtain said abruptly as Cole returned to work with the posthole digger.

Cole straightened and placed a hand on the small of his back. He looked directly at his father for the first time that morning. "You want me to ask my brother what he thinks about something?" He looked away and listened as several crows spotted the hawk and began hurling insults. "Attis enlisted," he said. He thought about his brother, before and after the war. For nineteen years he'd known Attis better than he'd known himself, and then after just one year he hadn't known him at all.

"They're going to draft you pretty damned soon," his father said, and Cole could hear something in Hoey McCurtain's voice. "You could go to Mississippi. Uncle Luther would hide you."

Cole looked up in surprise. Strangely, he'd found himself thinking about the old man lately, his father's uncle whom he hadn't seen since they'd moved to California when he was eight. It was the first time in years he'd thought about the solitary old uncle who'd raised his father, and now he recalled, too, the tar-paper sharecropper's shack where they'd lived close to the river. Daddy longlegs had crawled across the dark ceiling like delicate upside-down men on stilts, and an odor of things rotting had hung over everything. He remembered the bitter smell of the mud along the river and the acrid smell of the carbide lamps when his father would get ready to go hunting at night with Uncle Luther. And he remembered how Uncle Luther would appear like one of the swamp ghosts people talked about, beckoning his father out into the night.

"There ain't nobody going to dig you out of that Yazoo country," his father said, taking a plug of tobacco out of his jacket pocket and biting off a chew.

Suddenly Cole could feel and smell the place he hadn't seen in so many years—the deep river full of dangerous hidden things, a snake or a swirl or a shadow in the water that would disappear so fast you wondered if you'd really seen anything. It was a full-time, above-ground river as different from the Salinas as anything could be. And Uncle Luther had been short and as solid as the pecan tree in the yard, with long, stringy hair, dark as night under the big hat that hid his face, as if he, too, could have been one of the hidden things from the river. "Uncle Luther is Indian," Attis had explained back then. "That's why he only shows up at night and don't never talk. Indians are funny."

Cole had understood then that Indians came from tangled swamps to stand in front of one's porch and silently call one's father out into the night. The old man had frightened him deep down, and when he'd lie in the shack at night and hear the yowl of a hound or the sound of a rifle somewhere down toward the river or on the other side, he'd think of his father and Uncle Luther killing things in the dark. Across the river the thickest swamps boomed and cracked all night, and he thought of the two of them as lights trailing one another in the darkness. Sometimes he still thought of his father that way.

"I'll think about it," he said, puzzled by his attraction to the idea.

"Don't think too long." Hoey finished tamping a corner post. "I could drive you up to Frisco and you could fly to Jackson. There used to be a bus from Jackson to Waltersville."

Cole thought about his brother alone in a room in the hospital, and then he imagined his father alone in the house by the river. Back there in Mississippi, the old man was probably alone, too.

"Ought to start raining pretty soon," Hoey said, and Cole saw his father watching the clouds building up over the coast range. "It's damned near winter already."

Five

Mundo stumbled backwards from the railing and jerked the car door open. He grabbed the handle of the spotlight and shoved the light downstream, searching down and across and back again. But there were only shapes, black forms sliding and turning and spinning in the patterned water.

He leaned against the car. The river hissed below the bridge, and he heard the muffled wings of an owl. He wiped rain from his eyes and looked at the close water, thinking that it must be what he'd heard about, what so many of them had. Hallucination. Craziness. Post-traumatic stress. First the cat and now this. Attis McCurtain was in the hospital outside of town. Attis was out there seeing things, fighting the war again, taking the pills they gave him and waiting for Mundo Morales to pull him from the brown water of the Delta. He'd seen Attis in the hospital just a week before. Attis wasn't in the river.

He got back into the car and bent his head over the steering wheel, feeling the water on his back and shoulders and hearing the rain drumming on the metal roof. The drowned smell of the river had come into the car with him, and he switched off the spotlight and sat shivering, thinking suddenly of the ranch house behind him and the dead girl, Jenna. When he looked up again, the far end of the bridge leaped at him, and he grabbed for the keys frantically for an instant before becoming still again and forcing control over his body, beginning as he'd taught himself with the legs and moving upward through thigh and groin and guts and torso and finally down to the hands, the brain itself gradually assuming a stone hardness. When he felt himself to be the still point around which other things could move without effect, he started the car and drove across the bridge, turning along the opposite side of the river and climbing up out of the shallow drainage toward town. The road rose gradually for a mile and then curved around the base of Pine Mountain into the outlying homes and then the little town itself.

Six

The old man raised his head and listened for a moment. He smiled and waited for the knock on the door. When a stick pounded on the oak slabs of the door, he went to open it.

"You're sleeping, old man, wake up."

The old woman stepped into the cabin and leaned her oak staff against the table, then she stood beside the stove with her hands on her hips, looking about her suspiciously. Her hair was silver and hung free to her waist from a brilliant red turban. She squinted her eyes and stared like a magpie at the far corner of the room.

"I knew it, old man. It's here."

"I don't know what you mean. Invading a man's home and talking like a crazy woman. One would think *kashehota-*

25

palo had had his way with you in the forest."

The old woman turned with a smile. "Some old men have their way with no one, but can only make hog talk."

He snorted and looked at the woodbox to hide his grin. When he had shoved a stick of wood into the potbellied stove and turned back around, he saw that she was watching the corner again.

"It won't go," he said with a shrug.

The woman named Onatima, whom everyone called Old Lady Blue Wood, nodded her head, her wrinkled face softening in an expression of sorrow. "I felt it, old man. It wants the bones." She looked sadly at Luther. "Where are the bones?"

Luther shrugged. "It isn't simple. There is a river. The whites have broken it so that it runs only underground except when the big rains come. Then the river grows angry and when it is strong enough it rises up to revenge itself. When it is done, it goes back into its home in the ground. It has the bones."

The old woman pulled at strands of her hair and looked at him incredulously. "This isn't more mystical hog talk?"

"No." He shook his head again. "The river has taken the bones. There's a dark one who may help us, but he, too, must wait until the river goes to sleep again."

Outside the cabin an owl called once, and they both paused, waiting for the answering call that never came, confirming what they both knew.

She pulled a leather pouch from the pocket of her heavy wool coat. "I've brought cedar," she said.

He looked thoughtful for a moment and then shook his head a third time. "No, I don't think we should do that. The black *koi* has been around, looking for this one maybe. I don't think we can send this *shilombish* away yet. Maybe I should shoot that cat."

She looked sharply at him. "Don't be stupid, Luther."

They were both silent for a minute, and then he reached to touch her hair. "I know an old man who can still make old women happy," he said, the suggestion of a grin upon the downturned corners of his mouth.

She turned scornfully upon him. "Some old men are not like rivers who can rise from their beds."

"Ha!" he laughed loudly. "Let me bar the door, Old Lady Blue Wood." He nodded toward the corner. "This one won't mind an old man who isn't broken."

Seven

Mundo parked in front of the hole they'd given him for an office and sat for a moment in the car. The substation was in a corner of the town's only hotel, and the dark building loomed over the car like a bad dream. At either end of the block, one-fourth of the whole main street, street-lights showed a sulfurous yellow, and he listened as a truck geared up from the four-way stop where Amarga's two business strips intersected. He knew without looking which pickup it was and who was driving it and where the driver would be going at eleven o'clock on a Thursday night. He began to shiver and worked quickly to stop it before getting out and moving toward the office door.

"Psst!"

He jumped and looked around in the dark.

"Psst! Over here, hijo."

He followed the sound of the voice to a thin face in the entrance of the hotel.

"Something's happened, Ramon Morales. Something's happened."

He walked close to the doorway where the tiny old   27

woman wavered like a hallucination, clutching her gray robe close to her neck. Her brown eyes were sharp and set deep in the bony face, and the thin gray hair made a halo against the darker background.

"We thought you should know, hijo."

The second voice came from behind the first, and he looked more deeply into the doorway to see the other sister poised in an identical bathrobe in the moldy hotel lobby.

"Good evening, ladies," he said, feeling his heart still pounding. "Do you need my help?"

"Ramon Morales," said the one nearest him, "it's you, you need our help."

Mundo sighed, letting his abdominal muscles out slowly. "Ladies," he said, "it is late and I am very tired and I have business I must finish." He stepped one step backwards and made a slight bow from the waist and then, hearing the "Psst!" behind him, he quickly unlocked the door of his office and went inside, pulling the door tightly closed behind him. "Buenas noches," he murmured. "Chingada." He bent to pick up the mail where it had fallen through the slot in the door.

Somehow, somewhere generations back, the Moraleses and Mondragons were related. The sisters had told him that, and he'd let it remain a mystery, figuring that if they wanted to go so far back as all that probably everybody in the town was related, even the Indians, even Moraleses and McCurtains. There was a rumor that he'd had a Mondragon uncle. He flipped a light switch. The little office flickered out of the dark into a fluorescent half-light, and he jumped back, feeling his guts contract. For an instant there had seemed to be the figure of an old man in the far corner of the room, old and wiry like his grandfather but with long stringy hair and a wide-brimmed hat that hid the face. But when he looked again there was nothing.

He walked to a table against the right wall and touched his fingers to a Pyrex coffeepot, grunting when he felt the heat. He hung his dripping jacket on a hook near the door and turned back toward the table. There was a half hour until midnight, when he could go home.

Setting the cup of black coffee on the desk, he pushed aside a stack of blue forms and lowered himself into the swivel chair before picking up the coffee again. He lifted the cup and held it against his cheek until it began to burn and then lowered it, cupping his hands around it. Superimposed images of the cat and the face in the water came to him, and he shook his head to clear it. From outside came the frying of tires on wet pavement and then a long backfire as someone clutched down for the stop sign. There was a small shriek of compression scratch when the tires locked. "Clutch and tranny," he muttered aloud before he took a sip of the coffee and grimaced.

He tried thinking of the Mondragons. If what the viejo had told him was true, the Mondragon sisters had been hot numbers once. The viejo, in the cab of the pickup on the way to shoot a forked-horn buck, had confessed to having fucked one of the sisters, but the old man could no longer remember which one. He tried to imagine it. The old man not old and one of the sisters, skirt up or down, tit brown and wet from the old man's young mouth, eyes closed and small back arched out of the grass to meet the not-yet-old man's cock, wanting only that at that moment in life, being alive.

He felt an urge to put the last two hours behind him by going back outside to confront the old women, make one confess, to look for the feeling in the eyes that would push thoughts of Attis McCurtain further away. How strange it was that two people could meet in some secret place and do that, the most intense, alive thing they would ever know, and then go away and live other lives with children, dogs, grandchildren like him, Mundo, and even forget. The world was like that, full of hidden, half-forgotten things. Things like the baby that had appeared when the Mondragon sisters still lived in the old house on the fragment that was left of the grant. The baby, Rudolfo, had grown into

29

a man liked and admired by the town of La Luz. Rudy Mondragon had been the best mechanic in the town and even the town's mayor before the war. But no one, not even Rudy, ever knew which of the sisters was the mother. At PTA meetings, both sisters came to defend Rudy from society's attacks, glaring together with dark eyes at the imagined threat, imagined because neither society nor anyone else ever had a desire to attack the friendly boy. Rudolfo was "the Mondragon boy," and that was good enough for the town. The fact that the viejo spent many evenings on the sisters' porch, playing with the happy youngster, caused a few snickers, but the fair Rudy had turned out nothing like Antonio Morales. "Indios feos" the town's matrons called the dark and wild Morales tribe, nudging their daughters toward the handsome and genial Rudy and forgetting for the time being that the land they inhabited had once been part of the Morales hacienda.

How strange, Mundo thought, that the sisters, real beauties the viejo had said, should know the heat of life yet remain in the end unmarried and alone together, their one shared child dead in the big war, while the old man would marry a quiet woman and sire children, seven of them, remembering with simple curiosity and pleasure that time with the sister. Mundo thought of the women and girls of Amarga, the ones he had known in the back seats of cars or on a summer hillside. In some dark way those moments were more real than all the rest, more than his wife, Gloria, more than the daughter who was more important than life itself.

And yet sometimes everything got messed up, as it had for Attis. People did things that were acts of a moment, and those acts changed whole lives—acts as simple as a word or a look. Like squeezing the trigger of a rifle. And what if the old man had simply invented that story? What if, in the darkness of the pickup, warmed by coffee and smoke and the jolting country road and the anticipation of the hunt ahead, his grandfather had imagined it all? What did that change?

The county, led by Dan Nemi, wanted to condemn the old hotel and tear it down, so pretty soon maybe he wouldn't be in this building and he wouldn't have the sisters hovering up there on tattered wings to remind him of the past. The past was like a sore, he thought, and sores heal faster if they're covered.

"Attis McCurtain, right now, at this very moment, is in the Amarga State Hospital for the Criminally Insane," he said to the empty office. The hospital was south of town at the place where the river curved away from Pine Mountain. They'd sat in the visiting room together a week before, like they always did, Attis in a yellow Pendleton shirt that made his mixed-blood skin seem even darker than Mundo's.

"Still shooting hoops?"

When he asked the question, Mundo had watched Attis's eyes come swimming out of medicated depths.

"Point guard."

Mundo smiled. Attis McCurtain had been the best point guard the county had ever seen, a tricky ball-handler who seemed to be everywhere at once, dancing as he brought the ball across the time-line, driving the ball right up the gut of opposing teams, dishing off at the last second to somebody like Mundo, who was like Attis's big twin. At times, Mundo could have sworn that Attis made the ball disappear. Suddenly it would reappear in Mundo's hands and he would shove it through the hoop and people would cheer. Opposing teams hated the controlled chaos of Amarga's point guard. In the off-season the high-school team had scrimmaged against the hospital patients' team. More than once, Mundo had stepped out of the way of a psychopath driving for the basket only to see Attis take the charge with a grin. Attis had scholarship offers but had no interest in college. War was the new game.

"Pick-'n'-roll," Attis had muttered, his eyes going suddenly distant. *"Chahta isht ia."*

"What's that?"

31

"What?" Attis's eyes had come back again.

"What you just said, hermano." Mundo had tried to smile.

"Choctaw blood," Attis had mumbled before falling silent for the rest of the visit.

Mundo sipped the bitter coffee and concentrated on Attis McCurtain alive. The eyes in the hospital had been the kind of eyes Mundo had seen when he was on leave in Seattle, Indian eyes that evaded and hid. But Attis never drank, not even in high school when they all did. Not even in Nam and after. Not even before they found him with her in the motel room. Not "they," but he, Mundo.

He thought of the long, arcing line that had taken both of them from Amarga to Vietnam and back again, a red line you could draw on a big map and one ending with a phone call, a motel room, and something worse than Vietnam because it had been him, Mundo, Attis had phoned. A sex-slaying they had called it, using phrases like post-Vietnam-syndrome and post-traumatic-shock. He'd just stood in the doorway at first, waiting for the joke, the fake knife-in-the-heart, but then he'd smelled the blood.

"It's late."

For too many times that night Mundo jumped, jarring the chair away from the desk and spilling coffee on the paperwork beside him. Near the door stood Hoey McCurtain, the black collar of his wool coat turned up and the John Deere cap pulled low over his eyes.

"Jesus Fucking Christ, Hoey," Mundo finally responded. "How the hell did you get in here?"

"You don't lock your door." Hoey spat tobacco juice at a wastebasket near the door. "It never took much to sneak up on a Morales."

Mundo pulled a roll of paper towels from a desk drawer. As he blotted the spilled coffee he glanced up, seeing Attis's face in the face of Hoey McCurtain. He shook his head to clear it once more and tossed the wet towels at the wastebasket. The towels landed outside the basket an inch from where the tobacco juice had struck.

As Mundo started to speak, the telephone on the desk rang, startlingly loud. He grabbed it and then stiffened, focused on the voice at his ear. A minute passed before Mundo said, "I'll head out there right now."

When he looked up, Hoey McCurtain was standing with his hands in his coat pockets, watching him.

"When they going to give you a radio?" the older man asked. "Telephone ain't very professional."

When there was no reply, Hoey McCurtain said, "Something happened to my son. That's why I came."

Mundo nodded, the tightness in his throat like a bruise.

"I dreamed it—part of it," Attis's father said.

"They say he escaped," Mundo answered, looking at his visitor's good eye and avoiding the pale one. He heard a car drive by slowly, and then he thought he could hear the rain on the hotel roof two stories above.

"No." Hoey McCurtain was shaking his head. "No," he said again in an inflectionless voice. "He didn't excape."

Mundo held the receiver in his hand. "Is that what you came to tell me?"

"I been driving around."

Mundo set the phone back in its cradle. "I know what you've been doing. I didn't think anybody poached deer in this kind of rain."

McCurtain went on as if the deputy sheriff hadn't spoken. "You been at the river, so you know."

Mundo stood and looked across and down at the shorter man. 'They killed him,' he wanted to say. 'They killed him because he murdered their girl.' Pushed a knife into her heart so that all the blood emptied out. That was simple wasn't it? Nothing complicated about it.

He felt the weight of responsibility, and he closed his eyes, seeing the face in the river and the hand lifted by the chop of the fast water. When he opened his eyes, Hoey McCurtain was gone. And then the door opened again and another man entered.

33

"Where the fuck you been, Morales?"

Angel Turkus stalked to within three feet of the desk, and stood with his hands in his green deputy sheriff's jacket.

"I been trying to reach you for two fucking hours."

Mundo thought about the statement. The radio in his patrol car had been on the blink for a couple of days and he hadn't gotten around to taking it to San Luis to get fixed. "Looking for poachers," he said finally. "My radio must be on the blink again."

Turkus walked so close to the desk that Mundo could see the red hairs that sprouted from his ears and nostrils. Mundo looked at the pile of mail on his desk. There was an important-looking letter from the FBI, the kind he usually let sit for a few days, but because Angel Turkus was standing there he tore the envelope open and began to read.

"Well, we got us another dead hobo," Turkus said. "Somebody found him in the yard when they were switching cars. Dead as a doornail with a hole in his head. They figure he got plugged somewheres between San Luis and Paso."

Mundo looked at the way the other deputy's belly strained the green sheriff's jacket, and then he looked back at the letter. The FBI wanted Cole McCurtain for draft evasion. And they wanted him, Mundo, to locate Cole and hold him for them.

"San Luis told me to roust you out tonight and make sure that you went out to La Luz to check it."

Mundo looked up and nodded vaguely. "First thing in the morning. Unless you want to handle it. Paso is your territory, isn't it?" He knew they wouldn't find out jack shit in La Luz, but it wasn't hard to imagine what might have happened to the hobo. He also knew he couldn't tell them that a man had most likely been killed just for fun and that they'd never find out who did it. He could see a way it could easily have happened. The train ran along the edge of the river between the little town of La Luz and the bigger town of Amarga, and there were always kids hunting the riverbed with twenty-twos and four-tens. With the river flooded, the kids would be bored, looking for anything to shoot. Two or three kids would be out there, knocking off a thrush or bluejay, when the train comes along, the Southern Pacific swinging around one of those long, slow curves. One of the boys might point to a gondola full of new cars or farm equipment and say, "I bet you can't hit one of those fuckers."

Every kid in the county would want to take a potshot at a new car, or maybe ping a twenty-two slug off a new tractor. So the kids would take a few shots. Then they'd see a flatcar or boxcar with a couple of hobos or maybe one sitting there dangling his feet off the side watching the river. If one of the hobos had a red cap on he'd show up very well.

"Fucking hobos," one of the kids might say because he'd heard his dad talk about how worthless hobos were. "Bet you can't hit one of those sonsabitches," another kid would say, and that's how it could have happened. Afterwards, the kids would probably throw the rifle in the flooding river and run like hell for home. Nobody would ever know. Those kids would grow up together and never tell anyone. It was possible that he was wrong, that another rail tramp had done it. Maybe there'd been an argument over something. But the tramps seldom carried anything as valuable as a gun. And a 'bo never had anything worth being killed for except his life. The image of kids with a rifle depressed Mundo. The county was that kind of place, ass-deep in blood secrets.

"I don't speak Mexican, so they want you to do it. And they want you out there tonight, not tomorrow. By the way, Morales, that retard is out there walking around again. You ought to get him locked up before he attacks a little girl or something."

"Excuse me." Mundo picked up the phone and dialed.

In a moment he said, "Querida. Sorry to wake you up. I got some business to do tonight. Yeah. I don't know." He listened for a moment and then nodded. "It's about Attis. And a 'bo got shot on the train. Yeah. Daylight maybe, I don't know." He closed his eyes for a moment. "Te quiero, chiquita. Get some sleep."

He hung up the phone and turned to the other deputy. "I'll check on the hobo in the morning. Couple of other things have come up." He stood and shoved the federal letter in his back pocket. "Bobby's harmless. We grew up together. He walks around at night so he doesn't have to stay home. His old man drinks and his old lady just yells at him. He's sensitive." He brushed past Angel and grabbed his coat off the rack. "Gotta go. Lock up when you leave," he said as he went out the door.

Turning the patrol car south on the main street, he noted the reflected neon of the drugstore sign on the wet pavement and heard a dog barking nearby with painful monotony. A twisted shadow was dragging itself along with rhythmic irregularity on the sidewalk in front of the drugstore, and he stopped the car and rolled the window down.

"You okay, Bobby?" he shouted across the street.

The shadow paused, and the large head swiveled unevenly on crooked shoulders. Seeing the head nodding up and down, Mundo shouted, "Okay, Bobby, but you better get on home, bro. It's pretty late."

The head bobbed again, and then Bobby Bart began to move on the sidewalk once more, one foot swinging wide and slow with each step, one hand held up near the shoulders like a broken wing.

Mundo watched the steady crabwalk for a moment and then rolled the window up and accelerated. In the mirror he saw a light high up in the red-brick Memorial Building in the office of the north county supervisor, Dan Nemi.

He noted the time and swung the car around the building, seeing the rancher's El Camino pickup at the side entrance with a roll of barbed wire in the back. He drove past the building and the town park and headed south toward the hospital. After midnight, the town, with the exceptions of Bobby Bart and Dan Nemi, seemed asleep, the windows of the Amarga Market and Hong's Cafe black and dull, the two gas stations slick with oil and rain, their office lights pale as death. As he drove over the Amarga Creek bridge, he glanced down into the brushy creekbed. He'd fished the creek a few times with Attis and Cole and caught trout because no one else believed the fish were there and so didn't fish for them. He'd followed the brothers into dark places.

Though he couldn't see the water, he could feel how high the creek was and imagine what it would look like. Brown and sinewy, scouring itself out in the annual cleansing. Afterwards, when the river settled to a small, clear stream for a brief time, and the creek dropped back into its pools, the steelhead would have come upriver. Then, when the river ceased to run, there would be big, flashing steelhead in the deeper pools of the creek, trapped and nosing the rocky sides. He recalled the time that Attis had shoved his feet into empty smudge pots and jumped into one of the deepest pools. He'd walked on the bottom, grinning up at them through the clear water as if from another world. And then Mundo had had to dive in to help him get his feet out of the heavy pots.

The road swung in a long curve around the southern end of Pine Mountain, the solitary mound that rose over the town for a thousand feet. It must have been natural, he'd often thought, that the first settlers in the town would have looked up at the mountain and imagined burying the dead there. There had been bears on the mountain, but Angel Turkus had shot the last one five years before when it wandered bewildered into town and climbed a tree in panic. There had been a photo in the town newspaper of the little black bear staring down from the oak tree with an incredulous expression, like it had slept for a hundred years and awakened to madness all around. At the southern extreme of the curve, in a wide crease between the hill and the river, was the sprawling hospital complex.

After a quick conversation at the front gate he parked his car in the employees' lot, noting the county sheriff's car and two others with state license plates. The guard at the main door waved him toward the offices, where he saw blazing lights and men moving behind the bars. Walking toward the lights, he thought again of the scrimages against the patients' teams in high school. Once in the locker room he'd been approached by a young black man—after Attis, one of the best ball handlers he'd ever seen. "How you doing?" the patient asked. Mundo had been doing fine until the man said, "You know why they got me in here?" When Mundo shook his head, the black man answered his own question. "I raped and killed a little girl, a white girl. Can you believe that kind of shit, man?" He'd walked away, leaving Mundo staring at the floor. What did the whole mess mean, he wondered as he thought back. It was like a war.

Inside the central office five men stood around a desk, sipping coffee and glancing at a map spread across the desktop. Donald Wagstaff, head psychiatrist at the hospital, sat to one side, his three hundred pounds enveloping a small chair, his tiny, intelligent blue eyes sunk far back in his face as he studied the men studying the map.

Mundo looked from the shiny top of Wagstaff's head to the short, muscular man behind the doctor's desk. The two men seemed to complete one another somehow. Carl Carlton looked up as Mundo entered and then looked back at the map, tracing a finger along a wide blue line.

"We've got road checks north and south," the county sheriff said without taking his eyes from the map. "We've got men at the bus and train stations." He raised his head and seemed to see Mundo Morales for the first time. For several seconds he let his eyes, the color of fresh concrete, rest on Mundo, and then he shifted his gaze to the psychiatrist and back again to Mundo.

"Evening, Morales," the sheriff said. "How you like being a full-time deputy? Beats hell out of cleaning toilets, don't it?" Carlton smiled and added, "Then you sure as fuck better keep that radio of yours turned on so we can find your ass when we need you."

Mundo returned the sheriff's stare without expression. Without appearing to, he took in the rest of the group. Two of the men he recognized as deputies from the county seat. The fifth man was a stranger, a lean, sharp-edged man of about forty-five in a gray suit.

"Mundo knows this part of the county better than anyone else we have." The sheriff looked at the others as if waiting for someone to challenge his statement, ending with a brief gaze at the stranger. Then he ran a hand through his brown crewcut and looked back at the map.

"Okay, Mundo. We figure your buddy has headed along the river, north or south. The fence cut is on the south side, but that don't mean a whole hell of a lot." Carlton glanced up suddenly, in a practiced gesture. "Where you think he might have headed?"

Mundo stepped between one of the other deputies and the man in the gray suit and looked down at the county map. There was something about maps he didn't like. The first thing they did when they wanted to take something away from you was draw a map; that's what the viejo had said.

On the map the river was a blue the river could never be, a long, twisting line from the coastal mountains above San Luis to Monterey Bay a hundred and twenty miles north. The hospital's location had been marked with a red X. He put his finger in the middle of the thick blue line where it skirted the red X and bent around the east side of the contours representing Pine Mountain.

The sheriff's forehead wrinkled and he glared at Mundo. "There? The river? Mundo, did you hear me say that we figured McCurtain had gone either upriver or downriver? Tell me something I don't already know."

Watching the river on the map snake past the towns he knew—San Luis, La Luz, Amarga, Paso Robles, San Ardo, Santa Lucia, King City—he imagined Attis McCurtain at that moment, turning and slowly spinning with the logs and planks and other debris, maybe catching on one of the trees still above water, the brown flood lapping over him and turning him under. He'd seen other men die in Vietnam, and the simple fact was that every death was like that: alone and spinning in the dark, every man abandoned by the living in a single great leap away from death.

"He's in the river. I saw him tonight," he said, adding as an afterthought, "dead."

He studied the map with its close, wavy lines to indicate the high coastal mountains to the west and the gentle, far-spaced contours marking the low, grass hills on the east side of the valley. The map showed streams coming out of the western mountains to feed the river, dozens of them, two streams large enough to be called rivers on the map, Nacimiento and San Antonio. On the map the lines all flowed together in delicate, convincing patterns, converging in the thicker line of the river that carried them all out to sea. But both of those big streams had been dammed just like the Salinas, and below the dams in the summer months the river was dry. The headwaters of the San Antonio had been Attis's favorite fishing spot. They'd park Attis's pickup off the fire road on the north side of Nacimiento Summit and backpack the two miles down to where the little river threaded its way between boulders shaded by oak and pine and sharp-smelling bay. By day they'd drift nymphs or worms into the pools under cutbanks to catch eight- or ten-inch browns. At night the pine needles and oak leaves would rustle with the hooves of wild pigs that nosed around the camp, and they'd lie under blankets trying to name the stars and talking of girls they knew. Attis had known a few Indian stories, and those would become tangled with other stories and mythic tales of Amarga cheerleaders. "Brer Rabbit, you know," Attis had confided, "that's a Choctaw story that a white guy stole and wrote up like he'd invented it." A moment later Attis's voice would drift dreamily out of the dark, "That Becky's got some tits, you know." They'd laugh and listen to the rustling of leaves beyond the light of the campfire.

They were all watching him. The deputies had taken a couple of steps closer, and somehow, without seeming to move, the stranger in the suit had resurfaced on the opposite side of the desk next to the sheriff. Carlton had edged away a couple of inches.

"Dead?" The question came from the man in the suit.

The sheriff cleared his throat. "Mundo, this is Lee Scott, federal investigator."

Lee Scott leaned across the desk toward Mundo. "You want to elaborate on that?"

Mundo looked at the thin, dark face. Everything about the tanned face was thin, from the nervous gray eyes to the sharp nose, mouth, and chin. A blue stubble shadowed the sucked-in cheeks. Gray pouches of long duration hung under the eyes, and the close-cut graying hair showed a sun-burned scalp.

"I was down at the river tonight and I saw Attis. Floating. Dead." He told the story. When he finished, he saw Lee Scott exchange a quick look with the sheriff.

Donald Wagstaff shifted on his chair and emitted a heavy sigh. Mundo glanced at the psychiatrist and thought of one of the huge suckers that lay on the bottom of the creek in the summer. They'd tie red balloons to treble hooks and snag the dull-witted fish, releasing them again afterwards. Or sometimes they'd shot them with arrows and left them dying on the bank. He cringed at that memory.

"Are you sure that's what you saw?" Wagstaff asked sadly. "It couldn't have been something you imagined because of . . . fatigue?" Without waiting for an answer, the psychiatrist went on. "You and the escapee were in Vietnam together, I understand?"

Mundo hesitated. "I thought at first it might be something like that," he said at last. "But it wasn't. It was Attis, and he's probably ten miles away by now."

"And you didn't radio it in immediately?" Carlton kept his voice low and even. "You waited until just now to tell somebody?"

Mundo shrugged. "The radio in my car's busted again, and like I just said, I wasn't sure till now."

The sheriff walked around the desk and grabbed his green jacket off a coatrack on the wall. "You weren't sure," he said softly as he slipped the jacket on. He stepped close to Mundo and looked up at him. "That dead girl's father's the only reason you're not still douching toilets at the high school. Next time you report what you see, even if it's some motherfucking war-hero hallucination."

Mundo watched the sheriff's jaw muscles work. He thought of the old man, his grandfather. They'd sat together after the girl's death, the viejo sipping brandy and Mundo holding a can of beer on his knee. "They did something to that boy over there," the old man had said, studying the brandy, "put something into him. The kind of thing that has to come out some time." When he looked up from the beer, Mundo had seen that his grandfather was smiling a faint, ironic smile. "You was there and maybe they did it to you, too," his grandfather had said. "I don't know because I never went to none of them other wars they had. But you better be careful. Attis, he's an indio that don't even belong in this country, from some place down south Hoey told me, but you're a Morales and Moraleses used to own all this place where we are." The old man had waved his arm from the porch. "We was given it by a Spanish king. You remember that, Ramon."

And it belonged to the Indians and we sold it for a quart of whiskey, Mundo thought. That's all it had taken Dan Nemi's grandfather to get his cattle onto the grant and begin the takeover that would, in only ten years, make him sole owner of all the Morales land. Back when it was illegal for a Mexican or an Indian to testify against a white person in court. It was the grandmother who always told that part, reminding the youngsters that it was whiskey that stole their land, whiskey, and gringos.

"Let's take a drive down to that bridge," the sheriff said. "Might as well start there. Maybe another corpse'll drift by, or maybe we'll all start seeing cartoons."

Eight

A redtail hawk circled out of the pale sky to land at the top of a bare sycamore, turning its head to look down at the men. All three peered up at the big hawk's strange behavior as the bird spread its wings and fanned them in a slow pantomime of flight. Four times the bird spread the great wings and folded them, catching the brightening sunlight in transluscent feathering and drawing the light in toward itself. Then the redtail exploded from the branch and was lost in a long swinging arc down the river.

In one of the walnut trees a flicker started hammering, and Cole watched his father hunch deeper into the mackinaw and look out over the river. Already it was obvious that the river was falling, that the rainwater had leaked out of the mountains and was draining rapidly into the Pacific at the northern end of the valley. In a few days the river would be a small stream, and in a few weeks nothing would be left but the water behind the big dam upstream and beneath the sand of the riverbed.

Mundo went to lean against the '57 Chevy parked beneath the row of walnut trees. He ran his hand along the beautiful red metal-flake paint and looked through the

43

windshield at the rich black button-and-tuck upholstery. He'd gone with Attis all the way down to Tijuana to have that done. Now the car was up on blocks, a kind of memorial with a 283 bored out to 301, Holly four-barrel carbs, Hooker headers, a three-quarter cam, Hurst four-on-the-floor, four-eleven rear end, and mag rims. Maybe the fastest car in the county. At first a lot of guys had been after Hoey to sell the car. Now, the walnut leaves and greasy black-walnut husks were beginning to cover it, piling up behind the wipers and in every crevice and cranny. There was bird shit all over the windshield. He wondered about Cole; most guys his age would have somehow finagled their way into driving such a car. But Cole wasn't like most guys his age. Sometimes he reminded Mundo of one of the spaced-out priests they used to find walking the roads in Nam. Or one of those guys that lived on the island with the one they called the Coconut Monk.

"I saw him last night, in the river," Mundo said again. "He was dead."

Hoey McCurtain nodded and squinted toward the water. Mundo looked from Hoey to Attis's brother, and Cole looked directly back with hard green eyes. Mundo realized then that Hoey McCurtain and Attis had never made direct eye contact like that, that of the McCurtains only Cole would look straight at a person. He'd heard it was something Indians didn't do, but he didn't know whether it was all Indians or just some Indians. Maybe you had to be less than half to make eye contact.

"I seen him there," Hoey said, still watching the water, and it took Mundo a moment to realize it was the dream Attis's father was speaking of.

A flock of racing pigeons dipped and swooped over the river, their jerky flight brittle in the cool air. Mundo glanced from father to son and let out a deep breath.

"I'm sorry," he said. "At first I thought I was just seeing things, hallucinating. That's why I didn't tell you last night. They say that he cut a hole in the fence and escaped. That if I really saw him he must have tried to swim the river. But I don't think they believe me."

He could feel Hoey looking at him, and when he looked back he was surprised by a different kind of feeling in the good eye, the kind of thing you saw when you bent to look up into one of the caves animals made in wet parts of the river brush, a place you didn't get close to. He thought of the tiger then. They'd been on recon and he'd awakened with a breath in his ear. "Tiger," Attis had hissed. "There's a fucking tiger out there." And then he'd smelled it, right there, almost on them in the jungle. A smell of piss and death, something wilder than everything they'd been doing in the nightmare war. "A fucking tiger." And he'd realized that Attis was grinning, excited. And nothing had happened, death had just gone away. Afterwards, Attis seemed to live in search of the tiger. Waking at night, Mundo would find his friend gone into the dark, and he'd wait for Attis's return, rank with odors of night and sweat and, containing all the rest, infinite death. "They're out there," Attis had said on one of the first nights in response to Mundo's question. "I'm the only one who sees them. Me and Charlie. That's why Charlie hasn't killed us all. He's afraid to make more of them."

"To swim that river?" Hoey spat tobacco juice in the direction of the water.

They were all silent for a few minutes and then Hoey said, "He went to their war, like you did." His eyes followed a stump that bobbed out in the middle of the current. "They been doing that for a long time, using us to kill each other and then getting rid of us when it's done. I tried to tell him that, but he didn't want to be an Indian, just American." He looked back at Mundo. "They got away with all that before. They ain't going to get away with this one."

Mundo listened to the flicker and looked past Hoey McCurtain toward the river where a chicken house was floating by. On the ridge of the roof a scrawny and furious

45

fighting cock stood silhouetted against the flood. Mundo turned back and nodded toward Cole McCurtain, saying, "Can I talk to you for a minute?"

Cole looked surprised as he followed Mundo a few steps away from his father, who continued to watch the water.

Mundo pulled a crumpled letter from his pocket and unfolded it, holding it out toward Cole.

"Read this," he said. "Then I want you to give it back and forget you ever saw it."

Cole read the letter and then handed it back, saying nothing.

"You better do something about that, bro," Mundo said.

Nine

When Mundo pulled in beneath the white oaks, Dan Nemi was getting out of the El Camino pickup, his western suit still sharply creased and the cattleman's Stetson square on his head. The tall rancher unfolded upward and stood straddle legged, waiting, one hand on the top of the pickup.

"So you finally caught me?" Nemi grinned as Mundo booted the car door closed and walked toward him.

Mundo squinted and reached to scratch behind an ear. "Yeah. Felonious fellationus," he said, taking in the delicate pattern of oak bark on the ancient tree beyond the El Camino and then looking again at the richest man in the county. In the next oak behind the big one was a block and tackle they used to slaughter calves and pigs.

"Where'd you pick that one up?" Nemi smiled again. "You never learned big words like that at the high school."

Mundo's glance shifted to take in the big barn, the stacked hay bales between barn and corral and then the other long, sanitary-looking barn where the rancher kept his Arabians and Appaloosas. There was a sense of precision and efficiency about the ranch that he'd never felt in La Luz. He tried to imagine what the old Morales hacienda must have been like. It probably had dogs and kids and goats all over the place, fighting cocks on the porch and cats in the kitchen. They were like that. He studied the long, rectangular Nemi ranch house with its brown shutters. Beyond the house, the hillside rose in a comfortable arrangement of winter-dried grasses and dark scrub oak and buckbrush. The turning weather kept the damp alfalfa smell on the air. He looked back at Dan Nemi, admiring the economical way the rancher's words had reminded him that before becoming deputy sheriff he'd been nothing more than a janitor at the high school and that it was Nemi who'd gotten him this job. Vietnam meant nothing to anybody. All of that in inflection worthy of the viejo.

"You forget that I got to travel, free of charge," he said. "To educational places."

Nemi lifted his hand from the top of the sleek pickup and straightened so that he was slightly taller than Mundo. "Yes, we all owe you boys a lot, the ones that went over there. I just drove in from San Luis, and I'm anxious to sit down. Got time for a beer?"

"I got time for some coffee."

"Oh, yes. No beer on duty. Good man." Nemi slapped Mundo on the shoulder and motioned toward the house just as the front door opened and a woman stepped onto the porch.

"Well, hello, Mundo." Helen Nemi smiled with her whole face, the blue eyes switching on like two Christmas ornaments, and the dimples on either side of the full, slightly drooping lips deepening.

Mundo smiled back, meeting the rancher's wife's eyes for an instant before looking away toward the oaks. "Good

47

afternoon, Mrs. Nemi," he said, thinking of the daughters who, he thought, could never have what their mother had. Just an inch shorter than her husband, Helen Nemi wore her dark brown hair in a swirled crown above her head, letting the slender neck catch the light slipping over the oat hills. The white western shirt and tight jeans showed creases exactly where he thought they should, and he wondered how a man could leave Helen Nemi at home and go up the hill to Louise Vogler, the football coach's wife, which was where Dan Nemi spent afternoons when the football team had an away game.

Inside the house, Helen disappeared toward the kitchen, and Dan Nemi motioned toward a heavily padded chair.

"You look like you've had a long day. Sure I can't twist your arm and talk you into a beer?"

Mundo shook his head and sat down rigidly on the chair. He'd been in the Nemi house a couple of times, and it always surprised him. It should have looked and felt like money, but instead it was comfortable, all dark old wood and flowered wallpaper and leather chairs and a couch full of old cracks. There were plants on stands, and books were tossed here and there as if people really read them. It was the kind of house that didn't make you feel like you'd just tracked in dogshit.

Helen Nemi appeared with a cup of coffee with a saucer underneath it, and Mundo said thanks and balanced it on his knee, thinking of his grandfather slopping the coffee out of the cup so he could drink it from the saucer, a neat trick without spilling.

Helen set a glass of beer on the little table beside her husband's chair and then sat down on the long couch, watching Mundo.

"So, Mundo, what's up? You want the supervisors to vote you a raise?"

Mundo took a sip of coffee and said, "I came to ask you if you knew anything about Attis McCurtain's escape."

"His what?" Nemi looked at his wife.

"They say he escaped last night. That he cut a hole in the fence and escaped."

The rancher looked down the length of his brown slacks to his shiny snakeskin boots. He raised one hand to rub the blunt tip of his chin and then let the hand continue up one cheek and through his tight-woven gray hair.

"That's serious."

Before Mundo could speak again, Helen Nemi broke in. "Maybe they just lost him, you know, misplaced him out there in that great big hospital."

Mundo looked at Helen, noting that husband and wife seemed to exchange glances, though he couldn't be sure they had looked at each other at all.

"There's a hole in the fence and Attis isn't there, in the hospital." Mundo noticed that the weak northern sun was cutting through a window onto the delicate fronds of a fern. From outside came the sound of metal on metal and then a distant lowing. "Sheriff Carlton and some federal people are investigating it. And me—I'm investigating it."

Dan Nemi took a long pull on the beer and shifted one leg across the other. "I know Attis McCurtain was your friend, Mundo, but you have to understand how difficult it is for us to talk about this." His head moved faintly toward his wife. "Helen and I. . . ."

From another room came a blare of rock music and then silence again. Diana Nemi appeared in a doorway opening off the living room. She wore a black leotard top and a long skirt that clung to her narrow hips and nearly touched the floor. On the skirt was a pattern of pine trees.

"Well, it's the policia." Her smile was harder than her mother's. "Somebody rustling my father's milk cows?"

"Mundo has been asking about Attis McCurtain," Helen Nemi said, looking from Mundo to her daughter.

"Attis who?"

"Attis McCurtain, dear." Helen glared at her daughter.

"Why?"

"They say he escaped last night."

Diana reached one arm up and leaned against the door frame, her cheek against the long muscle of her upper arm and her nipples prominent through the black top. She lifted one foot so that the knee pushed against the skirt. Her brown hair framed an oval face and dark eyes, the lashes so long they gave the appearance of makeup.

Diana yawned and smiled apologetically. "Please excuse me. I had a long night." Her eyes flashed past Mundo's, and the knee moved beneath the thin layer of cotton.

"Did you see or hear anything last night?" Mundo asked, looking at Dan Nemi.

Nemi seemed to think for a moment. "Well, I heard some bad music. You see, I was in the Tiptoe Inn last night. Had an Association meeting yesterday and went to Jessard's to unwind." He exchanged glances with his wife.

"That's funny," Mundo said. "I could've sworn I saw your car down at the Memorial building last night."

"Oh. That was me," Helen Nemi said quickly. "I had to type up a report for the Library Society, so I dropped Dan off and was using his typewriter." She touched her cheek with two fingers. She seemed to concentrate for a moment. "That big owl that lives in the middle oak was hooing again last night. I think. And I heard some cats, maybe. And, of course, the coyotes up on the hill."

Mundo heard Diana laugh from across the room and then Dan Nemi said, "The river, too. You must have heard that, Helen. This time of year it always makes noise you hear all night, a kind of grinding." He looked satisfied with his speech.

In the doorway, Diana laughed softly again. "I heard some things, but they're secret. Felt some, too." She smiled at Mundo and turned and disappeared down the hallway.

"I'll bet he's still out there at the hospital," Helen said reassuringly. "Just misplaced. I'm always amazed at the things I lose around this little house."

"Hell, yes," her husband added. "Just last month I lost one of my studs. One of the boys put him in the wrong pasture—with a bunch of Guernseys—and it took a week to find him. And, don't forget, McCurtain's sort of an Indian and you know how they are; they just melt right into places and you never see them. Stoic, don't talk, no broken twigs, that sort of thing. Hide in a linen closet as easy as you or I drink a cup of coffee."

Mundo watched as husband and wife exchanged satisfied looks. Finally he said, "I noticed that your barn lights were on pretty late last night."

"Mare was foaling. Had one of the hands up all night with her. Arab-quarter cross. Fine little colt." Nemi relaxed.

"You know, I've always felt very bad about what happened," Mundo said. "I should have known. It didn't have to happen. I saw it in him over there, and I should have done something to help. But I guess I didn't want to admit it."

"Hell, it wasn't your fault, Mundo. You told everything you knew at the trial. You and the shrinks saved Attis McCurtain's life." The rancher's eyes hardened. In a voice near a whisper he said, "It was a sickness, something that's maybe so big we can't even see the extent of it."

Mundo watched Dan Nemi's shiny boots cross and re-cross, and he wondered about the strange note in the rancher's voice. Now that the sun wasn't cutting through the window any longer the room was becoming shadowed. From outside he thought he could hear the river just like Nemi had said, a sliding, heavy sound of things going away never to return. The big wooden house seemed to settle into itself. From the recesses of the house came the wiry guitar lines of something he thought might be "Plastic Fantastic Lover."

"I saw Attis last night," he said. "In the river."

Husband and wife looked at each other and then at Mundo.

"Attis? In the river?" It was Helen Nemi who spoke.

Dan Nemi sighed. "In my war some of the boys got hit pretty hard, too. We called it shell shock then, or battle

51

fatigue." Mundo started to speak but Nemi waved him quiet. "Now I guess they call it something else, some psychological term or other. But it's the same thing. You see things, hear things. The mind plays bad tricks. After the islands, you know, there was a lot of that. Ever wonder why the casualties were so one-sided toward the end of the war? Why, we went right into their field hospitals—"

"I wasn't hallucinating. It was him."

Helen Nemi said, "You poor boys who had to go over there. I'm so lucky I had girls." She put a hand to her mouth and looked down.

"We all owe you a lot," Dan Nemi put in. "A debt we can't ever repay. When I think of the draft-dodgers that. . . ."

"It was him."

"I'm sure you think it was, that you thought it was him," Nemi replied. "But maybe you ought to talk to one of those doctors at the hospital. I understand the stress—whatever they call it—can crop up any time, even years after it's over."

Mundo drew in a deep breath and held it for a moment. "Attis killed your daughter, and I saw him in the river last night. Those things happened. It won't do any good to pretend they didn't." He set the cup and saucer on a little hexagonal table beside the chair and stood up. "I was there."

"Mundo." Helen still held a hand over her mouth and looked with shocked eyes. From the back of the house came a tatooed drum solo.

"Now, Mundo. There's no need to upset Helen like that." Dan Nemi looked at Mundo through narrowed eyes.

Mundo walked toward the door and then turned around. "I'll find Attis," he said. "And I'll find out. What was done and who did it." He listened to the sliding river and the sound of drums from Diana's room. "Murder is against the law, no matter why it's done. I'll find out."

Ten

Cole McCurtain lay on his back and held both hands above him, toward the light. Between the thumb and index finger of each hand he held an arrowhead. In the right hand was a long point of black obsidian, with a white lightning bolt shot through the middle of the stone. In the left was a pale brown flint, the edges more finely and delicately fluted than those of the black point. He lifted each arrowhead toward the light and studied it in turn, remembering the cave they'd dug in the hillside behind the family house when they lived in the coast range. "Look at this Indian stuff," his brother had yelled from the deepest part of the hole, and when Cole tumbled down there Attis had been holding both arrowheads and a white stone doll about the same size as the points. The doll was as crudely formed as the arrowheads were fine, its face and limbs merely suggested by the carver. That night, a bear had chased their border collie, Rex, onto the porch right through the screen door.

Cole looked at the doll on a shelf over his brother's bed. On the nights when he couldn't get to sleep, he would look over at the shelf and imagine the doll and the arrowheads together there in the dark. He would think about the people who had made them, trying to imagine their lives in the coastal hills. Chumash, a people who seemed to have vanished into the pale hills the way the river disappeared into the sand. He'd heard that there were a few of them left somewhere, but he'd never seen one of them. And then he and Attis, who were Indians too, sort of, came to dig up what those vanished people had made. It was funny. He would try to understand the convergence, what strange design could have brought Choctaw blood so far from Mississippi to find these Chumash things.

Finally, exhausted, he would try the trick his brother had taught him, making a black cave of his mind and putting all of his thoughts in that cave. Then he was supposed to imagine a great round stone and roll that stone into the mouth of the cave. "Then you stop thinking and go to sleep," Attis had said. Cole wondered if his brother had been able to make a black cave big enough to hold all the thoughts that must have kept him awake the last couple of years. "Yea, though I walk through the valley of the shadow of death, I shall fear no evil. For I am the meanest motherfucker in the valley." The words on the jacket reminded him of Choctaw things Hoey McCurtain had told them. Stories he'd only half listened to. The shadow of death and the valley of death. "If Mundo saw my brother in the river," he thought, "then I can't say my brother's name." Bone pickers came walking from the deep woods, or the house next door, the people opening paths for what they imagined them to be. To clean the bones and put them away. Afterwards they presided at a feast in honor of the dead, their long fingernails clicking over the guests. Did they smile, he wondered, or grin there above the food, knowing what they knew? For years after the Choctaws had been forced to stop doing that, there were bone pickers wandering from town to town, begging, useless, clutching at passersby with their long nails.

Attis had tried to kill him in this room. Coming in late, when the house was dark and still, he'd removed his boots at the back door and tiptoed to their room. He had swung the door all the way open without a sound, when he saw Attis rise from the bed like a spirit, the knife in his right hand and his unseeing eyes locked on Cole. "Attis!" he'd screamed, and at the word, Attis collapsed, awake suddenly and weak with nausea. "It's good you yelled my name," Attis had said later. When Hoey reached the room, he'd found them sitting together on the bed, Cole's arm around his brother's shoulders. Was that what happened with her? He tried not to imagine how it had happened.

He rose from the bed and picked up a leather pouch from the shelf beside the doll. He slipped the arrowheads and doll into the deerskin pouch his brother had made, and he put the pouch in the pocket of the jacket hanging on the closet doorknob. After his return, Attis had walked the dry riverbed every day, his hands in the pockets of the fatigue jacket and his eyes empty. Cole had followed, unseen, wondering where his brother's steps were taking him.

They left in the morning, heading up Highway 101 in the pickup and then cutting west through the Jolon Valley. They forded the little San Antonio River and followed a one-lane road past the run-down mission church through thick forests to Nacimiento Summit. At the crest of the coast range, Hoey pulled the truck under the shelter of a massive pine and they sat together for a moment staring toward the sea and smelling the sharp bay trees of the canyons.

"Remember that time you got lost hunting pigs up here?" Hoey grinned at Cole. "I found you halfway down to the ocean."

"And I didn't even hear a pig grunt all day."

"Ha. And they say Indians ain't never supposed to get lost. You ever try making a fire by rubbing sticks together, Cole?"

"They taught us how to do that with a little bow and a stick in Boy Scouts. They said that's how Indians always did it."

"I forgot you was in Boy Scouts. They teach you any more Indian stuff?"

"How to mash up acorns and make flour. I was only in for a few months. It was too expensive."

Hoey nodded. "How'd that acorn stuff taste?"

"Like shit," Cole said.

Hoey nodded. "I always thought it must," he said quietly. Then he got out of the truck and walked alone into the forest of madrone and ponderosa. Through the windshield of the pickup, Cole watched the line of fog out over the Pacific and smelled the fragrances of the damp mountains, remembering what it had been like down in the canyon. He hadn't really been lost. He just hadn't wanted to retrace his steps all the way back up along that black creek where the sun never reached. So he'd kept walking downstream, dangling his rifle carelessly, following a thread of trail that must have once been a wagon road for the men who came up to cut the old-growth redwoods. It was cool and quiet down there, and he couldn't make himself turn back. Until he heard his father's shouts and began to climb slowly up through the tall trees.

In a few moments, Hoey returned, and Cole saw that his father's hair was hacked off in a jagged line just below the ears. When Hoey got back into the pickup, he slid the hunting knife beneath the seat.

For a long time, they sat staring at the blanket of fog that hugged the green coastline and climbed the mountains in spindly fingers. Without looking away from the white plain below, Hoey said, "You know, I guess I don't understand how to be Indian anymore. When I was a kid back in Mississippi, I never thought about it. Out there with Uncle Luther it never occurred to me. I'd listen to him and my mother talking Choctaw in the kitchen while he was helping her churn butter or something when my dad wasn't around, and it was just the way things was supposed to be, even if I couldn't understand what they was saying. I never had to think, 'Indians act this way or that way,' or 'Indians look like this or that.' They used to argue about my hair, with him always trying to get her to leave it long and her always cutting it, but I never thought that had anything to do with being Indian." He leaned toward the windshield and seemed to study the swath of pale blue sky that lay over the fog. Then he settled back in the seat.

"I've been reading books and remembering how it was back then and trying to figure out how to act and think. But books can't tell you things like that. Remember when

I took you to that powwow them Indians had in San Luis? It was like a circus to me. I didn't know beans about what them dancers was doing. Your grandfather was Irish, and he wouldn't let your grandmother talk Indian in the house. He told me he'd whip me if I talked it. I guess he loved my mother and me, but now I think he must of been ashamed of marrying an Indian."

He was silent for a few minutes, and Cole watched shreds of fog creeping up through the redwoods and pines in the knife-thin canyon.

"Now I wonder why my dad let me go off with Uncle Luther like he did. I guess maybe he knew I could learn a lot about the woods, or maybe that was the one thing he gave my mother, the one Choctaw thing he let her have. I never used to think about it, not until your brother come back. Then I got to wondering about the ways a man can live so such things don't happen. I started remembering some of the things Uncle Luther told me. What it boils down to is respecting your world, every little piece of it. When I poach does at night, it's against the law. Mundo looks the other way, but he'd have to arrest me if he seen me. But what I'm doing ain't wrong if you look at it in an Indian way. I pick out old does past their prime. They're tougher, but not as tough as those four- and five-point bucks white men are always trying to kill, the ones that are legal. And I leave the best breeding bucks and does alone. That ain't like the poison that chicken plant dumps into the creek, the stuff that kills the fish, or all the rest of things people are doing to the earth."

Hoey pushed the starter button and the Dodge ground into life. As he swung it into the middle of the little road and started down, he kept talking. "You know what it says on my birth certificate? White. I never knew it till I went in the army. I asked Uncle Luther about it and he said that because my dad was white, he figured he had a choice of what to have them put down, so he told them 'white.' It's funny, ain't it, to think a man can just choose like that? He

57

was probably worried about me, because being Indian in Mississippi back then was almost as bad as being a nigger. But colored people can't choose. The way people think in this country, one drop of colored blood makes a white person a nigger. But the same people think it takes a hell of a lot of Indian blood to make somebody a real Indian. I figure I got the same right to choose as my dad, so I chose Indian. Those Choctaws down there in Mississippi don't even know I'm Indian, the ones that run that new reservation they got. Uncle Luther told me a long time ago that they started up the dances and everything again, and I don't know shit about any of that."

"What does that make me?" Cole asked after a long silence. "At least somebody looking at you or my brother could tell you were Indian of some kind. I don't look like anything."

Hoey downshifted for a tight bend in the road, and the truck's differential shrilled. "During the war some guys thought I was Italian. I've thought about that, too. You don't look Indian, but then you don't exactly look like your average white man either. You got them Indian eyes like me and your grandmother and Uncle Luther. An Indian could probably tell you was Indian, but a white person might think you're just funny looking. I remember once a teacher asked your mother if you was part Russian. And when you was little, other kids used to ask if you was Chinese or Japanese. Remember that?"

Hoey chuckled and Cole grinned out the window. "Looks don't count. Indians look all kinds of ways. Some look Mexican and some look black or white or Chinese; you can't never tell. Think of it this way. You can't just ignore the fact that your grandfather was white. Uncle Luther says he was proud of being Irish. And your mom's mom was a quarter Irish, too, but she was proud as hell of being mostly Cherokee. Your mom's dad was Irish and Welsh and French or something like that, but he made damned sure nobody thought he was Indian. Now what do you do with all that mess? You just got to decide who you're going to be."

"What about you? You just cut your hair off like an Indian for mourning, and you've always been telling us how Choctaws do things. But you just told me it says white on your birth certificate. Why do you have to be just one thing or the other?"

Hoey downshifted again and tapped the brakes on the steep road. The fog had climbed up from the ocean through the redwood canyon and boiled over in streamers onto the road. The truck bumped slowly over a small limb across the road.

"Like I said, I thought a while back that there must be some way to live that was better than I was doing. I remembered Uncle Luther. So I been trying to remember more things, and read things, things that are Indian. I guess if I grew up over in Ireland and knew more about being Irish, I might choose that. I'm not pretending I'm not a half-breed. The damned trouble is I don't know very much. I didn't listen well enough back then."

He touched Cole on the shoulder. "You got a chance to listen to him now. Maybe you can learn some of the things I never learned. You're smarter than me, and you're smarter than your brother, so maybe you can learn something. Just watch and listen, and remember that the old man don't teach only by talking. He sure used to like to talk though."

An hour later, they stopped beneath the broken cliffs of Big Sur to buy cups of coffee and headed north again, Hoey holding the coffee close to his mouth.

"I seen a picture of your grandmother when she was sixteen. She had hair to the floor and must of been the most beautiful woman in Mississippi. Her father was a full blood and he wanted her to marry a full blood like him. She married a dirt-poor white cropper out of spite, and that was your grandfather. Uncle Luther told me all that. He also told me that there wasn't a man in Mississippi could of been better to his wife than my dad was, except for being ashamed she was Indian."

59

"I wish I could have met them," Cole said.

"She could of taught you some things," his father answered. "But you still got Uncle Luther. You got a world in that old man."

The coast highway was a shining black ribbon flung against the cliffs. Cars piled up behind the old truck and passed them on the few straight stretches, horns blaring. Hoey didn't seem to notice the furious drivers as, for the first time in his life as a father, he emptied himself in language. The fog curled up the cliffs and over the berm of the highway so that they breasted it like a flood.

Eleven

The fog rose off the water, though he couldn't see the water, and hovered in the air so that it was the air, a gray close to black so thick that only the movement of the water could have told him his direction. Even three feet away the man was only a suggestion in the fog, a darker shadow that moved rhythmically, rocking in time to the flat sounds of the river. A birdcall ricocheted across the water, and Cole recognized the *kree* of a kingfisher, the sound skipping tentatively before disappearing in the fog. All the time he felt the steady push of the current, stronger in some places and seeming to bend strangely at times but always the same

steady force. He hunched inside the fatigue jacket and

shivered, feeling the damp next to his skin and remembering the brittle gray skeletons of trees that had spread across
the land on either side of the road as far as he could see
until the road had swung closer to the river and the woods
had gotten suddenly thicker, darker, impenetrable looking.

On the bus he had felt still the drone of the plane, and
here in the boat his back and neck vibrated with the movement of the bus as the old man rowed him deeper into the
fog, the outline of his shoulders bobbing in time to the
slapping of the water.

The store had been where Hoey McCurtain had said it
should be, a brown-gray, bare wood thing leaning in upon
itself under a pair of big pecan trees, with the ancient black
man on the porch looking the way Hoey had said he would.
And behind the store then, in the time when a winter day
darkens quickly, Cole saw not the river but the fog climbing
up through the trees and bare vines toward the building.

"Shu," the small, shrivelled man had said finally, after
minutes of watching the buckled wood of the porch floor.
The uncle was still there, in the shack across the river, and
this black man that Cole's father had called only Jobe would
take him across, tonight, in his own boat.

Jobe had stood up and stuck the ten-dollar bill somewhere in his overalls under the old dress coat and then,
saying nothing, walked around the side of the store into
the fog. Cole had watched him disappear and then walked
quickly after him, wondering if he was supposed to and
afraid to walk too fast into what he couldn't see until he
realized he was on a trail between walls of limbs and brush
and the trail dumped him out where the black man stood
in the thickest fog. He could hear the river close behind
Jobe, and he could see the dark bulk of the boat at his feet.

And now he thought back along the route that had
brought him at last into the middle of a river he could hear
but couldn't see with an old man who looked merely like a
darker portion of the suffocating fog. At the airport his
father had shaken his hand, and before that, up the wind-

ing coast highway through Big Sur, he'd talked about Uncle Luther, the river, the swamps he remembered around the uncle's cabin, reminding Cole of the brief time Cole and his brother had been there by the river, too, so that after he'd talked a while Cole remembered the smell of death and rot along the river, the way the mud flaked in patterns when the river went down. The long-hair who came at night to stand in front of their cabin and wait for Hoey McCurtain.

The old man spoke a second before the boat hit the riverbank, and the voice and jolt came at the same time, waking Cole to the fact that the fog had thinned enough for him to see the heavy outlines of the face and dark eyes.

"Luther Cole's cabin right up that trail few hunnerd feet. Stay on the trail you cain't miss it."

Jobe stood and stepped out of the boat and Cole saw the line of shore underneath him. Cole rose carefully, feeling the boat slip beneath his feet, and swung his brother's duffle onto his shoulder.

As soon as Cole stood beside him, Jobe climbed into the boat and started to back it away into the current neither of them could see.

"That ten dollars tells me I ain't never laid eyes on you," he said just before he slipped back into the fog.

Cole listened to the sound of the oars until he couldn't hear them any longer, and then he turned away from the river toward the tall outlines of trees slightly darker than the dark air. Through the fog now he caught a trace of wood smoke, and looking down he could see the black thread of the trail Jobe had mentioned. He took a step and then stopped, realizing all at once that he was scared and that the shivering he felt was from more than cold. Off in the trees beyond where the cabin was supposed to be he heard a screech owl, the call shrill and jagged through the fog. And then he saw him just before he spoke, standing a few feet away on the trail and nothing more than a line of black in the fog.

"I thought you was Hoey," he said, the voice soft and

the words run together. "You felt like him."

"Uncle Luther?" With the question, Cole felt his voice to be brittle and out of place. The old uncle's hat was the same as in his vague, dreamlike memories, and he could see lines of long, straight hair, but the face was hidden.

"I have a fire," Uncle Luther said as he turned and headed away into the darkness.

Cole hurried after the old man and found himself staring at the lighted window of a small cabin. Uncle Luther stood in front of the cabin, and from the dark around him a pair of hounds came spilling and baying.

"You, Yvonne! Hoyo!" the old man said almost quietly. At once the dogs quieted and crouched together six feet from Cole, their faces in the dim light reminding him of deer.

"Come inside." Uncle Luther pulled a leather strap to open the door, and the hounds tumbled in around him so that he had to catch the edge of the doorway to balance himself.

A kerosene lamp lit up the small room and threw shadows across the two plank beds on opposite sides. Uncle Luther dragged a wooden chair from a small table near the door and pushed it toward the potbellied stove in the middle of the room, nodding from Cole to the chair. When Cole leaned the duffle against the table and sat down, the old man pulled off a ragged mackinaw and hung it on a nail in the wall behind the stove. Then he sat on the edge of the bed that had blankets on it. The dogs crouched beneath the bed, watching Cole with incredibly large brown eyes.

"I'm Hoey's son, Cole."

Uncle Luther took off the hat and set it on the bed beside him, and Cole saw that the long hair was heavily streaked with white and that the face was lined with vertical wrinkles like old scars. Parted in the middle, the hair was pulled away from his forehead, and the sunken eyes slanted toward a blunt nose. The lips were thin, his cheeks drawn in and, like the chin, marked by a few long white hairs. The 63 brown eyes caught a glint from the lamp and watched Cole without blinking.

"I have a letter from my father," Cole said.

Uncle Luther nodded and, when Cole unzipped his jacket to pull the letter from his shirt pocket, waved the paper away.

"I know why you're here. We'll read the letter soon. You're the baby, the little one Hoey had across the river."

The old man stopped on the edge of another word, and Cole waited for him to go on. Through the cracks in the stove the fire glowed red, and Cole took off the jacket and hung it on the back of the chair.

"Hungry?"

When Cole nodded, Uncle Luther went to the table and lifted a cloth off a plate of corn bread. The he removed what looked like an upside-down cake pan from a cast-iron skillet.

"You like possum?"

When Uncle Luther grinned, Cole saw that half the front teeth were missing, the ones still there a yellowish brown.

Cole stared at the gray meat, smelling the old cabin, the hounds and grease and years of an old man's life, the thick odor of the river outside. The fire began to scorch his side, and he shifted the chair in front of the stove.

"I don't know," he said finally. "I haven't had possum since we left here."

Uncle Luther grinned again and lifted a chunk of the yellow bread onto a plate, forking the stringy meat beside the bread and then uncovering slices of potato from beneath the possum.

"I thought you was Hoey," he said again, handing Cole the plate. "I felt you coming from the other side of the river, and I expected you but you felt like Hoey." He shook his head in amazement and then sat back on the edge of the bed and scratched the hound named Yvonne between the ears. "I'm slipping."

"Now you can give me that letter from Hoey, and I'll

read it while you eat."

Cole handed him the letter and then started on the corn bread, surprised at how hungry he was, working his way slowly through the pieces of potato toward the possum.

The old man went to a shelf over the table and returned with a pair of wire-rimmed glasses. He hooked the glasses over his ears and read the letter slowly, holding it up so the light from the lamp would fall across it.

"It's good you came," he said finally. "Even back here I heard of that new war they got. Hoey should not give two sons, not even one. It's that President Jackson." He held the letter up and looked at it again. "But that ain't the reason I called you back here."

Cole looked up in surprise, with a forkful of the gray possum meat halfway to his mouth.

"But—"

The old man held up a palm. "We'll talk about these things by and by, nephew. Ain't many men likes to talk as much as me, but I don't get too many visitors nowdays. I ain't used to so much talking all at once. How about cards? Hoey teach you to play poker?"

Cole nodded "yes," as he saw his father's face in the odd angles of the old man's, and he thought that the old uncle was Choctaw, really Choctaw, what he, Cole McCurtain, could never be. As he looked back down to his plate, there was a thin, distant sound outside like a violin string just touched, and the dogs growled beneath the old man's feet and then started to whine. There seemed to be a stirring in the corner of the cabin behind the other bed, and then the old man said "Hush!" and the room quieted.

Uncle Luther grinned the crooked, yellow-toothed grin and said, "We got another visitor out there."

Again came the faint sound, reminding Cole this time of the sound of a baby in another room. "What is it?" he asked, swallowing the last of the corn bread and setting the plate in his lap.

"*Koi*," the old man said. "Painter."

He stood up while Cole watched him and went to a wooden trunk at the foot of the other bed, opening the trunk and pulling out a couple of brown wool blankets.

"Maybe that poker'll have to wait." He poked his chin in the air toward the bunk. "This here bed's yours. Hoey used to sleep there." Seeing the plate in Cole's lap, he added, "You look like you need some sleep. You can wash that plate in the morning."

Cole set the plate on the table, seeing the dogs' eyes move with him, and then he looked back at his father's uncle, wondering how old he was and knowing he couldn't guess closer than twenty years. The face had shrunk back until it could go no further against forehead and cheekbone, and the eyes had the hard black edge Cole had seen sometimes in his father's good eye. The old man moved in slow, gliding steps, as if he walked on water, before standing beside the bed and lowering the overalls to his waist, pulling off the boots and stepping out of the bleached overalls. As Cole stood there, the old man slipped under the blankets and turned his face to the wall and was still, neither sound nor movement suggesting that he breathed.

Cole felt in his duffle bag and pulled out a plastic sack with a toothbrush and toothpaste in it. Dipping a cup of water from a bucket on the table, he opened the door and stepped outside, pulling the door closed behind him. As he brushed his teeth, he smelled and listened to and felt the place where his life had begun. The cold air was thick, and the woods that formed a dark wall around the clearing seemed eager to come nearer to the little cabin, leaning anxiously inward.

He rinsed his mouth and spat on the ground below the steps, and an owl shrieked close by. Feeling fingers of ice in his back, he turned and reentered the cabin. As silently as possible, he unfolded the two blankets and looked at the musty mattress on the bed. Remembering the old man's long underwear, he realized he'd have to sleep in his pants and shirt. He memorized the terrain of the room, and then went to the table and turned the wick of the lamp down until the flame fluttered out. In the dark, he took two steps to the plank bed and sat on the edge and began to unlace his boots. Outside, the sound that had been deep in the trees moved closer, and he heard the cry of a man in pain, the sound muted and liquid.

"*Koi*," the old man had said. A panther. Cole had seen mountain lions in the coast range, and he'd felt them close by, but he'd never heard them and never felt them the way he felt the panther outside the cabin. A panther was a freak, a black accident that happened sometimes to cougars so that the burning gold of the lion turned black and cold.

The panther screamed again, closer now, and Cole looked toward the uncle's back and saw no sign that he had heard the cat. And when he pulled the blankets over himself, he realised that he was stiff, steeled to the next sound and probing the dark room for shapes, forms of things. Again, he sensed movement in a corner beyond the old man's bed, but gradually, when the cries outside came no more, he felt his mind drifting away from the cabin clearing, the river and swamp, raising images of his brother in the dark room. He imagined the push of the current in that other river, shifting, spinning, uncovering things, and his whole life was a singular journey to this moment in a clearing in a place he didn't know. At the edge of the clearing Attis stood, his face wet with rain, his long hair tangled, his eyes dark and wondering, and then Attis stood with Jenna Nemi at the border of trees, and Cole couldn't see his brother's eyes any longer but only Jenna's, matching the color of the rain that had begun to fall.

Then Attis was alone again, his hands in the pockets of the fatigue jacket, his face and eyes dark and focused now. One hand came out of the pocket and reached toward Cole, opening slowly. In the palm lay the arrowhead, the lightning bolt slicing through the black stone. "I shall fear no evil," Attis said. "So I give you these things." Jenna moved up beside Attis, mouthing words Cole couldn't understand, until Attis smiled and said, "You don't owe the bastards nothing. They made Pushmataha a general." Attis began to laugh, the rain pouring heavily off his face and streaming hair. And then Attis began to cry, weeping like a baby until Jenna joined in, the wailing merging in a single cry that became a scream and Cole heard his own voice blending, rising above the others until Attis began to shake him, trying to drag him away.

"Wake up, boy!"

Uncle Luther's face was a few inches from Cole's, and Cole could smell the familiar sweetness of chewing tobacco mixed with the sour stench of old age. Behind the old man the screaming went on, cutting through the cabin like torn tin.

"You been hearing that cat."

And then Cole realized it was the panther, close now, just outside the plank walls of the cabin and shrieking. Huddled beneath the bed, the dogs growled and whined.

"He's mad," the old man said. "Fool white man over to Satartia tried to shoot him last week."

He straightened and remained standing by Cole's bed for a moment and the sound of the panther died away. After another minute, the old man turned back toward his bed, saying, "He's gone now."

Cole waited, but the scream did not come again. Uncle Luther lay down and pulled the blankets over himself, and gradually Cole heard the other sounds return outside the cabin, the hooing of a large owl and the shrill of a smaller one, and then answering calls that sounded deep and comforting. And from far off a sound he connected with vague memories of the alligators that had risen to the surface of the river when he was a child.

Attis came again, holding a hand out toward Cole and smiling in a way that seemed sad and angry at the same time. In the hand was the other arrowhead, the brown flint, and it seemed to throw off heat there in the cold palm. Slowly Attis raised the other hand, opening the closed fist to show the stone doll, pale and dead looking.

Then Attis's face disappeared in a flood of dark water that cut and gouged at the earth, slicing at the edge of the graveyard on Pine Mountain, the dull slapping of oars echoing across the water.

Twelve

When he awoke, the old man was frying bacon on the wood stove. A stack of cornmeal pancakes kept hot in a tin plate on the edge of the stove top, and the coffeepot sat next to the cakes so that over the iced air of the cabin the aromas of all three mixed with the smell of wood smoke. Cole saw that Uncle Luther had tied his long hair back with a piece of red yarn and that below the overalls he wore a pair of rubber slippers with a toe protruding. Neither of the dogs was in the room.

When Cole swung his feet from the blankets and sat up, the old man pointed toward a tin bucket beside the stove. "You can wash if you want to." He stirred the bacon and then forked it onto a tin plate on the table.

Cole stood and peeled off the flannel shirt that smelled of the long trip in the Dodge, the plane, the bus, and Jobe's boat. Shivering, he walked cautiously to the bucket, touching the water and expecting ice. But the water was scalding hot and he jerked his hand away in shock.

When Cole looked up, the old man was laughing silently. He motioned Cole toward an apple crate near the table. "Use one of them washrags," he said, and Cole went to the box and found a stack of ancient, threadbare cloths.

As Cole scrubbed the trip from his face and arms and chest, Uncle Luther watched skeptically. "You better drop your drawers so's you can wash your pecker and everthing else," he said. "I run a clean establishment here."

While Cole did as he was told, the uncle turned back to the stove and slid corn cakes and bacon onto the two plates. When Cole began rummaging in the duffle for a clean shirt and pants, the old man poured coffee into a pair of matching blue enamel cups.

Feeling in the bag, Cole found a pair of Levis and slipped them on. Next he dragged out another flannel shirt like the one he'd taken off, one that had been his brother's. When he pulled the shirt from the dufflebag, something heavy fell out of the folds of cloth onto the floor. He reached down and picked up the leather pouch, feeling the sharp edges and rounded stone inside. When he looked up again, Uncle Luther was watching him, his eyes on the pouch. Then the old man turned quickly back to the coffee, spooning three teaspoons of sugar into one of the cups from a crumpled blue bag at the rear of the table.

Cole started to drop the pouch back into the duffle and then, instead, he slipped it into the pocket of the fatigue jacket, hanging the jacket over the foot of the bed.

The old man sat in the straight-backed chair and poured thick molasses over his corn cakes, motioning Cole toward an upright piece of log that Cole thought must have been a footstool.

"You done some dreaming last night," Uncle Luther said as Cole began to cut the cakes with the edge of his fork. "That's good."

Cole wondered what the old man had heard from the dreams, and he remembered the panther.

"You said somebody shot the panther," he said, trying not to watch as the old man maneuvered a piece of bacon toward the teeth he had left.

With no expression on his face, Uncle Luther said, "Fool named Reese." He chewed for a moment and added, "He didn't know about this *koi*. Thought he could shoot him."

"If it's wounded it's pretty dangerous, isn't it?" Cole tried to keep his voice flat, but underneath the words he heard a trace of the scream during the night.

The old man kept chewing, without answering, and Cole looked up at the ancient bolt-action thirty-ought-six hung on nails above the table. "You going to hunt him?" he asked.

The old man straightened from the plate and looked at him, the eyes nothing but surface now. "A man could try. But maybe it's soul-eater out there. You don't hunt *nalusachito*," he said. "Soul-eater hunts you."

Cole laid the fork back on the plate. "You think this panther is *nalusachito*?" He felt himself begin to shiver again, remembering the river, the shadows down there. "*Nalusachito's* a myth," he said, "an old superstition." The Choctaw word was rough and heavy on his tongue.

"Maybe so. But even if it ain't him, there ain't no reason to shoot a cat. Pretty soon he'll forget he's mad and he'll go away. There's still enough room for all of us. If it's just a painter out there." He walked to the trunk where he'd found the blankets and poked around inside it for a moment. When he came back to the table, he held out a thin leather thong.

"You best wear that medicine you got," he said as Cole took the piece of leather. Then the old man stood up and took a second bucket from beside the stove and went outside while Cole thought of the pouch Attis had made. Was it a medicine?

He had finished the corn cakes and swallowed the last of the coffee by the time Uncle Luther came back in with the bucket full of water and set it on the stove.

"You wash those," the uncle said, pointing at the plates and skillet. "Then I got something to show you cross the river." He went back outside, and Cole heard the hounds come in a long baying arc through the woods, their voices like a blend of joy and terror.

71

He placed more wood in the stove and went to look out the dingy window on the side near his bed, seeing a shed wall covered with drying pelts and the old man emerging from the door with the small, naked body of a raccoon which he threw to the dogs.

Finding a deep pan in the cupboard, Cole divided the hot water, washing and rinsing and setting the things on the table to dry. All the while he thought of his father, trying to imagine Hoey McCurtain as a boy in the cabin, standing by the same stove. Abruptly the distance his father had traveled was sad, tragic, and he knew all at once what his father must have known for many years. They'd all gone too far, and Attis had been right. None of them, not even Hoey McCurtain, could ever go back. It was more than a mix of blood, and his father must have known it all the time he was remembering and reading, trying to teach his sons how to be Choctaw, growing his hair long. The panther that haunted the cabin wasn't *nalusachito*. The soul-eater came from inside. The cat was only what Cole had already imagined it to be, a genetic accident that had come to this place only to be angered by a white man who, like Cole, knew what it really was.

He finished the dishes and went to the jacket, finding the pouch and carefully tying one end of the leather thong to each drawstring. Then he slipped it back into the fatigue jacket, seeing his brother's words on the back of the coat.

Outside the cabin, the fog had slid down toward the river and hung in a thin line over the muddy Yazoo. Around the cabin a half acre had been cleared and was littered with dried cornstalks and melon and squash vines. On the back side of the coon shed a fat Plymouth Rock hen was scratching her way out through a hole in the wire front of a chicken pen.

Uncle Luther stood with his arms folded in the middle of the husks of vines, watching the hen.

"Fox 'll get her," he said, shaking his head. Going to the pen, he shooed the hen back through the hole and bent to tie the chicken wire closed with a piece of string.

Cole hunched his shoulders against the cold, wishing he'd worn a sweater under his brother's jacket, then he followed the old man to the river a hundred feet away where a muddy rowboat nosed up against a small wooden pier.

Uncle Luther stepped out on the suspicious-looking wood and reached for the rope, saying over his shoulder, "Old Jobe can't never find this at night. Colored folks can't see at night the way Indians can, even colored folks that's part Indian, like Jobe."

He stepped into the back of the boat, setting the oars in the oarlocks, and motioned for Cole to shove the boat from the pier.

Out on the river the fog drifted in wisps, leaving the brown water and tall, bare trees exposed between sheets of gray. The smell of the river was sharp and rancid, a blend of wet and rot and musty earth, a disturbing odor Cole had never smelled in California.

Like the old black man, Uncle Luther bent deeply with each oar stroke, moving rhythmically with the slip of the boat over the swirling, dirty water. Cole looked back at the wall of swampy forest around the cabin and thought of his father again. This had been his river, and even in Cole's lifetime his father had followed the old uncle at night in that forest.

On the other side of the river Cole jumped onto the muddy bank and tied the boat to a wooden landing about twice as big as Uncle Luther's, recognizing by feel and smell the place he'd set out from with the man called Jobe. Up the trail that led from the water, he could make out the dark rectangle of the store's back wall, and he started up the trail when he felt a thin, hard hand on his arm.

"This way." Uncle Luther pointed toward a nearly over-grown trail that angled off to the south of the store into thick trees and skeletons of brush and vines.

For half an hour he followed the old man's curved back, 73

protecting his face from the brush with raised arms, and then the trail emptied onto a dirt road. Across the road was a brown, bare wood cabin, squatting on top of log rounds like fat pilings, the windows broken and the yard overrun with weeds and rusting cans and broken glass. The tar paper on the roof was peeled back in ragged flakes, and the great pecan tree behind the house rested a broken branch upon what had been the house's tin chimney.

"Thought you'd want to see the place you used to live," Uncle Luther said as they stood looking across the road. "Place you was born."

Cole remembered then the damp shack that, at five and six years old, he'd thought of as a house. The wood stove and buckled floors and black-papered walls, the kerosene lamps that smoked and flared yellow, the water barrel that had disappeared from the front porch and the outhouse he knew would still be back there out of sight. He remembered his brother's gap-toothed grin and his own surprise as Attis lashed without warning with the cane pole, cutting a gash that had become the scar Cole wore on one eyebrow. And then, for the first time, he remembered that it had been the old man beside him who had carried him up the steps to the house, tearing one of his mother's dish towels to stop the blood. Beside his memory of the shadow who came to call his father to the river now was another memory of being lifted and carried by that shadow with strange, soothing words in a language he couldn't understand. He thought of how he had just come from the place his father had gone to back then and stood where his father must have stood when he walked back before daylight to his family.

"Do you remember your name?"

The old man was looking at him curiously, and when he didn't respond, Uncle Luther added, "The name I give you here."

Cole could see what was becoming the familiar beginning of a grin at the corners of the old man's mouth. When he shook his head, Uncle Luther said, "When your brother hit you that time you was bleeding bad. All over everything, like a stuck shoat. But you never cried, never made a sound. So I give you a Choctaw name then. Not the regular way to do it, but I done it anyway."

Cole waited and the old man began to grin the jack-o-lantern grin once more. "*Taska mikushi humma*," he said, pausing for a moment and then adding, "I think that's right, but I ain't positive, it's been so long and I don't hardly talk Indian no more. Means something like Little-chief-warrior Red. Because you was bleeding all over but you was brave like a warrior."

The old man was grinning widely now, and Cole thought he must be enjoying himself as much as he'd enjoyed anything in a long time. In the pocket of the jacket, Cole fingered the leather bag, running his thumb along the hard edge of one of the arrowheads. He thought of what Uncle Luther had said. A long time before, men had sat on a hillside in California and made the two points in the bag, chipping an idea of who they were into obsidian and flint, and somewhere nearby someone had picked up a white stone and imagined the figure in the bag. And now the old uncle was telling Cole that he had an Indian name, a Choctaw name. A name that had come to him through an act of his brother's, but a name that set him forever apart from Attis, as though he were stone shaped by the old man's words. "Little-chief-warrior Red," he thought to himself, if that was right.

He knew the answer to the question before he asked, but he still had to ask. "Did you give my brother a name, too?"

Uncle Luther looked away. "A man earns his name," he said. Then he turned and started back along the trail they'd come on.

For a moment Cole watched the falling cabin, seeing the two of them playing in the mud of the front yard, remembering how it had smelled and tasted and felt to be a child with his brother there. He remembered Attis boosting

75

him so he could peer over the edge at things in the rain barrel, and he remembered trailing his older brother into the woods along the river. A deep pang of love stabbed through him, nailing him to the spot. Then, with great effort, he turned and started slowly after his father's uncle, letting him stay just out of sight, knowing that he would have to go back for his brother.

Thirteen

Cole rowed the boat toward the little cabin and the swamps, the old man chuckling as Cole awkwardly fought the heavy, sluggish current that tried to spin the boat away. The fog had lifted completely, and in both directions he could see the long curve of the river, as slow and solid as the earth itself, moving only in shifting angles and riffles.

"Up there," Uncle Luther pointed upstream with his lips and chin, "in that deep pool is where the *oka nahullo* live. They got white skins all slippery like fish. They catch you, they turn you into one of them. That ain't a good place to be at night."

Cole glanced up to where something like a big whirlpool deepened at a curve in the river, and then he had to fight to straighten the boat. When he looked back at Uncle Luther he could see the humor in the old man's eyes.

"Are there any other monsters I should know about?" he asked, looking past the old man to the slight wake they left in the brown water.

Uncle Luther was quiet for a moment as if considering, then he said, "Monsters ain't the right word, but I spose you ought to know a little about *bohpuli* and maybe *kasheho-tapalo* so's they don't surprise you in the woods. That first one, he's a little guy, about this big." He held his hand a foot above the edge of the boat. "He likes to have fun, throwing things and confusing people. Some call him a hide-behind. He ain't no danger, don't have a mean bone in his body. That second one, he's a man and a deer and he likes to scare folks when they're out at night." He looked at Cole and grinned. "Even that one wouldn't scare the meanest fucker of mothers in the valley."

Outside the cabin, Cole sat on a round of oak and watched the old man stacking coon skins for the trip to Jobe's store. When the skins had been stacked, Cole helped load them in the boat and shoved it out into the current. From the shore he could still feel Uncle Luther watching him.

When the boat was across the river, Cole went back inside the cabin. One of the hounds whined at the door, and he pushed the door open to let both dogs into the room. They went to their places beneath the old man's bed and lay with their heads on their paws, sagging brown eyes watching him as he went to lie on his bed. Almost immediately he was asleep and running. The black cat sprang effortlessly behind him, while the mud sucked his feet deep into the swamp and threw up vines to trip and hold him. The panther cried like a woman in pain, and Cole heard himself crying also. He wanted to turn and comfort the beast, but when he turned it was Attis who stood there with arms reaching toward him. Cole clutched the pouch at his neck, and his brother lowered the outstretched arms and stood watching him with a terrible longing.

Fourteen

Mundo drove out of the rancher's gate and turned onto the asphalt, slowing again to look at the wide, roiling Salinas where it disappeared and reappeared on either side of the bridge. The water had dropped ten feet, and in the weakening daylight the river looked serene, the shifting, identical prisms of waves edged with yellow froth sliding north toward the sea. A few sycamores and cottonwoods stood three-fourths out of the water in midstream, debris lodged high in their branches. Downriver the trees thickened with shadows and the brush along both banks encroached on the water so that the islands of growth and flotsam seemed to stretch nearly across the water in a tangled sieve. In the bowl formed by Pine Mountain on the west and the sloping rise of the oat hills to the east, the river muscled its way gently downstream, looking as if it might always be such a river and that it had no thought of retreating into the sand again in just a couple of weeks.

Rolling down the window, Mundo took in a chestful of the winter air, with its slight edge and smell of decay. The muddy stir of the river gave the air a heavier aroma than usual. He thought about the Nemis. Everything had been wrong. He thought of Diana stretching against the doorframe, the fall of the light skirt against her long thigh. There had always been something about the Nemi women; they radiated it, a kind of dangerous-feeling sex. Smart sex, he thought.

Leaving the river and curving into town, he drove past Jessard Deal's tavern, the Tiptoe Inn, with its red gabled roof. In front of the tavern Jessard's black Ford pickup nosed against the wall.

On impulse, he pulled the patrol car in under the over-hanging eaves and went into the bar, pushing the heavy oak and steel door open with his foot and working to adjust his eyes to the empty room.

"The moral world comes to deal. It's about time, Mundo. I've been waiting."

The voice was a deep-throated growl from the back of the room near the beer box, while on the other side of the room the form of Jessard Deal reared up to its six-feet-eight-inch height. Disoriented, Mundo spun from the figure to the voice. Then Jessard Deal stepped out of the mirror behind the bar and approached from the opposite direction of the beer box across the room. Mundo saw the thick reddish-brown beard first and then the entirely bald head and the black eyes like chipped glass, and then the outline of the tavern owner came into dim focus in a gray sweat shirt and overalls.

"What would you like, Mundo?"

Mundo watched the land of sky-blue waters ripple in the electric sign over the beer box, the man in the canoe paddling his endless way across the light waves, somebody's idea of heaven. He thought of something Hoey McCurtain had told over beers when the river had flooded the winter before, something about Indians putting their dead up in trees in canoes. Air canoes. He thought of gun ships in Nam swinging in graceful arcs over the padded jungle.

Against the third wall of the bar the jukebox lights glowed softly, with a red, buttery warmth. At the far end of the room, close to Jessard, the pool table soaked up light with its dark green, the cue ball a spot of gray.

The Tiptoe Inn was Amarga's toughest bar, the county's toughest bar, maybe the world's. Jessard Deal crouched in his bar like a trapdoor spider, waiting for customers as if he'd picked his place and built his bar knowing it would be irresistible to the farmers and the truck drivers off the highway and the abalone divers who came twenty-five miles from the coast to drink there. Seething quietly, Jessard

Deal waited for his customers, waited for the noise and spilled beer and shouted threats across the pool table. From behind the bar on Friday and Saturday nights Jessard rehearsed the room like an orchestra, drawing out the extra desperation from desperate men, whetting the cutting edge of his customers. And when the wild edge had been honed to a killing point, Jessard Deal would come out from behind the bar and start to take all the meanness into himself. Mundo had seen it when he was younger, had felt himself sucked into Jessard Deal's violence in the old days so that when it was over and they'd all blown apart and smashed against one another, he had been vaguely aware that the bar's owner had wished it and brought it all to an exact pitch with care and precision. It was known all over the county and as far away as Portland and Las Vegas that periodically, on a Friday or Saturday night, Jessard Deal would come raging out from behind his bar and attack his customers. All of them, any of them, friends or strangers. Jessard groomed them, fed them fine pretzels and stout beer, honed their dull-edged violences until collectively their violence might meet his own, and then he flung himself against them. And they always came back, nervous, drinking hard and fast because any night might be the night, drawn toward Jessard Deal as if he represented some dimly sensed ritual, frightened almost to death of their host.

"You heard anything about Attis McCurtain lately?"

Mundo leaned an elbow on the bar and watched Jessard unfold to his full height, the light from the beer sign rippling across the shiny flesh of his skull.

"You asking me as a cop or McCurtain's friend?"

Mundo hesitated, rubbing a finger along the brass on the bar rail.

"Both, I guess."

Deal moved behind the bar and reached down to grab two glasses from the shelf. Holding both glasses in one hand, he pulled on a draft beer lever and then set a spilling glass in front of Mundo. Reaching again, he came up with a plastic bowl filled with little candy bars.

"Halloween," Deal said with a shrug. "My favorite holiday, and nobody came. Sad, isn't it? I had a mask." The bar owner tore the red and white wrapper from a miniature Baby Ruth and pushed the candy bar into his huge mouth, chewing slowly and then taking a swallow of beer while motioning toward the bowl with his chin.

"I . . ." Mundo began and then, seeing Jessard Deal's eyes, he picked up the dripping glass and took a long pull.

"Christ," Deal said, reaching for another Baby Ruth when both glasses were empty. "I threw your asses out of here when you were both just punks. And now you're the fucking police and McCurtain's. . . ." Chewing reflectively, he looked past Mundo toward the jukebox.

"He's what?"

Deal picked up his own empty glass and pushed it into a basin filled with oily water.

"He's out there in that fucking looney tunes."

Mundo tried to catch the big man's eyes but failed. Hearing the sound of paper, he looked down and realized that his hands were unwrapping one of the little candy bars.

"You hear anything about Attis escaping?"

Deal shrugged and looked beyond Mundo toward the back of the bar. Taking a bite of the Baby Ruth, Mundo got the impression that the enormous man had suddenly shrunken as he watched.

"I haven't heard a thing." The bar owner looked at him and then away again. "I don't hear anything. Who's fucking who, that's all. Whose old lady's getting hosed by his best friend, who's laying pipe. Who cares?"

"Attis liked you." Mundo watched Deal's face.

"Attis didn't have a clue." Now Deal's eyes met Mundo's, and behind the beard was a fragment of chocolate-smeared smile that appeared and vanished in an instant. "Funny thing though, he was tough as chewed leather before he went off to Vietnam and soft as pie when he got back. Not worth a goddamn after he got back." The eyes became dark glass again. "You either. Not worth a good goddamn since you got back." His teeth showed in a mean grin. "I thought Vietnam was supposed to make all you boys tough. Just made looney tunes and cops. Same difference."

Mundo ran a hand through his hair, feeling the sweat and grease. He watched the face in front of him.

Jessard Deal's big hand rifled the bowl of candy and emerged with a Mars Bar. "McCurtain was your buddy, right? That guy out there playing with his pecker at the funny farm wasn't your friend." He tore the end of the wrapper open and pushed the bar a half-inch out of the paper, taking a delicate bite with his front teeth. "That ain't your buddy, Mundo. Your buddy didn't come back from Nam, Mundo. He ain't out at that hospital and he ain't never been out there, get it?"

Deal's chest swelled under his sweat shirt, and he stuffed the remainder of the candy into his mouth, talking around the lump. "Hell, you hardly exist yourself anymore. You walked through that door, I thought I'd just made you up. Like I fucking invented you, know what I mean?" Back to his true size, he stalked to the beer box, levered the door open, and disappeared, pulling the heavy door closed behind him with an implosion of air.

Mundo remained leaning against the bar, watching the man in the canoe paddle across the mirror, the dip of the paddle setting off lemniscate motions, circles circling back upon themselves, the tree-studded islands dark and very clean looking, the empty sky a lighter blue than the rippling waters. He tried for a moment to find a pattern, to locate that precise moment when the first ripple began to set in motion the second, some kind of cause-and-effect thing, but each seeming motion was simultaneously the beginning and end of other motions. He imagined a fish breaking the surface of the sky-blue lake, coming unexpectedly out of those reflected depths to rearrange, to change the story. The paddler in the flannel shirt was a figure of certain

82

knowledge, one who obviously wouldn't tolerate that kind of thing.

As he walked toward the door he heard the beer box open. The bar owner spoke to his back. "You ever read poetry, Morales?"

He turned toward the voice and shook his head. Poetry made him think of the Shakespeare he'd had to read in high school, and that was like trying to read Japanese or something.

"You ought to try Robert Frost," Jessard said, tossing an empty cardboard box on the floor. "Problem with poetry is the right people never read it, and if they do they don't know how to read it right. Why don't you come back to-night, Mundo? You might learn something. But if you come back, be ready to deal."

Mundo turned in time to see the heavy door close again. He took a step in that direction and then stopped. With a shrug he spun and went out the front door of the tavern. As he walked toward the patrol car, he was surprised to find the creamy wrapper of a Milky Way in his fist. Bunching it up, he pivoted on one heel and set for a jump shot, feeling the weight of his body rise upward as he soared, squared to the basket, elbows in and hands cupped, candy wrapper delicate on the fingertips. At the apex of his leap he felt his bootheels almost leave the gravel, his incipient belly lift and fall, and then he came to earth with an expulsion of gas and the faint slap of the holster against his leg. The balled candy wrapper arced to a stop and bounced off the door into a small puddle in the gravel. "Seven years out of school," he thought.

To the west, a sliver of sun showed through what must have been the pines along the crest of the Santa Lucia Mountains, and as he watched that sliver blinked out and the mountains were simply a dark, uneven line against a rapidly graying sky. As if wired to the disappearing sun, the half-dozen lights along the main street began to snap on, winking several times before reaching full, dim lumi-

83

nescence. The blinds of the tavern rose to expose a lighted room and Jessard Deal standing with a cord in one hand and a towel in the other. Deal stared blankly for a moment and then turned to walk around the pool table and disappear. As he watched the tavern owner, Mundo heard a supercharged engine gear down suddenly at his back. He swung around but the street was empty, the only motion the hyphenated neon arrow of the Camino Real Motel across the street. He shook his head to clear it, thinking, "I'll be out there in a padded room pretty soon." From north of town came the pleasing, high-pitched whine of ascending gears: second to third—pause, dying sound—third gear rising in steady, growing contralto to the point of despair—third to fourth with a quick inhaling of breath and then a three-quarter cam geared to a steadily powered rocket going away with a deep, unfamiliar growl. An owl screeched from the trees along the creek.

"Learn anything, Mr. Morales?"

Lee Scott, the FBI agent, stood on the other side of the patrol car, wearing a blue rain parka with the hood crumpled around his neck. Even in the near dark, it seemed to Mundo that he could see the man's sunburned scalp.

Mundo turned to watch a Chevy Impala glide by with girls in front and back. Seeing the cheerleaders from Amarga High cruising like that sent him back in time for a moment. One of the girls waved and he thought it was Theresa Lopez, a distant cousin of his.

"Tunas. Chicks. Burgers. Isn't that what you call them? Don't you call it 'Cruising for burgers'?" Lee Scott was grinning. "I checked you out, Morales. High school, Nam, everything."

Mundo narrowed his eyes and looked at the investigator.

"You're a suspect, Mundo. You ought to know that. It's logical. The missing man's last known visitor, best friend, maybe the ex-boyfriend of the girl he killed, father of her unborn child perhaps."

84   Mundo started around the car.

"Hold it, Morales. I said perhaps. Nobody even said she was knocked up when he killed her. You'd been in Nam. It couldn't have been you even if she was. And probably she wasn't. I made that part up. But you have to admit you're as good a suspect as we have."

Mundo stopped halfway around the front of the car. "What about Dan Nemi?" he said. "The father of the girl he killed."

"Pillar of the community. Man without a stain on his record, unless you call diddling the coach's wife a stain."

He could see Lee Scott's teeth, and he felt like he'd turned over a rock he should never have touched.

"He's a man without a record. You understand that? The man simply has no record. He has never ever done anything wrong, unless you believe in sins of fathers and all that. Isn't that incredible? How can we suspect him? Besides, Dan Nemi was in this tavern last night, airtight alibi. You, on the other hand, with a record like yours I don't see how you got in the military in the first place." Lee Scott reached behind his neck and scratched beneath the parka hood. "Of course we were in a war and they needed everybody they could get for the body counts, even a Mexican with a pretty impressive juvenile record—not anything big, just stuff like petty theft, underage driving and drinking, buying prophylactics under a pseudonymous title."

Again Mundo saw the teeth flash.

"I was over there, too," the man continued. "Intelligence. Kept an eye on guys like you. I know your type."

"Everybody in Amarga has a record like mine," Mundo said. "Kids do those things."

"But not everybody, at the precocious age of twenty-five, becomes a deputy sheriff and the only law enforcement in his little town. And what about all those poor girls, Mundo, the ones whose virtue you stole?"

Mundo stared in amazement at the man who had become just a bulking shadow now. On both sides of the town, the hills were black, uneven lines, and the half-dozen street-lights simmered in an exact north-south line. Through the window of the Tiptoe Inn he could still see the rippling blue of the beer sign.

"You see, one theory is that you cut the hole in the fence for your friend and helped him escape. That you know where he is right now and are going through with this charade to throw us professionals off the track. A subtle thing to do. But there's another theory that you not only helped Attis McCurtain escape but once he was out you murdered him and threw his body in the river in revenge for what he did to that poor, innocent girl. Sure, maybe she fucked a lot, Attis McCurtain and maybe even a few other guys while you both were serving your country, but she was an innocent just the same. In fact, she fucked precisely because she was an innocent, like all these small-town girls. It's a question of power, like the vc. We use what we have— what we're allowed to have. And you, Officer Morales, did what you did in revenge for a sex-slaying—something no one could blame you for and many, in fact, would thank you for. You could confess."

"You're nuts, pendejo." Mundo turned and walked back to the driver's side of the car. "I have to go."

"Dan Nemi was in Jessard Deal's tavern, but we don't know where you were, Mundo. You say your radio was broken and that you were driving around down by the river looking for poachers. But nobody knows what you were doing down there."

Mundo stopped with his hand on the door.

"I was over there, too," Lee Scott said. He had both hands on the top of the car and was leaning across toward Mundo. "Special Forces advisor from '60 to '62. Lead ARVN patrols. Jungle all the time, the whole three years. Had an Indian as point man, a young brave from one of the pueblos in New Mexico. I've always been fascinated by Indians. Made a study of their traditions when I was younger. They're raised not to show pain, you know. It's a shame they're all vanishing. A noble way of life goes with them, something valuable and essential in all of us. This one was a short, quiet fellow, good with a knife, like most of them. We walked into a Montagnard village together, just me and him. Charlie'd hung the pregnant women from trees lining the road to the village and they'd cut their bellies open. The Indian just looked, never said a thing. But I cried like a baby. Later, they got the Indian, but here I am, looking for another Indian. Incredible, isn't it? I'm telling you all this because a man should always know his friends and enemies."

Fifteen

He awoke to the whining of the hounds and sat up. The dogs were at the door and watching him expectantly. Sliding from the small bed, he rose and opened the door and they ran for the woods.

He looked around the little room, seeing something he hadn't noticed before. On a shelf over the table, a thick, green book sat on top of a coffee can.

He lifted the book down and read the title on the spine: *History of the Choctaw, Chickasaw and Natchez Indians.* He opened the book. "I often heard the Choctaws, when engaged in their ancient dances at their former homes east of the Mississippi River, utter in concert and in solemn tone of voice Yar-vo-hah, Yar-vo-yar-hah!"

"Yar-vo-hah," he said tentatively, wondering how it was really pronounced. The book said it was the Great Spirit, but he remembered Hoey McCurtain calling the Great Spirit "Aba."

The door pushed open and Uncle Luther came in carrying a paper sack. "I brung back some pork chops," he said. "Thought you might like pork chops almost as well as possum. I got a funny story about this pig, too." He lifted the newspaper-wrapped chops out of the bag and set the parcel on the table.

"You reading that book?"

Cole closed the book self-consciously. "I just got it down," he said. "It looked interesting."

"Hmph." Uncle Luther held out a hand and Cole gave him the book. "This is a good book. Tells us all about ourselves. " He took his glasses from the shelf and put them on. Then he began to thumb through the book, stopping finally with a satisfied grunt. "This here writer was a man of rare intelligence. For a white man," he said. "Listen to this." He began to read, obviously enjoying the way the words rolled off his tongue. "The Choctaw warrior, as I knew him in his native Mississippi forest, was as fine a specimen of manly perfection as I have ever beheld." He looked up with a grin. "He seemed to be as perfect as the human form could be. Tall, beautiful in symmetry of form and face, graceful, active, straight, fleet, with lofty and independent bearing, he seemed worthy in saying, as he of Juan Fernandez fame: 'I am monarch of all I survey.' His black piercing eye seemed to penetrate and read the very thoughts of the heart, while his firm step proclaimed a feeling sense of his manly independence. Nor did their women fall behind in all that pertains to female beauty."

The old man paused and looked at Cole with a wide grin. "Now there's a man that hit the nail on the head." He seemed to reflect for a moment. "Though he sure must have never met a Choctaw woman like Old Lady Blue Wood. You ever heard of this Juan Fernandez? Us Choctaws didn't get along too good with Spanish people in the old days. Remind me to tell you about Tuscalusa."

Cole shook his head. "Alabama?" He had an absurd vision of the old man at a football game. After a moment he added, "I've never heard of him—Juan Fernandez."

The old man sat down in the chair and tilted his head back. "Onatima—that's Old Lady Blue Wood—she'd make this fellow think twice about them Choctaw women. Listen to what he says." He picked the book up again and searched for a moment before reading. "They were of such unnatural beauty that they literally appeared to light up everything around them. Their shoulders were broad and their carriage true to Nature, which has never been excelled by the hand of art, their long, black tresses hung in flowing waves, extending nearly to the ground; but the beauty of the countenances of many of those Choctaw and Chickasaw girls was so extraordinary that if such faces were seen today in one of the parlors of the fashionable world, they would be considered as a type of beauty hitherto unknown." He placed the book on his lap again and removed the glasses.

"Now parts of that sound like Onatima. That unnatural part, and that part about broad shoulders. She ain't never had a carriage that I know of. And she's more likely to light into anybody that's close than to light 'em up."

Cole laughed out loud and Uncle Luther grinned back at him.

For a moment the old man turned inward, and then he said softly, "You know, truth is Onatima was like that. When Onatima was a girl she'd come into a room and light up that whole room. She was her daddy's pride. Lived in a big house down toward Natchez, with colored servants. Her momma was a white woman from up north, and she wanted Onatima to get a white education, so she sent the girl to school in Jackson. All the men wanted to marry Onatima, Choctaws and white men both, and not just because her daddy was rich. But when she was still a girl she run off on the river with a gambling man—white man. Her daddy, he was a Choctaw, went after them with a gun all the way to New Orleans and brung her back. Then nobody would have her. Her daddy made her marry Old Man Blue Wood to punish her. Her momma just sort of dried up then, living with that old Choctaw man and all that hate. She died a couple years later. Old Man Blue Wood didn't live much longer himself. Got drunk and fell in the river one night. There was people thought Onatima done it with medicine because the Old Man used to get drunk and beat her."

Uncle Luther seemed to surface slowly from those other times. He smiled at Cole. "Onatima brung me that book. She brings books all the time. Says medicine's got to go beyond these swamps now, got to go all out through the world. Because the whole world's out of whack and people like us Indians is the onliest ones that knows how to fix it. So she brings me these books so's I'll know what the world out there is like. I tell her that a man that can dream don't need books. But I like to read anyway, to see what the storytellers in the books say. She brung me a book about a *hanta* whale, a great big white fish. The man that told the story thought kind of in a Indian way. He knew the world had to be balanced, and he knew a man's job was to keep awake and watch everything and know the witchery that was loose in the world. He was on a ship that had the name of a tribe they wiped out a long time ago, and the captain of that ship was out to kill the witchery, something the storyteller knew he couldn't do. The giant fish, like them giant white cannibals that us Choctaws killed out a long time ago, finally takes the captain down to the bottom of the ocean just like the *oka nahullo*. You see, that captain didn't know you can't kill evil, that you just got to see it and know it like the storyteller did."

He pondered for a moment. "But you know, it was a white man's book. There was a Indian man in it who smoked his pipe with the storyteller. A hatchet pipe like ours. At the end, the white-man storyteller come bouncing up to the surface of the ocean on that Indian's coffin. You know, grandson, us Choctaws signed nine treaties with the government, smoking the pipe nine times, and evertime it's just like this book. The white man comes riding to the surface on a Indian's coffin."

"What if a man's white and Indian at the same time?"

The old man looked at the young man for a long time, his eyes narrowed. Finally he nodded, and his eyes met Cole's. "That storyteller in the book forgot his own story," he said. "You see, a man's got to know the stories of his people, and then he's got to make his own story too. A man's got to live in balance, inside and outside, and that man in the book who said he had a eagle in his soul went and killed off his brother. He come riding up on that coffin, but he wasn't complete no more." He reached to place a hand on Cole's shoulder. "You got your brother inside you. You don't need to ride no coffin."

He was quiet for a moment, and when he spoke again his voice was still slow and measured. "That storyteller had a name out of the bible, a name that belonged to a man who had to live alone with his brother's hand against him, in desert places. That's what we say happens to a bad man who dies. When you think about what that storyteller did, you can see why it was like that. He was in bed with the Indian, and they shared the Indian's pipe, and that made them one thing then, like they was man and woman all the same. And that's a kind of balance, you see, Indian and white and man and woman, two bloods in one. When that white storyteller come bouncing up on the Indian's coffin, he killed off half of himself and he lost his power but didn't know it.

"I like to read these books because they're always making up stories, and that's how they make the world the way they want it. This storyteller understood the way the world really was, with everything in balance, good spirits and bad ones and all, but then he changed the story. You see, we got to be aware of the stories they're making about us, and the way they change the stories we already know."

Sixteen

He heard and smelled the river before he saw it, a heavy, fast-moving mass there in the dark, smelling of wet forests and fresh earth, a deep, gutteral sound rising from its broken struggle with trees and brush. The rain curved out of the black sky in thin, sharp lines, striking him in the face and running down his black hair and pricking the backs of his hands. The wool shirt was soaked through, and his jeans were black with water that ran into his boots. He wiped rain from his eyes and looked around in the dark, wondering what reason he had to be there and what purpose he could discover in going anywhere else. Then he remembered, and he looked more eagerly into the darkness, listening for the sounds of their movements.

He'd found the hole in the fence right where the orderly, a conscientious objector serving in the hospital, had said it would be. There'd been no staff people, no guards to challenge him when he slipped out into the yard and ran half-bent across to the fence. The yellow yard lights had refracted in the slanting rain, combining with the medication to bring dizziness and a sense that he ran at odd angles to the earth. Once through the fence he had run toward the river, where the orderly had said they'd be.

At first he'd just shaken his head. He had no desire to leave. There was something loose out there beyond the walls, something terrible that couldn't come into the gray place he was in. If he left, he'd have to confront what was out there, and he wasn't strong enough.

"No," he'd said. "You don't know what's out there."

The orderly had looked nervous, sweating. "It's your chance," he'd said. "If you don't take it they'll keep you in here the rest of your life. They don't trust Indians. They'll keep frying your brains with electricity until you've got tapioca behind your eyes." The short white boy seemed desperate, and Attis had watched him with curiosity.

"Your father will be there. And your brother. They'll take care of you."

Attis's mind sharpened. His father would know what was stalking him out there and would know how to deal with it. And his brother was stronger than him, a warrior who could give him strength. Something out of the jungle, out of that nightmare triple-canopy jungle, had followed him back from the war, and it was out there, crouching and waiting, sniffing after him. Watching the orderly's pale eyes, he remembered the snake. They'd been on patrol in elephant grass, fifteen feet high and sharp as knives. He'd been the first to see it as it rose slowly and gracefully above the grass, its hood spreading and the yellow eyes searching. For a moment he'd just stopped to watch it, amazed by the beautiful form that death could take, and then another man had seen it and screamed and they all began to run. Later they'd said that it had been a real snake, that cobras in that war could be eighteen feet long and rise up like a reminder of what awaited all of them. But he'd known it was something they created, a simple distillation of all their fear and hate conjured out of the land to destroy them.

In his dreams it was blackness. He'd dream of fishing, of a meadow with a blue stream in it and yellow cottonwoods and the smell of lupines and he'd be incredibly happy, and then the blackness would rise up in a corner of the dream and begin to grow and move inward until he woke croaking for breath and moaning. He would sob and wait for the night man to help him wash and change.

When he nodded yes, the orderly seemed relieved and happy. When he padded back to his room to wait for dark, the orderly watched him go and thought that it would be a good thing to help the Indian escape. Maybe he could return to the wilderness and live naturally. Some of them, he knew, had forgotten how to live that way, but probably 93 not this one. And he, who would have been in medical school except for the war, deserved the money he was being paid to arrange the thing.

So Attis crouched there beside the river, listening to the enormous strength of the water and tasting the rain on his lips, trying to penetrate the total blackness of the air to see them. He hunched, listening for the sound of boots in the mud, of breath, the voices of his father and brother. And then it was there in the dark with him, slipping through the drowned grasses and mud, its breath hard and fast in the rain. He had no fear of death. It was something much worse than death that he put his hands out to fend off, but it was all around. He felt it crouch, ready to spring as he stooped and then squatted close to the muddy earth.

Attis stared up wide-eyed at the face looking out of the depths of a hooded parka. A cat's head stared back at him with yellow eyes. He felt the bullet enter his heart, striking suddenly to his center, and he fell backwards into the water.

And then he began to float down the flooded river with logs and old boards and tires and tumbling trees. He wondered why the rain had stopped and why he was no longer cold. An owl flew overhead, heavy winged and slow, its call remaining with him when the bird was gone. A shadow rose from the water and moved slowly away from the drifting body, and its going left him naked and frightened in the knowledge of death.

Seventeen

"How do Choctaws worship the Great Spirit?" he asked, sipping the old man's thick coffee and feeling the warmth of the stove. "Hoey never told me."

Uncle Luther stopped combing his long hair and looked thoughtful. "We don't," he said.

"Don't?"

Uncle Luther shook his head. "Why would we do that? The creator ain't never told us to do that."

Cole considered the new information. He'd never thought before that people only worshiped God because God told them they'd better. Or else.

"It ain't like them holy rollers down to Satartia. They have a good old time whooping up a jamboree and all, but then they go home and they're scared that god of theirs is gonna get mad over some little thing they done. I like to see 'em dance and hear 'em talk in all them different voices, but I wouldn't want to live scared like that."

Cole watched the old man run the plastic comb through his hair. "I have to go back," he said.

Uncle Luther nodded and pushed the hair behind his shoulder. "Soon as you're ready. Did I tell you about that pig? Seems old man Jobe was going to visit a lady friend and not paying much attention when that pig stumbled out of the woods and he run over it. Right off he knew whose pig it was, so he turned his car around and threw it in the trunk and drove home. Had a pig roast behind the store a couple nights ago with twenty or thirty people there. Old Jobe said, 'When a man's eating another man's pig, he better eat fast.' " He grinned widely. "He says he saved us them chops because he was too busy to come across and tell us about the roast. I think he was afraid I'd scare off his other guests."

"Let me tell you about Choctaws," the old man went on. "You ever hear about dueling, the way white people was always doing it in the old days?"

Cole nodded.

"You ever hear of Choctaw dueling?" When Cole shook his head, the old man said, "Well, Choctaws went about it a little different. Let's say a Choctaw challenged another Choctaw to a duel. They agree when they're going to do this and where, and then they both show up with what the white people call seconds, usually a relative or a friend. Then when it's time, each second kills his friend. Don't nobody survive a Choctaw duel. You see, it's a test to see who's ready to die and who ain't. A warrior is always ready to die." He looked very serious. "That kind of dueling kept a town pretty peaceful."

Cole watched the old man's eyes, waiting for something that would tell him it was a joke.

"One time a French man challenged a Choctaw man to a duel." Uncle Luther pronounced the word with a pause, emphasizing "French." "When the French man showed up, the Choctaw was sitting on a keg of black powder holding a match. 'Where's your keg?' he says. Ha!"

The old man's laugh filled the cabin for an instant, and then he was serious again. "Hoey thinks he's got to revenge his son's death," he said. "That's the way he thinks it's 'sposed to be. Us Choctaws you know, have always believed in blood revenge. Somebody kills your relative, you got to kill that person or one of his relatives. That was ironbound, and a man had to do it if he was going to keep living amongst people. Of course such things become complicated. You see, Hoey's son killed that girl and so her folks killed him. They was acting like Choctaws. Now Hoey thinks he's got to revenge their killing. So it won't end. But my nephew is wrong. You must go back and prevent this thing or else it will go out into the world. You throw a rock in the water and it sends little waves everywhere. That's what this world is like, you know. It don't never stop. Now there's a kind of balance. They put a terrible medicine in Hoey's other son, and then he done a terrible thing. And now somebody else done a terrible thing, and it's got to end. I been dreaming this story, and I brung you back here so's you could learn your part in it."

Cole stood up and set the half-empty coffee cup on the table. "I. . . ."

Uncle Luther looked hard at him and he fell quiet. "It used to be simple, but it ain't anymore. You got to go back and stop Hoey from doing that. There's something loose in the world now, something bigger than soul-eater even. Soul-eater's just a little thing now. What your brother was doing in that war, that was part of it. They're doing it everywhere in the world now. And what he did to that girl, that was part of it, and she was part of it, too. Us Choctaws made up stories that told us about these things, stories like soul-eater, so we could have words for such things and watch them carefully. If we didn't have the stories we couldn't live in this world. Like that storyteller in the book about the white fish knew, it takes stories to keep the balance. Only he forgot his own story, like I said. Now Hoey is part of their story, and he forgets who he is. He thinks he must act like a Choctaw, but that's just something he made up like a card game. And he don't know how the world is changing.

"The world is screwy. They took that river and built a wall across it, locking up all the water so it can't run like it's supposed to. Now it's all cockeyed. When the river can't stand it no more, it rears up and starts smashing everything. Then everthing's confused. Fish swim up from the ocean like they been doing forever, but because the river's broken, the water all goes back in the ground and the fish die. I've dreamed it. The fish laying all over that white sand, drying out and dying every year. It's part of a circle, you see, and they broke the circle when they broke that river. And they're doing that all over the world, breaking all the circles."

Cole thought of the steelhead that slipped flashing over the shallows when the river ran, how they caught the sunlight and sent diamonds of water upon the sand. Then he remembered them dead and coated with the dried river moss under muddy cutbanks, so many that the cats and racoons couldn't touch them all.

"There's something else you must do, grandson. When our people came here from the west we carried our bones with us, so many that we had to carry a load and put it down and go back for the rest. It was hard and sometimes we thought about stopping. It took a long, long time to come here to where the pole stood straight, but we made this country our home with our bones, you see. A Choctaw's bones must not be lost."

Cole waited, hearing very faintly the cackling of a hen from the chicken pen and feeling a stirring behind him that he dared not turn around to see.

"You have to find the bones," Uncle Luther said. "And bring them back here. Your brother cannot go on until you do this thing."

The old man again reached to touch his shoulder. Then he stood up and began to unwrap the pork chops.

"Onatima's coming for dinner," he said. "She'll talk to you about books."

Eighteen

The ticklebug's fingers sought the soft muscle inside the little girl's thigh, twisting lightly and causing her to writhe in a torment of giggles.

"Don't, ticklebug," she shrieked. "I don't like that."

Mundo drew his hand back with a mock frown. "I'll make the ticklebug stop, then, chiquita."

"I like the ticklebug," she said, beginning another giggle.

Mundo tickled his daughter's belly as she lay in his lap, causing more hystirical shrieking.

"I still don't understand why you have to."

Gloria stood in the doorway to the kitchen, a dish towel in one hand and a wooden spoon in the other. From the kitchen came the spicy aroma of green chile stew, a recipe she had brought from her childhood home in Santa Fe.

"I can't tell you more than I already did," Mundo said over his shoulder as he petted his daughter's curly black hair. "I'm trying to find some things out, and I think Jessard might help."

"From what I hear, Jessard Deal's never helped anyone." Gloria disappeared into the kitchen and returned with a can of beer.

"Here," she said, handing it to Mundo. "You drink this and save your money on the beer at that bar."

Mundo sighed. "Thanks," he said, taking the beer. "It was Attis I saw in the river, and Jessard knows something. I think if I don't screw up I might find something out tonight."

Gloria came to stand behind his chair and massage his neck. "I wonder how many wives have listened to their husbands say they had business in a bar." She echoed Mundo's sigh. "Even if it was him, Mundo, maybe you should just let it drop. I know Attis was your friend, but look at what he did. You said there was a federal man on the case. Let him figure things out. If it was Attis, you can't help him now." She paused. "You couldn't even help him when he was in the hospital. You tried enough."

Mundo jiggled his daughter on his knee and took a drink from the can. "I didn't try enough. No one tried hard enough, but I was the one that should have understood. It started over there, and I watched it. One time. . . ." He smiled at the little girl and lifted her from his knee, holding her close with his chin touching her hair. "I can't let it drop, Gloria. I keep feeling like there was something that brought me to the bridge right when he was there. Like I was there for some purpose. And the only thing I can do is try to find out more. And there was something odd about the Nemis. They know something. Jessard Deal knows something."

He picked the little girl up and stood, setting her back in the chair where she started to swing her legs. He took another drink and said, "Maybe everybody in this goddamned town knows about it but me." He looked at his wife. "You know anything I don't?"

Gloria gave him a disgusted look. "I'm a cop's wife, remember. People don't tell Gloria Morales what they used to tell Gloria Altamirana." She stood with her legs slightly apart in tight blue jeans, the towel tossed over her shoulder. Her brown hair hung over her red blouse and halfway to her waist, held into a ponytail with a silver-and-turquoise comb. Mundo watched her and marveled yet again at her beauty. Her dark hair framed the brown eyes and fair complexion of a New Mexico Spaniard. She no longer had the girl's body she'd had when they met—her breasts had grown heavier and her hips had rounded into a woman's— but she was if anything more beautiful. The mocking glint in her eyes and angular set of her cheekbones had not changed, and he felt again that he had been incredibly lucky to attract such a woman, especially when her parents had looked with scorn upon a dark-skinned California Chicano. They had told him immediately that they could date their ancestors back to a seventeenth-century Spanish expedition into the New World. When he confided that his ancestors had once owned a large portion of California in a grant from a Spanish king, they had warmed a little. They knew what it was like to be down on your luck for a few generations.

"Go ahead and do your research, Officer Morales, but watch what you probe." She looked at him with arched eyebrows and he smiled. She knew he'd done his share of probing in the county before they met. But then, Gloria had not been innocent of research.

"Querida mía," he said. "Te quiero más que todo."

"Don't try that sophisticated foreign stuff on me. If you do, you'd better lisp a little, like they do in Barthelona." She came close and kissed him on the cheek. "Just be careful down there."

"Come, Maria," she said as she bent and picked up the girl. "We must send our daddy off to do his research."

Mundo sat at the bar watching the reflected land of sky-blue waters once more. The man in the boat reminded him of the land baron who'd had himself pulled in a boat across thousands of dry California acres so he could claim the area as swampland. It was part of the systematic land theft that had made a few white men rich, but he still couldn't help seeing something funny in it and admiring a man that smart.

Behind the bar Jessard Deal and his assistant bartender set out beers and shots of bourbon. The assistant, a thin, pale man in his sixties with sparse white hair and the face of a frightened titmouse, rushed about as if in mortal fear. Mundo watched the old man and the beer sign simultaneously, amazed that the terrified-looking bartender was almost as precise as the boatman in the rippling sign. Again and again Mundo thought the old man would drop a tray or spill a beer in front of a customer, and apparently the old man thought the same, for his timid bird-eyes rolled wildly at such times, but the drop or spill never came.

Jessard Deal glanced occasionally at his assistant with an ironic expression, and then he would shift the same expression to Mundo. From the bar, a pair of identical blondes with dark-rooted hair and leather complexions danced their bony frames between the tables, eyeing the customers with experienced boredom. The rumor was that Jessard had brought both women back from a whorehouse in Juarez.

Mundo saw that Jessard kept it all within the frame of his vision. Behind Jessard the big mirror reflected his shining skull and broad shoulders and beyond Jessard the slow, deliberate movement of the barroom.

Jessard floated down the bar toward him, a shot glass in his huge fist.

"Glad you could make it, Mundo." Jessard set the glass of whiskey in front of Mundo, and when Mundo opened his mouth to refuse, Jessard's stare hardened.

"Guests must accept my gifts," Jessard Deal said. "It's an old tradition with us redskins."

"Thank you," Mundo said, hearing his voice come out in something close to a croaking whisper.

This time Jessard smiled openly, and Mundo realized just before he could respond that the smile was directed toward something over his shoulder. In the mirror he saw what it was. At a small table a very large man was beginning to stir. He had a much smaller man by the shirt collar and was holding him up out of his chair with one hand. Mundo could see the big man's mouth move, and he could see the other man's face contorting with words, but he could make out nothing that was said. In the background the jukebox wailed a Hank Williams song about crawfish pie and big fun.

Just as Mundo thought Jessard might come around the bar, he saw the big man set the little one down and then reach to pat the victim's head. In the mirror the little man said something and smiled timidly, and the other man bent his head toward the ceiling and roared a laugh that Mundo heard above the jukebox, pool tables, and assorted noises. The back of Jessard Deal's skull wrinkled into his line of vision, and then he realized Jessard was leaning on the bar and staring into his face.

"A truck driver from Oklahoma City," Jessard said with a nod toward the room behind Mundo. "By special invitation." He signaled to one of the blondes and then pointed at the truck driver. The blonde came to the bar, where

Jessard poured a double shot of Jack Daniels and matched it with a beer. The blonde turned without expression and carried the shot and chaser to the truck driver's table. The big man said something, and with a bored face the waitress nodded her head toward Jessard Deal and then moved on to another table.

"You got to treat your best customers right, don't you think?" Jessard looked at Mundo with a conspiratorial grin.

Mundo turned around on his stool to look at the truck driver, who was now in earnest conversation with his victim. He glanced at the other tables, where men, almost exclusively men, were drinking hard and fast and talking in low, tight voices. Probably half the men in the county who had a significant criminal record were in the bar. He turned back around to see Jessard Deal at the other end of the bar talking with Dan Nemi. Beside the rancher was Lee Scott.

With his hat on the rancher stood a head taller than the federal investigator and every other man there except Jessard Deal. In his western-cut sport coat and slacks Dan Nemi stuck out amidst the truck drivers and ranch hands, and Mundo saw a number of them swivel very slowly to eye the rancher with contempt. He waited for Nemi to turn so that he could see his face, expecting the rancher and county supervisor to be frightened, as anyone in his right mind would have been. But when Nemi turned to scan the bar, his expression was one of amusement. His eyes took it all in, and then he saw Mundo. With a wave and a nod toward Jessard, he moved down the bar with Lee Scott close behind.

"Mind if we join you, Mundo?" Nemi said with a friendly smile.

Mundo shrugged and looked at his beer.

The rancher took off his hat and set in on the bar. "You know Mr. Scott, don't you, Mundo?"

Mundo turned from the beer and looked at Lee Scott. To his surprise Scott looked very frightened. Sweat stood out

103

on his forehead, and even as he nodded to Mundo his eyes shifted to take in as much of the bar as he could. One hand was inside the lapel of his sportcoat.

"I met Mr. Scott out at the hospital," Mundo said.

"Oh yes, the hospital. Of course." Nemi signaled to the old man who was now behind the bar, and when he approached, the rancher ordered two draft beers. "Strange how Attis McCurtain just disappeared like that, isn't it?"

The rancher was smiling broadly, his even, white teeth glinting from the light of neon signs.

Mundo considered for a moment. "A body disappears pretty fast in a river."

Nemi placed a five on the bar and picked up one of the mugs, shoving the second one toward Lee Scott on the stool at his back. "So you still think you saw him?"

"That's right."

"How do you think he got in the river?"

Lee Scott was off his stool and standing at the rancher's shoulder, craning to hear the conversation. His face was red and sweating furiously.

"I think somebody put him there."

Nemi shook his head. "Murder?"

Mundo nodded.

"You have any clues, any tips, any idea who might have done it?"

"I have an idea it was you. Who else had such a good reason?"

Nemi laughed out loud. "Okay, you're right, I did it. But how are you going to prove it? Did you find the body yet?"

"I will."

"Now just a minute, Morales," Lee Scott broke in, speaking rapidly. "You can't just accuse the most important man in your county like that. You don't have anything to go on. Mr. Nemi has an ironclad alibi, with a number of witnesses." He looked from Mundo to Nemi and back again, taking a handkerchief out of his sportcoat to wipe his forehead and cheeks. "The federal government has an interest in this, and we're convinced McCurtain has gone into hiding."

"Where?" Mundo turned for the first time toward the investigator.

"Well, we know the McCurtains are Indians and have Indian relatives down in the south. We think he might have gone down there, to hide out with his Indian relatives. We have some men on their way back there."

"The only place Attis has gone is down the river," Mundo replied.

"Suppose I really did it," Nemi said. "Suppose I told you right now that I did it. What could you do about it? I could deny it five minutes from now, and you wouldn't have a thing to go on. Besides, no one in this town would blame me if I had, would they?"

Jessard Deal appeared in front of Mundo with a shot glass and a mug of beer. The tavern owner winked at Mundo and moved away down the bar. In the mirror, the rippling man seemed to be having trouble with one oar.

"Okay, Mundo. I did it. I killed your buddy and dumped him in the river. Now what do you do?"

Mundo downed the bourbon and took a pull on the beer. "I arrest you and have this fed here testify that you confessed."

"But, Mundo, I didn't confess. I don't know what you're talking about. Do you, Mr. Scott?"

Lee Scott was watching two men beginning to argue at the pool table. One hand had crept back inside his coat.

"I don't know what he's talking about," Scott said quickly. "I was over there in Nam, you know. Special forces, Navy. Saw a lot of fucked-up brains, men having all kinds of hallucinations. It wasn't a war, it was the god-damned Twilight Zone. The dead walked those jungles in the screwed-up brains of their buddies. Long lines of walking dead, tramping through their buddies' minds. The dead walked in daylight. So many we couldn't count them all. A country full of corpses and trained dolphins."

"It wasn't a hallucination." Mundo spoke to the two faces in the mirror, while behind the faces a man was swinging, slowly and carefully, a pool cue down on another man's head. Other faces swiveled in the mirror to watch. The man in the boat seemed to be moving in erratic circles. An enormous hand intercepted the cue stick before it reached the amazed face toward which it was aimed. The truck driver flexed the muscles of his chest and snapped the cue stick, while the ranch hand who had wielded the stick backed away in and toward the mirror. The trucker tilted his head back and roared, and the little man he had been choking earlier appeared beside him in the mirror. With a casual motion the big man backhanded the smaller man across the face and sent him limply into the pool table.

Two men stood up from another table, each as hard edged as a splitting maul, both dressed identically in blue jeans and denim shirts and work boots, with hair cut high above the ears. The two approached the big man in the mirror, and Mundo could see that one of the men had wrapped a rodeo belt buckle around one fist. Behind the two men the blonde waitresses stood poised together with trays of beer and shot glasses, watching with bored expressions.

"It was me, Mundo. I did it."

Dan Nemi leaned close and spoke in a whisper and Mundo began to get up from the stool to face the taller man when, out of the corner of his eye, he saw the little man rise in the mirror beside the pool table. In his hand the man held a red ball and, as Mundo stared at the mirror, the man's arm moved back and began to launch the ball toward Mundo's head. Just before the release, half of a cue stick caught the little man beneath an ear and lifted him onto the green felt table. Mundo watched the arc of the red ball as it spun through the rippling blue waters, past the surprised boatman to disappear behind Mundo's head. The last thing Mundo saw was the great, buoyant body of Jessard Deal soaring above the bar.

Nineteen

Mundo sat in his car watching the river carry yellow foam and trash toward the ocean. The flood had fallen to half its former size, and debris hung in the tangled branches of trees and lay heavily atop the mat of brush between the trees. Limbs quivered with the force of the brown water, but the menace had gone out of the river. Overhead, the distant winter sun shone through a vaguely blue sky. He had driven thirty miles of back roads, through the ranch country east of the river, to sit at this bridge and watch the river coming toward him.

Underneath a small bandage the side of his head still throbbed, and he thought bitterly about the little patch of hair they had shaved off to stitch up the cut. When the bandage came off, maybe he'd buy a hat. He pictured the Stetson he planned to get. Bigger than Nemi's Cattleman.

It could be between this bridge and the other bridge fifteen miles upstream, or it could be between this bridge and the ocean a hundred miles to the north. Would it float indefinitely, he wondered, or did bodies eventually sink? He flinched at the image of Attis's body tumbling and bumping along the bottom of the river, just another item in the immense amount of flotsam the river collected in its passing. Once he'd seen a photograph of a body pulled from an Alaskan river. Every orifice had been packed with river silt. The river had treated the body no differently than it would have treated an old tire.

He wondered if Hoey McCurtain would wait until the body was found, if it was found. He didn't think so. Anger mounted at his friend's father for complicating the picture. He'd have to find Attis's body to prove the murder, and he'd have to prevent Attis's father from committing another

107

murder at the same time. He wished the government hadn't been after Cole, because Attis's brother might have been able to help him.

He looked upstream to where the river came sweeping in a dizzying braid of brown streams between islands of trees and brush, and then he turned to watch the water move steadily away in the same striated pattern. Somewhere there was a body. Would hounds help, or did such a body lose its smell? In the movies, fugitives waded rivers or floated downstream to evade the hounds. So how the hell could it be done? He shook his head and winced at the pain. He'd wait until the water was all but gone, and he'd search the river. In the meantime, he'd find Hoey McCurtain.

Twenty

Old Lady Blue Wood removed the wool shawl from her head and laid it carefully on the end of the old man's bed. When she turned toward him, Cole was shocked by the beauty of her face beneath the red turban with its dangling hawk feathers. He felt that he'd never seen eyes that shone like the brown ones in the wrinkled face, as if light came from an unimaginable depth. The infinitely wrinkled skin of the face, stretched over sharp cheekbones and a delicately shaped nose and chin, seemed also to glow, and her smile uncovered a fine, even line of white teeth. Framing the face was long hair of pure silver. When she removed the heavy overcoat, he saw that she wore a man's red wool shirt tucked into black wool pants held up by suspenders the same color as the turban.

"You're Cole McCurtain. Why aren't you in school?"

Caught off guard, Cole stammered, "I graduated."

"I don't mean piss-ant high school," she replied, looking him up and down. "I mean college. It's time one of you McCurtains made something of yourself."

"Onatima went to college," Uncle Luther said from the stove where he was inspecting a pot of hominy. "And she don't let nobody forget it."

"If I hadn't gone to college, old man, you'd be reading shoot-'em-ups instead of the stories that count." She swung back to Cole. "He used to read those cowboys-and-Indians novels he borrowed from that old colored man across the river. I told him that those aren't the real stories, the ones we have to pay attention to, the ones they use to change the world."

Uncle Luther turned with a pot lid in his hand and winked at Cole. "She don't understand that it's them cow-boys-and-injuns stories that really count. I tell her that it's all them kids we got to worry about—Billy the Kid, the Comanche Kid—all them kids in the shoot-'em-ups." He set the lid back on the hominy. "You see, grandson, white people don't really want to grow up, so they tell these stories about kids that go around acting like they never heard of growing up. They don't have no homes, and they don't know about taking care of mother earth or any mother at all. That's the story we got to worry about, all them kids that white people make heroes out of. There ain't nothing more dangerous than a man or woman that digs their heels in and won't grow up."

He seemed to reflect for a moment and the old lady watched him with amusement. "That's what the white peo-ple wanted to do to us Indians, you know. That's why they made up all that great-white-father stuff, to turn us into kids so's we couldn't know who we really was. And that's why they thought they could just send all us Indians out there to what they called Indian Territory. To them one place was as good as another. Sure, they wanted Choctaw and Chickasaw land here because it was so good, but they really thought we shouldn't care where we lived. These white people been packing up and leaving some place as long as they could remember. They mostly don't even know where their people's bones are."

"What I tell this old man is that there are bigger stories, the ones that they make up to change the world. Those are the ones this old man's got to read."

"An old man dreams," Uncle Luther said as he turned a skillet of corn bread out onto a plate.

"An old woman dreams, too," Onatima countered. "But there's more to it than dreaming. Did you tell him about the bones?"

Uncle Luther was pulling a skillet of pork chops off the stove, and he stopped and stared at the old woman, holding the skillet in one hand with a washcloth around the handle.

"You never was a woman wasted time," he said finally.

"You didn't tell him." She glared at the old man who turned and forked the chops onto three plates.

Onatima turned from Uncle Luther and looked hard at Cole until he began to shift nervously where he had been standing since she came in.

"Sit down, boy," she said gently.

Cole sat back on the edge of his bed, feeling once again a movement in the shadows at the far end of the other bed. When he turned to look, there was nothing there.

"You know about the *shilombish,* grandson?"

When he shook his head she glared at the old man and said, "You and that nephew both have neglected this boy's education." She began in a patient voice.

"Every person has two shadows, grandson, an inside shadow and an outside one. When a person dies, the inside shadow, the *shilombish*—that's kind of like what white people call the soul—goes to wherever it's supposed to go. Most people's inside shadow goes to a good place where there's always plenty of game to hunt and it's never cold and people play ball games all year round. A person who's murdered someone can't go to that place. That person's *shilombish* goes to a different place where the earth is hard and dry and nothing grows. The inside shadow is taken down a black river full of snakes to a place where all the trees are dead and the people cry and suffer all the time." She paused and studied Cole for a moment. "Now I'm not speaking metaphorically. You've been raised differently and this may sound strange to you. But think about it. Is it any more strange than a religion that says one day angels will come blowing trumpets and all the dead will rise out of their graves? I've always found that idea rather revolting."

The old man began to speak but she waved a hand to silence him. "Now the outside shadow, the *shilup*, is different. It stays around the dead person's body and scares people. It's similar to what white people call a ghost. That's what you've been noticing stirring around over there in the corner."

Cole looked quickly over his shoulder. In the corner behind the old man's bed he could now see a shadow gathered, slightly darker than the other shadows in the room. It seemed to shift as he watched.

"Don't be afraid," Onatima said. "It's not something like soul-eater for you to be afraid of. It's the *shilup*, that's all. And it's waiting for its bones."

Uncle Luther stepped close behind the old lady and motioned to Cole with a crooked finger. "I wonder if Onatima ain't got those words backwards. It's a tricky language. Our dinner is going to get colder than a old lady's heart if we don't eat," he said.

Onatima turned and glared again at the old man. Then she moved to the little table and sat in the straight-backed chair. Uncle Luther pushed a log stool up to the table for Cole and moved another one into place for himself on the other side of Onatima.

"Old Lady Blue Wood's done give you a whole education in ten minutes," Uncle Luther said as he broke a piece of corn bread off and spread molasses on it. "You see, grandson, the world's both more simple and more complicated than most people know. It's simple because all we really got to do is stay awake and keep our eyes open. That means we got to watch out for our animal relatives and human relatives both, for the waters and the earth we walk on. That part's easy, because a person knows without thinking what the right way to live is. It's when people start thinking too much and messing with things that we get in trouble. Now the complicated part comes because we got to be awake all the time. Most people's asleep all the time, just walking around in their sleep, fighting in their sleep, making children and dying without ever waking up. Wars like that one Hoey's other son went to is fought by men in their sleep. They shoot and stab and die without ever waking up. And they don't dream in that sleep. What they think is dreams, when the dead come to them, is just part of the same thing they think is waking. Most people think dreams is only for the time we're asleep, they don't know that dreams is how we see in the dark, when we're most awake. The great spirit don't want churches and hullabaloo, he just wants us to stay awake and look with more than our eyes. That one in the corner there, he's awake now, and that's what he ain't never been before."

Cole looked over his shoulder at the corner of the room again. What was there wasn't Attis. He could feel that. It was something beyond Attis, something that had existed when his brother did not and that existed now that his brother was not. And he could feel a terrible loneliness emanating from that part of the room, a yearning he thought he could almost reach out and touch. It occurred to him that this shadow must have been there with his brother all the time. When they climbed golden, oat-covered hills after sunrise to smell the ocean just over the coast range, when they took turns in the pools of the little, twisting creeks, this shadow had been there with Attis, crouching with Attis, sniffing the sea air with them. And

Attis hadn't known because the two had been one then, *shilombish* and *shilup*, inside and outside shadows. Only in death did one become two. He thought of the old man's description of the storyteller, spinning atop his brother's coffin. Was the survivor then a ghost?

"You know, Onatima brung me another book a while back that got me to thinking about the difference between white people and us," the old man said after several minutes while they all ate in silence. "It was about this boy and a colored man that run away down the big river on a raft. The colored man was a slave that wanted to get free, and the boy was running away from all the witchery in the white world that made him think wrong. Funny thing is, they had a wigwam in the middle of that raft and they felt safe there. Then at the end of that book the boy thinks he's going to light out for Indian Territory all by hisself, like that's the onliest way he can live right, being out there all by hisself. I got a terrible feeling thinking of that good boy out there all alone. Of course some Indian family would take that boy in, and maybe that's what he wanted. But you know the boy kept making up stories about different families he wanted and then killing them families off in the stories, so I think that white boy knew he was part of something that wouldn't let him live with no Indians. It's like these white people want to keep killing off everything so's one day they'll be alone, no parents, no family, not even mother earth. Just one kid out there all alone somewhere."

"You have to find the bones, grandson." Onatima paused with a piece of corn bread in her hand. "He's waiting for his bones, and he can't go on until we bring them back." She took a bite of the corn bread and looked from the boy to Uncle Luther. "This old man, you see, couldn't leave him out there in the cold on that river. So he did a dangerous thing. He spoke that boy's name out loud and brought the shadow back here."

She looked admiringly at the old man. "It was a brave   113 thing to do, you know, because a shadow is very lonely and always wants to take a loved one, or anyone, with it. But this old man has powerful medicine, the most powerful there is, and he won't let that *shilup* take nobody."

Cole shifted his gaze to Uncle Luther, who chewed methodically while looking at his plate. When the old man finally looked up, he said, "Onatima's right, grandson. You got to go back for them bones. I can help you."

"There are two men coming here, to this cabin," Onatima said. "Coming in the dark and seeking that one in the corner."

Uncle Luther looked at the old woman with his eyes half closed. "You dream that, old lady?"

Onatima looked meditative for a moment. "Old Jobe told me they were snooping around his store a couple of days ago. He says they say they're from the government. Jobe didn't tell them anything, but they know who you are, old man, and it won't take them too long to find out about this cabin."

Uncle Luther nodded. "I seen them." Turning to Cole, he said, "Us Indians always end up on the short end when government men come around. These two are having an interesting experience right now. Something they can tell their grandkids about." He grinned.

"Isn't his grammar terrible?" Onatima said, grinning at Cole. "You'd never know this old man had gone all the way to Haskell and been the top student in his class." She spoke as if the old man wasn't in the room. "You see, I know why he speaks the way he does. He thinks that if he talks like all the other backwoods Indians and colored and white trash around here they won't be so scared of him. But people are always going to be afraid of a man with power. Or a woman."

She looked back at Uncle Luther. "What are you doing to those poor men?"

He closed his eyes for a moment and creased his lips. "It
114   ain't nothing so terrible, Onatima. Just a little night walk."

Onatima glared and then looked back at Cole. "Old man ain't going to hurt those men any. He never hurts anything."

Cole thought about the coon skins Uncle Luther had taken to Jobe's store.

"The animals understand," the old lady said.

Cole looked at her in surprise and she smiled kindly. "Choctaw people have been living right here for at least two thousand years according to the books," she said. "If we had not respected this world and treated it with care, we would have long ago destroyed it. You see what white people have done in only a few hundred years?"

She ate the last piece of pork chop on her plate and turned in the direction of Uncle Luther. "You can't leave those poor men out there all night. You know why they've come, so now you'd better go get them."

Uncle Luther sighed like a henpecked husband, and when he looked at Cole one eye winked subtly. "These here is government men, old lady."

"So? Those tribal bigbellies that give you your money are government men, too. Would you leave them out there?"

Uncle Luther seemed to think for a moment. "Yes, I believe I would."

"Luther Cole, you get out there and find those men."

Wiping the last of his gravy up with his last piece of corn bread, the old man sighed again. "You see, grandson, women is the ones that's always run this tribe. They used to pretend men was in charge, but nowadays they don't even pretend."

Cole tried to smile, but his confusion trapped the smile halfway, so that he thought he must look like he was about to cry.

Uncle Luther stood up and pushed his plate back on the table. "Would you care to come with us, Miz Blue Wood, or do you want to stay and wash these dishes?"

The old lady snorted. "You put those men out in the swamps in the middle of the night, and I'm not about to go

115

wading around out there to help you find them. And I'm not going to wash your dishes either." She smiled sweetly at Cole. "I'll just stay here and do some reading while you help Luther." From the pocket of the overcoat she pulled a small paperback that said *The Crying of Lot 49* on the cover.

"You want us to go now?" Uncle Luther asked with feigned surprise. "It ain't really a swamp, you know, just some wet woods."

"You bring those men back here so they can dry out. I'll make some tea."

"Better get your boots on, grandson," the old man said.

Cole sat on the edge of his bunk to lace up his boots and then stood and slipped his brother's jacket on, glancing nervously at the corner of the room where the shadow seemed to stir.

Uncle Luther had his own boots and heavy coat on. He reached to tie his hair back with a piece of yarn, and then he lifted the big floppy hat down from its nail and placed it carefully on his head. He looked critically at Cole for a moment and then said, "You better wear that medicine you brung."

Cole found the leather pouch in the jacket pocket and placed it around his neck and zipped the fatigue jacket over it, turning the collar up.

Uncle Luther lifted the rifle from the wall and slipped three cartridges into the chamber, placing the remaining shells in his coat pocket. Then he pulled the door open and stepped out into the moonless night.

"Should I bring the flashlight?" Cole asked from the doorway.

"Lights make targets," came the reply from outside. "These government men might be a little jumpy right about now. I doubt their guns work too good, but we'd best not take chances."

As Luther spoke they heard two quick pistol shots from somewhere deep in the woods.

Twenty-one

He stared in amazement at the thick, quivering surface. Seconds before, his companion had tripped on something and done a belly flop there, and now he was gone. The black-looking liquid shimmered like a foul jello in the beam of his flashlight, the witch's concoction that floated on the surface making it look just like the rest of the woods, something between liquid and solid. There, where Hicks had disappeared, it was obviously more liquid than where he stood three feet away.

He edged toward the soup, keeping the light on the ground in front of him and testing each step with the toe of his boot. Behind him he heard the sound again, and he whirled with the light. Only the shadows of tree trunks and the tangled web of vines and brush showed. When he shifted the light back to the liquid, a head was rising slowly, trailing a veil of lacy black.

"Jesus H. fucking Christ," Hicks tried to scream, but the words came out in an incoherent sputter. He sat up in the stagnant pool, his head and neck showing above the surface. When Harwood put the light on the head, he saw a mess of twigs and stringy vegetation with a face behind it.

"Help me out of this fucking cesspool," the man in the water finally shouted, shoving a hand toward Harwood from beneath the surface.

Harwood shifted the flashlight to his left hand and extended his right, grasping the hand and pulling. The other man surged out of the liquid, landing on the firmer ground beside Harwood who backed up with a grunt and wiped his hand on his pants.

"You smell like shit, Hicks."

"You stick your head in there and see what it smells like. 117

Gimme your handkerchief."

Harwood pulled a large bandana from a pocket of his fatigue pants and handed it to Hicks, keeping an arm's length away. "Man, you fell into some pool of shit there."

Hicks shook his head, sending debris flying into the dark. Then he wiped his face slowly and carefully.

"We'll just take the nigger's boat and go get the Indian. That's what you said, remember." Hicks glared through the dark at his bigger companion. "Piece of cake, right? "

From the wall of darkness around them came a jagged scream.

"Holy shit," Hicks sputtered. "That sounded like a woman."

"That's no woman," the other answered. "You've never heard a big cat, have you? That's a big one. Must be one of the pumas that live in these woods. Funny, I thought they'd all been hunted out a long time ago."

They stood in the dark listening for a moment and then Hicks began brushing debris off his jump suit.

"You know," Harwood said, "people are usually afraid of wolves. People have a primordial fear of wolves. But the fact is there's never been a proven attack by a wolf on man in the continental United States. Never. On the other hand, there have been numerous documented attacks by pumas, or cougars, or whatever you want to call them. They've been known to kill and eat children."

"All I fucking need right now is a goddamn lecture on the eating habits of whatever's out there," Hicks sputtered. "Let's just get the fuck out of this swamp. To hell with the Indian. To hell with you and the whole thing."

"You should be grateful I made you wear that jump suit," Harwood said. "You probably didn't get too much water inside it, did you?"

"Not more than fifty or sixty gallons. I had the god-damned zipper open."

"Not too bright, Hicks."

The scream came from the dark beside them, cutting

through the night like a broken bottle, a shattering wail.

"Shit!" Harwood yelled, swinging the flashlight in the direction of the sound and framing the coiled body of an enormous black cat, the eyes a burning yellow and the face infinitely blacker than the surrounding darkness. The cat screamed again, its lips curled back over teeth like daggers.

In an instant Harwood had his pistol out of the shoulder holster and aimed, one-handed, at the panther.

"Shoot," Hicks screamed just as Harwood squeezed off two fast rounds from the nine millimeter.

Then the panther was gone. Harwood stared at the circle of light where the cat had crouched, trying to remember the moment the animal had turned and ran or leaped into the brush, or something. But all he recalled was the fact that it had been there and now it wasn't. I must have closed my eyes when I fired, he thought, knowing that in his entire life he had never closed his eyes when he fired a gun.

"Where did it go?" Hicks now had his own gun out and was peering at the spot between tree trunks where the cat had been. "Where the fuck did it go?"

Harwood tiptoed to the place where the panther had been, shifting the light back and forth, to each side and deeper into the woods. As he got closer, he widened the circle of light, keeping the pistol in front of him. When he was there, he shone the light all around, trying to penetrate the thick growth, and then he moved the light close to the ground.

"There's no blood, no hair, no nothing," Harwood said.

"How could you miss that sonofabitch?" Hicks had moved closer behind his partner. "I wish to hell I hadn't lost my flashlight in that hole."

I couldn't have missed him, Harwood thought. There's no way I could have missed him. "I couldn't have missed," he said.

"Great. Now we've got a wounded cat out there who didn't like us to start with." Listening to Hicks's voice, Harwood thought his partner was about to cry.

Harwood fished in a pocket of his parka and brought out

a small compass. "It's time to just get the hell out of here," he said. "We can get some local assholes to find that old man's cabin."

"You're going to get us out of this shit hole with a Boy Scout compass?"

"Look," Harwood said patiently. "We came due east from the river, I checked all the way. It's simple. Now we head due west and we'll get back to the boat."

"After three fucking hours lost in this shit, you tell me we can just turn around and walk straight back to that stinking boat?"

Harwood held the compass out and shone the flashlight on it. The needle on the compass was spinning in slow circles. He turned the housing, shook it, held it out again. The needle spun very slowly.

"Know what, Hicks?" he said. "You're right. We're totally fucked. The compass is busted."

"We're going to die in the asshole of the world," Hicks moaned. "If we don't drown in this sewage or get bitten by a fucking snake, we're going to be killed by a giant goddamned black cat you wounded."

"I've never seen a compass do this," Harwood muttered, more to himself than to Hicks. "Not in Korea or Nam or anywhere. Not like this."

"So what are we going to do, mister survivalist?" The sarcasm in Hicks's voice gave it more strength, and Harwood looked at the other man approvingly.

"For a while there I thought you were just going to piss your pants and start crying," Harwood said softly, adding, "What we're going to do is build a fire and wait for daylight."

"Build a fire in this fucking quagmire?"

"Shut up and start looking for dry sticks," Harwood said. "And watch what you're grabbing. There's a lot of snakes in these woods."

Hicks had been reaching for a clump of what looked like twigs, but at Harwood's words he jerked his hand back as if he'd touched fire.

"You've got the flashlight," he said. "You find the fucking wood. I'm going to stand right here."

Harwood sighed and began probing the edges of their little clearing, shoving the light close to twigs and downed branches before picking anything up. Every few minutes he returned to where Hicks stood and dropped a half-armload of wood. After twenty minutes he had a good-sized pile and he began pulling the trailing moss from the branches of trees overhead.

"This stuff's better than newspaper," he said as he set about making a pyramid of sticks over the moss.

When he had the pyramid neatly built, with larger branches over twigs and several sizable chunks of dry wood ready to add when the fire got going, he reached into a pocket of his fatigue pants. Finding nothing, he tried another pocket and then he began patting all the pockets of his pants and coat. Finally he was silent.

"I lost my lighter, Hicks. Let me have yours."

"Lost your lighter? I thought you were some big special forces guy, green beret or something."

"Give me your goddamned lighter, Hicks."

Hicks began searching the pockets of his jump suit, starting slowly but soon patting all over the jump suit frantically.

"It's gone," he said. "I had it in this pocket, but it's gone."

Harwood sighed. "Great. We have to walk a hundred yards from the river to an old man's cabin, and we get lost in the goddamned swamps. A black panther decides to have us for dinner and when I shoot it, it disappears. My compass, the best one there is, starts going in circles just like we've probably been doing for three hours. And now both our lighters disappear." He shook his head. "Hicks, do you realize how this will all look on a report? If we get back alive."

"If," Hicks replied pointing his gun toward the dark around them.

"For chrisesake, Hicks, put your gun away before you

shoot your nuts off."

Hicks put the pistol back in its shoulder holster.

"We're doomed, Harwood, fucking doomed. Can't you rub sticks together or something? I read somewhere that cats are afraid of fire. Snakes, too."

Harwood sank to the earth, sitting with his hands around his knees, eyeing the black circle around them.

Hicks stood, shifting his vision from one point to another in the dark tangle.

"Don't shoot, whitemen."

At the sound of the voice, Harwood sprang to his feet and both men whirled, Harwood illuminating the old man in the circle of the flashlight.

"What—" Hicks began, but Harwood cut him off.

"Put that rifle down, old man."

Harwood had his pistol out and pointed at Uncle Luther. From behind, Cole saw the old man lower the ought-six so that the rifle butt touched the ground, the barrel in Uncle Luther's hand.

"That gun don't work," Uncle Luther said.

"I don't care if it works or not, old man, just keep it where it is." Harwood edged closer.

"I mean that gun you got in your hand there."

Cole stepped up beside Uncle Luther and watched the two men, one of whom had approached within three feet of them and was pointing a pistol and a flashlight in their direction.

"Like hell it doesn't." Harwood turned the pistol toward a tree trunk to one side and squeezed the trigger. There was a click. He squeezed again and then again. Each time the gun clicked faintly.

"What the hell?" Hicks was staring from the gun to the old man.

"Seems like your cartridges must've got damp or something," Uncle Luther said.

Harwood looked at the old man with a lopsided smile. "I should've known," he said. "I should've fucking known."

"Known what?" Hicks was staring at Harwood now.

"Shut up, Hicks. And leave your gun in your holster. It doesn't work either." Turning to Uncle Luther, Harwood said, "Okay. Can you show us how to get out of here?"

"That's why we come," Uncle Luther replied. "Old Lady Blue Wood sent us to bring you home so's you can have a cup of tea and get dried off."

Cole watched the man who seemed to be in charge smile back at Uncle Luther with a strained, skeptical expression.

"Thank god," Hicks said. "Let's get out of here. Who's Old Lady Blue Wood?"

"Shut up, Hicks." Harwood turned on his partner with a hard smile. "Let's just go with our hosts and ask no questions."

Uncle Luther turned and started back through the woods with Cole behind him. All the way, Cole had marvelled at the old man's ability to find his way unfalteringly in the dark, stepping precisely around and over roots and logs that Cole only saw at the last second, and easily skirting the standing waters. Now, following the old man in the dark, he resented the light from the man behind him. It seemed to obscure the trail, throwing shadows across tangled roots and making each step more difficult. In front of him, Uncle Luther walked steadily, paying no attention to those who followed.

"Ignore the light, grandson," the old man said without turning. "If you see only the trail, it will become clear."

Cole concentrated on the path behind Uncle Luther and, as it had all the way, the trail began to be clear, a thread somewhat lighter than the surrounding dark. Behind him he heard the white men stumbling and cursing in their haste to keep up.

Twenty-two

W hen Uncle Luther pulled the leather strap to open the cabin door, the two hounds came tumbling at them with loud bays. The old lady scolded the dogs, and they went at once to lie beneath the bed.

"You found them. How nice." Onatima stood beaming near the wood stove, the lantern light shining on her silver hair and the red turban gleaming like a jewel. She smiled beautifully at them all as they filed into the cabin.

"Welcome," she said, looking from one of the white men to the other. "Come and stand by the stove so you can warm up. I've made some tea for you."

Hicks crowded close to the stove and held his hands out over the glowing cracks. His teeth were chattering and he concentrated his whole being on the stove's warmth.

Harwood edged near the stove but kept his eyes on the old woman, marvelling at the beauty of the ancient face. The eyes seemed to burn with light. When she held out an enamel cup filled with hot tea, he took it wordlessly and wrapped both hands around it. After a few seconds he nodded and muttered, "Thank you."

Hicks accepted the tea with a nod and immediately began to sip it, recoiling from the burning cup but taking another sip at once.

Uncle Luther set the rifle back on its nails and then hung the big hat on another nail in the wall above the table. Cole shrugged off the fatigue jacket and hung it on the end of the bed, noticing one of the men looking at it curiously, and then he turned and tucked the pouch inside his flannel shirt, self-conscious about the bulge it made but unwilling to take the pouch from around his neck.

"You poor men. You must have had a terrible time," Onatima said in a clucking voice. She cast a quick glare at Uncle Luther.

Harwood looked around the cabin and then back at the old woman and old man. He turned his gaze toward Cole.

"This tea is a lifesaver," Harwood said to Onatima. "We're grateful. And we appreciate being rescued." He turned another skeptical smile toward Uncle Luther. "My associate here is extremely grateful," he added, nodding toward Hicks who stood shivering over the stove.

Hicks nodded at them. "I was afraid we weren't ever getting out of there," he said. "There was a big—"

"That's a very interesting coat you have there," Harwood said, looking at Cole. "I saw a number of coats like that in Vietnam."

"It was my brother's," Cole said as he reached for the tea Onatima held out. "He was over there."

"I know." Harwood shook his head disbelievingly as he spoke. Turning back toward Uncle Luther, he said, "I worked with mountain tribes in Nam, and I saw some interesting things." He sipped the tea while the old man and woman both watched him with friendly, expectant expressions. "I know what was going on out there in the woods, old man, and believe me, I'm impressed. But one thing I can't figure out is why you brought us back here. You must know what we're here for."

Hicks had turned from the stove to watch his partner with a look of confusion. "What the f—excuse me." He looked at Onatima, who smiled back, and then he turned to Harwood. "What are you talking about?"

Harwood looked from Hicks to the old couple and then swung around toward Cole. "This gentleman has brought us right where we wanted to go," he said. Motioning toward Cole with his head, he added, "That's Attis McCurtain's brother."

As Harwood spoke, there was a movement in the corner of the cabin behind the old man's bed. Harwood looked sharply at the corner. Seeing nothing but shadow, he turned back toward Cole.

"Isn't that right?"

Cole looked at Uncle Luther and the old man nodded his head. From behind Harwood, Uncle Luther said, "That's right. This one is Cole, the younger one."

"I appreciate your hospitality," Harwood said. "But I'm afraid I still have to ask you to turn over Attis McCurtain. He's a federal fugitive and considered dangerous."

The shadow in the corner of the room began to move and this time they all turned toward it.

"That's it," Onatima said. "You should be careful not to say its name anymore."

Harwood stared at the gathered shadow. It had moved slowly from the corner and now stood against the far wall of the little cabin, looming there in something like the form of a man.

Cole stared at the shadow and then looked at the old couple. "That's okay, grandson," Onatima said. "It's just restless."

"What's going on here?"

Hicks had backed away from the stove toward the door, staring at all the shadows that shimmered across the room.

Harwood, too, backed up toward the door. "Make it go back, old man," he said.

"That's the one you come for," Uncle Luther said. "Onatima's right."

"Okay, old man," Harwood said. "If you show us where our boat is we'll leave." He stared at the shadow as he spoke. "It's clear the fugitive isn't here." He glanced at his partner and saw that Hicks was pale, with one hand on the handle of his pistol.

"Leave the gun alone, Hicks," he said. "Don't be an idiot."

Onatima stepped close to Cole and put a hand on his shoulder. "It's time you returned," she said. "Remember what you have to do. Don't forget that."

Harwood nodded toward Cole. "I almost forgot," he said.

"Cole McCurtain is wanted for draft evasion."

"What?" Hicks stared at Harwood.

"That's right. He wasn't our primary target, but we're supposed to bring him back if we find him, and I guess we found him."

Cole looked desperately from Onatima to Uncle Luther. The old man nodded.

"It's okay, Cole," the old man said. "This is the way it's supposed to be. You don't have to worry."

Harwood fixed a strange expression on the old man and then spoke to Cole, being careful to keep his gaze away from the shadow. "I'd say you can trust your grandfather. If he says you don't have to worry, I'd say you got it made. But you'd better get your things together right now. I don't intend to spend any more time here than I have to."

When Cole saw Uncle Luther nod in agreement, he picked the jacket up and slipped it on. When he reached for the duffle bag at the head of the bed he realized it was already packed. He glanced questioningly at Onatima who smiled back at him.

Uncle Luther came and put a bony arm around Cole's shoulder. "You'll come back soon, grandson. Don't worry. This is part of the story. Just remember what you are supposed to do." He turned toward Harwood. "Take that path outside the door. It goes straight to the river. Your boat's right there."

When Uncle Luther moved away, Cole swung the duffle onto his shoulder and stepped toward the two federal agents.

"I'm ready," he said.

Harwood pulled the door open and held it while Hicks stumbled out. After Cole had gone out, Harwood stood for a moment watching the old couple with a thin smile. "You two are good," he said. "I wish I knew what the heck it is you're up to."

Uncle Luther smiled back. "You ought to read that book called *Moby-Dick*."

Behind Harwood, Hicks muttered between clinched teeth, "Let's get the hell out of here."

Harwood pulled the door closed after him and followed Hicks toward the river. Cole walked between them, feeling a mixture of sadness and relief. A little bit of Attis was back there in the cabin, and he felt a strange poignancy in leaving it. What he was going to find and bring back would not be Attis at all. He wondered what story his father's uncle had in mind, how he would free him from what the two federal agents represented. He had no doubt that Uncle Luther would make sure they did not interfere with the search, but he wondered how that would be accomplished.

"It was a fucking ghost," Hicks said, his teeth chattering again. "A motherfucking ghost."

"You're hallucinating, Hicks," Harwood said from behind Cole. "You've had a hard night. Get hold of yourself."

Cole heard the man behind him chuckle. "Witch," Harwood said very softly. "Witch, witch, witch, witch, witch, witch, witch." He chuckled to himself again.

Twenty-three

Mundo thought of water. Where it came from, how it collected, ran together, trickles making streams running into creeks that all aimed toward a river that sought the ocean that laid itself out before the sun so that it could be sucked up and spit back at the mountains again so that trickles would make streams. What was it that made all that water stick together? And how much force was there when a river rose out of the ground like that? Where did all the rabbits and possums and skunks go? Were sea creatures shocked when the flooding rivers brought their cargo from the land, disgorging drowned cattle and sheep and chickens and dogs and cats and deer and rabbits and snakes like a broom sweeping trash out the door? And the bodies of men? Did the creatures of the sea come and taste these new delicacies from ashore, sampling this and that?

He had spent an hour upstairs, in the apartment of the Mondragon sisters, and his head ached from the stifling air of their rooms and the unblinking stares of the sisters.

What had they meant when they'd said something had happened, that he needed their help? He'd asked the question over tea and cookies as dry as dust balls.

They could not remember. Something had disturbed them. Dreams, perhaps. But now the memory was faint. Fresher was the fact that wire-boned hobos had been prowling the shadows of their rooms, men in swallowtail coats and pointed beards who stalked them through the nights speaking ornate Spanish unheard in many years. Suggesting the most impossible things and combinations of things that made the sisters wince and look at one another. Would Mundo come and lay in wait for the wire men who bent so low when they crawled the walls that the sisters thought they would bend right through themselves?

The sisters had forced him to think again of the hobo on the train in Paso. There were no clues. No one knew anything or said anything. The dead man had bent into himself completely, the circle closed, and that was that. They'd never know how or why, but did it really matter? The 'bo would have been dead soon for one reason or another, drinking sterno or falling off a flatcar, rolling into his own campfire. Hobos were like that, like the rags of paper that blew up against chain link fences along the highway. Their lives should matter, but they didn't.

So he thought of the movement of water. How did it flow underground? Was there a river down there just like a river would be above ground, running through underground channels like a pipeline through the earth, or did it sift through and between rocks and sand? Why didn't the earth wear away and collapse into the underground river, making it an aboveground river in a sudden canyon? He couldn't believe he'd lived next to this particular river all of his life and knew nothing about it.

How many things like that did a man live with in such ignorance? Like Attis. The gentlest boy he'd known, growing up. He couldn't remember Attis McCurtain in a fight, or even raising his voice at another person. On the court, Attis would walk away from trouble, as if it were not merely distasteful but simply uninteresting. Twice when Mundo had stood up for his friend, kicking the shit out of a couple of guys in the process, Attis had disapproved, silently and patiently. And the girl, Jenna Nemi. They'd seemed to be in love. From the last year of high school, when Jenna had started wearing Attis's letterman's jacket, through the two years before he and Attis joined the marines, Attis and Jenna had been together almost every minute. Mundo remembered his own feelings of jealousy. Graduating a year before Attis, he'd worked at the mushroom farm and waited. They'd planned it out. As soon as Attis graduated, they'd join the marines on the buddy system. But then Attis hadn't wanted to leave Jenna, so they'd both worked at the mushroom farm for another year. It was only when Mundo was about to be drafted that Attis gave in. They enlisted together, and in Nam, Mundo got his best friend back again, in spades. Was Lee Scott right? Had Jenna been screwing other guys while Attis was in Nam?

The change had begun almost as soon as they arrived in Nam. In the beginning, Attis had seemed strangely excited by the whole thing, the nearness of death and the unbroken presence of death. Like the tiger, the smell of death had seemed to awaken Attis to a new awareness. Attis's eyes were abruptly sharper, more focused. And as Mundo became more and more terrified and outraged by the probability of his own destruction, Attis settled into what Mundo could only think of as a state of excited anticipation, what Mundo could remember feeling before a big game. That excitement ended when Attis began to see the dead, the lonely ghosts of the long-range recon men wandering the jungle, ghost patrols marching forest trails, swift boats manned by the dead, dead men on search-and-destroy. And at night, in whispers, he would describe them to Mundo, explaining how the dead never left, how the war was becoming crowded with the dead who kept fighting the war in their death-sleep. He'd talked of shadows, and wondered aloud. "There's a slippery log, Mundo. Most people can get across and find the bright path to a good place, but murderers can't get their footing. They fight to stay on, but they always slip. They try to hang on, but their hands won't hold. They fall into a black river full of snakes and dead things, and they go into a whirlpool that takes them around and around until they wash ashore in a terrible, dead place that they can never leave.

"Warriors always used to go to the good place. But what I can't figure out, Mundo, is the difference between a warrior and a murderer. If we're warriors, why do the shadows walk? Sometimes I think we all fell off that log, all of us together, and washed ashore here. This is the dead place. We'll never leave. We'll just kill each other over and over, forever."

Mundo felt her before he was aware. It was a feeling he associated with triple-canopy jungle and air too full of oxygen, the kind of intoxicating night air that made you breathe too deeply and rapidly. Where there were always hidden things, looming in the darkness.

She leaned in the doorway almost the way she had at home. One arm was raised and bent so that her head could rest against it. The other hand touched the belly of her thick purple sweater. Instead of a skirt she wore pants so tight he knew he could have read the date on a dime in the pocket.

"He's dead, isn't he?"

131

He sat up straighter in his chair and placed both hands on the desk, watching Diana Nemi's green eyes. There was a sadness on her face now, but it was mixed with another emotion he couldn't fathom.

She walked over to the desk and smiled at him, a poignant smile so completely unlike what he'd seen in her parents' house that he remained in perplexed silence.

"Can I sit down and talk to you for a few minutes?" Diana asked. "I'm not interrupting anything important, am I?"

He shook his head and motioned toward the chair.

"Yes," he said. "I think so."

"And you think my father did it?" She leaned back in the chair, with her hands on the chair arms, looking directly at him.

He closed his eyes against her for a moment. When he opened them, he nodded. "Yes, I think your father did it, but I don't know how. You see, your father was at Jessard's when it must have happened, so I don't know. Maybe he paid somebody else."

She shook her head. "He wouldn't pay someone to do that. Are you sure he was at Jessard's? Do you believe Jessard Deal?"

Again he nodded, somewhat introspectively this time. "Jessard doesn't lie, and there are other witnesses, people I trust."

"It's a terrible thing, isn't it?" It was a question. She wanted his opinion.

"Attis did an awful thing, but he was my friend." He shrugged. "Murder is a terrible thing." He thought of the hobo's body in the freight car all the way from La Luz where it must have happened. It was a rough stretch of track, no longer maintained for passenger service, and the body would have jarred and bounced in the freight car close to the open door. There would have been nothing to cushion the bare head. He frowned.

"I guess if Dan Nemi did it he would think of it more as revenge than murder. That's how I would think of it."

He was surprised to hear her use her father's name the way someone else, someone like Carl Carlton, might have. He'd heard Attis refer to Hoey McCurtain that way. "He probably would," he replied, uncomfortably conscious of the girl's physical presence across the desk. She gave off an aroma that was sharp edged and sweet, unlike any perfume he'd ever smelled.

"You know, I admire you, Mundo. You're the only person I know who actually cares about what's right and wrong."

Mundo looked away from her toward the picture of a man wanted for bank robbery. That part was easy, he thought. Sorting it all out was the hard part.

"He killed my sister. In a horrible, horrible way." She leaned forward and placed her palms on the desk so that her breasts rested on the edge of the desk top, and he became more disturbingly conscious of her. "She loved him. Don't you think he deserved to die in return?"

Mundo noticed the FBI letter about Cole McCurtain open on his desk. He casually folded the letter and slipped it into a pile of mail.

"No one deserves to die, hija. We all die, but not one of us deserves it."

He stood and walked to the coffeepot. Patting the side of the pot to test its heat, he said, "How about some coffee, Diana?" Without waiting for a reply, he pulled two mugs from their hooks on the wall and filled them with the very black liquid. He walked back to the desk and set a cup in front of her.

"Milk or sugar?"

"No thanks," she said, her face alert and waiting.

Mundo sipped the bitter coffee. "I thought about it a lot. I saw some people killed, quite a few. It came to me that we don't have anything to do with being born; we just wake up and there we are. And right off we find out we're going to die. Then we spend our lives doing every damned thing we can to keep from dying any sooner than we have to. Sometimes we even kill other people so we don't have

133

to die too soon. It's a mess, but it's not our fault, you know. It's sad. We don't deserve to die, none of us. We don't deserve any of the rest of this shit either." He sipped the coffee and watched her. "No, Diana, Attis McCurtain didn't deserve to end up in that river, no more than Jenna deserved what Attis did to her."

When Diana smiled her sharp cheekbones caught slivers of shadow. She leaned closer across the desk.

"That's too easy, Mundo. Attis himself told my sister that we have to accept responsibility for our lives, for everything within us and around us. She said that Attis said it was an Indian way of looking at the world. He told her about balances in the world. Attis wouldn't have believed what you just said."

Mundo became intensely aware of her aroma as she bent even closer. He sipped the awful coffee to counter the effect.

"I think Attis would have believed that he deserved to die," she said. "I think he wanted someone to do that for him. Now things are balanced." She cupped both hands around the coffee and sat back from him a little. "I've thought about it, too, Mundo. We aren't alive very long, and then we die. It isn't such a big deal to die a few years before you would anyway. Twenty years, fifty years, it's not even a blink of an eye in time. So what matters is how we die, don't you think? Sometimes I walk up the hill behind our house, and I climb up on top of that big water tank up there. I lay on my back and look up, and there's nothing there. There's nothing up there, Mundo, and it's scary. Why did he do that to Jenna? She was the same age I am right now. It's like she was just something he could break, like she wasn't real.

"Men are like that. They break things, and they think women are just more things. I tried to tell her, but she wouldn't listen. My mother knew, and I tried to get her to tell Jenna, but she was afraid. I think you're just taking the easy way out, Mundo. That's what men do, isn't it? But aren't you different? Aren't you the only one here who does care about right and wrong?"

He shook his head. "No one deserves to die. But we all do."

Diana sat all the way back in her chair and placed both hands behind her head.

"I guess you can't prove who did it unless you find his body."

He nodded. "Probably not."

"I like you, Mundo. You're sweet." She still smiled. "As my mother would say, you are a sexy man. As my mother, in fact, has said."

"How old are you, Diana?"

She lifted strands of her hair with both hands and brushed it behind her shoulder. "Almost nineteen, officer, legal. I'll be a freshman at Berkeley next fall. Ever had a coed?"

Mundo toyed with his cup. "How come you waited a whole year before you started college?"

"I had things to take care of." She raised her eyebrows.

"You are a very sexy woman," Mundo said. "So is your mother."

Diana laughed. "An interesting thought."

"I understand why you're confused, Diana, but things aren't balanced." He leaned back in his chair and folded his arms. "You see, Hoey McCurtain thinks he's an Indian, and he believes he has to revenge his son's murder. Naturally, he thinks your father did it."

"My father didn't do it, besides he can't prove it."

Mundo shook his head. "Hoey won't need to prove anything. He may not even wait for a body." He watched her for a moment. "Hoey saw what happened to Attis in a dream. He dreamed his son's death."

Diana raised her eyebrows again. "Well, Officer Morales, I guess you'll have to protect the Nemi family. Maybe it would be best if you moved into the guest bedroom." She looked at him through half-closed eyes. "It's right next to my room, so you could protect me every night. From the

135

Indians. I'm sure your wife would understand."

She rose from the chair. "I have to go now, can't be late for dinner."

He remained seated, watching her walk toward the door, where she turned and said, "I'd love to talk to you again, Mundo. Why don't you come and interrogate me? The kind of in-depth investigation I'm sure you're wonderful at."

He heard her laugh again as she pulled the door closed behind her. He took a deep breath and picked up the phone. In a moment he said, "Querida, I just wanted to check in. Of course. I'm heading out to the McCurtains' to talk to Hoey. Yeah, I'll be a little late for dinner."

He set the phone back in its cradle and watched the door, letting out another long breath and then rubbing a hand over his eyes. "Stupid pendejo," he said. "She's trying to convince herself of something. And she wants me to help her do that."

"A bruja? Is that what you're thinking, niño?" The viejo sat on the edge of the narrow table that held the coffeepot, his skinny legs dangling. Muno jumped and then swiveled the chair toward his grandfather.

"Goddamnit, old man, that's about the tenth time in the last couple of days I've almost had a heart attack. You have to stop doing that."

The old man grinned beneath the enormous white moustache that seemed to hover over his mouth. His chestnut-brown eyes gleamed with the fluorescent light from the ceiling.

"Should I knock first?" The viejo swung his legs slightly in their baggy suit pants. Mundo saw that his grandfather seemed to have lost weight. The pinstriped suit coat was much too large, bunching at the lapels and across the chest and stomach. The old man had taken off the tie they'd put on him, and the thin white hairs of his chest and neck showed through the open collar of the white shirt. The white hair on his head stood in a wild, sparse halo. The leathery brown skin of his face had sunken further so that the cheekbones, chin, and eye sockets stood out more sharply. The hands that gripped the edge of the table were brown bones, the skin like parchment.

Mundo shook his head and walked to the table with his coffee cup. As he poured coffee from the Pyrex pot he said, "I guess you don't drink coffee now?"

The old man sighed. "No, hijo, and I miss it. A cup of coffee—real coffee, not that poison you drink—in the morning, that was the great pleasure in one's life."

Mundo sipped the coffee and looked at his grandfather. "*The* great pleasure, old man?"

The viejo smiled beneath the moustache again and waved a hand vaguely. "Let us say *one* of the great ones then." He was introspective for a few seconds. "I miss that one also."

"Hmph," Mundo grunted.

"Maybe a bruja," the grandfather said. "You have a complex problem here, niño. What are you going to do?"

Mundo shrugged and made a face as he sipped more coffee.

"That coffee will shrivel one's huevos, boy." He looked at Mundo with concern and added, "But a delicious bruja, no? Such a face. If I were a young man. . . ."

"You mean if you were alive, old man. No one has forgotten the Sanchez girl."

"She was in love with me, niño. We swore endless devotion."

"She was sixteen, viejo. And you with a foot in the grave already."

The old man smiled happily. "She taught me much, that one. How is she doing?"

Mundo rolled his eyes. "She got married. She has a child now."

The viejo nodded. "This bruja Nemi is a dangerous one, Mundo. She is no wise innocent like that Adelita Sanchez. But I think there's another one who may help you. *Un indio.*"

Mundo looked at the oily swirls in his coffee. "Diana is

137

no bruja," he said. "She's a young girl who's troubled. Besides, the only Indian I know, grandfather, is Hoey McCurtain, and I have to stop him from killing someone else." When he looked up again, the old man was gone.

He dumped the remaining coffee from his cup into the steel basin in a corner of the room and hung the cup back on its peg. Grabbing his coat from the rack by the door, he went out and locked up the office. Then he drove slowly out of town toward the McCurtain house and the river.

When he reached the house, he saw Hoey McCurtain's back curving over the fender of the battered pickup. A trouble light hung above Hoey's head, creating a yellow circle in the shadow of the truck's hood. He parked the car and got out, closing the door quietly, and then he leaned against the fender of the patrol car, with his hands in the pockets of his coat, waiting for Hoey McCurtain to look up. The shrill whine of the grinder shredded the edge of the short day, causing him to clench his jaws and look away toward the river behind the house. He took in the worn path that led to the riverbank, the empty chicken coop that sagged against a pair of black walnut trunks, the lovely, cool sweep of sycamore trunk and branches, a head gasket hung randomly from a broken branch, the abandoned block of a V-8 engine shackled by weeds, the empty rabbit hutches near the back door, the television antenna lying along the rear wall of the house, the screen door loose and limp on its rusted hinges, the scattered oilcans, deflated basketball, chewed boot, rusting bicycle, bald tires, and deer antlers that jungled in the dead weeds beside and behind the house, and the Chevy. The river was dropping fast. Now the right word for it would be "flowed." It flowed in a small stream, barely thirty feet across, toward the Pacific. In the sky, mares' tails held a tattered sunset.

Hoey finished honing a cylinder of the pickup engine and straightened out from beneath the raised hood, with the drill and honing bit in one hand. He squinted past

138

the trouble light hanging from the hood. When he saw Mundo he stepped back from the truck and spat near the front tire.

"How you doing, Hoey?" Mundo stood with his hands in his pockets, conscious suddenly of the weight of the gun on one hip.

Hoey watched him for several seconds without replying. Finally, he laid the drill on top of the engine block and looked toward the house. "Come on in and have a beer," he said.

"I'm on duty."

"Shit."

He followed the short, stocky man onto the back porch. When Hoey stopped to take off his muddy boots, Mundo slipped his shoes off and set them on the porch beside the boots.

Inside, the house had a musty odor of disuse. A dismantled carburetor lay spread across a newspaper on the kitchen table. An open jar of peanut butter sat beside the newspaper with a needle valve inside the jar's upturned cap. A pocketknife lay next to the jar with peanut butter on the blade.

He went to the refrigerator, jammed a screwdriver into the hole where the handle had been and, when the door jumped open, grabbed two black cans of beer with gold on the labels.

"Brew 102?" Mundo said with a frown. "Hoey, this stuff'll kill you."

Hoey turned one of the cans upside down and stabbed holes in the bottom with a beer opener. He held the can out and, when Mundo accepted, he opened the second can in the same way.

Mundo held the beer, feeling the tab on what was now the bottom of the can.

Hoey sat down in an overstuffed chair covered with a chenille spread. Mundo sat on a sagging couch and noticed that most of the little tufts of the chenille had been worn away, leaving a nearly transluscent cloth over the black chair.

"So, Mundo, I don't suppose you stopped by for some of this fine beer?"

Hoey's good eye looked a little past Mundo, almost but not quite making contact.

"How's Cole?" Mundo sipped the beer and watched the other man's expression.

Hoey shrugged. "I don't know. He ain't been around for a little while. Maybe he went backpacking."

"In the winter?"

"Maybe he went on a vision quest."

Hoey smiled slightly.

Mundo nodded. "I came by to ask you not to do anything crazy. I'm trying to find out what happened to Attis. Give me some time."

At the sound of his son's name, Hoey closed his eyes. When he opened them again he looked at the can in his hand. "This ain't such bad beer. It's cheap."

Mundo waited, watching his friend's father. For several minutes neither man spoke, while Hoey considered a window that opened onto the side where he'd been working on the pickup.

"There was this Frenchman once, down in Mississippi way back when there was still a lot of Choctaw people there. He got worked up one day and challenged a Choctaw to a duel."

He took a drink of beer and Mundo waited, accustomed to Hoey McCurtain's way of telling a story.

"You see, that Frenchman thought the Choctaw would refuse because Choctaws never believed in white people's way of dueling. But the Choctaw said all right. Then he said he believed that the one that was challenged got to pick the place and the kind of weapons. The Frenchman got a little worried, but he figured the Choctaw couldn't hit much with a pistol, so he swaggered and said that's right."

140   Mundo waited again while Hoey took a long pull from

the black and gold can and looked out the window for a few seconds.

"The Choctaw watched that Frenchman swell around for a while and then he said, 'Okay. We'll use rifles. Tomorrow morning at sunrise you have your second take you to that big oak tree on the east side of the trace pond. My second'll take me to the biggest oak on the west side.' He stopped to watch the Frenchman start to get nervous, and then he smiled the special way Indians smile when the joke's on somebody else. 'Then we'll hide behind them trees and start hunting each other.' "

Mundo grinned along with Hoey. "They say the Frenchman moved to Alabama."

Hoey rubbed his fleshy chin and glanced at Mundo and then back at the window.

"You see, the Frenchman knew a Choctaw always gets what he hunts."

Mundo turned the can on his knee, looking at the place where boots had scraped the linoleum to licorice in front of the big chair. He noted that the living room was very neat, with hunting and fishing magazines stacked precisely on an end table and the throw rug perfectly aligned with the contours of the room.

"You know what gets me sometimes?" Hoey went on. "It's the names of these damned teams. The Cleveland Indians, Washington Redskins, the Braves and all that. There ought to be teams like the San Francisco Whitemen, or Detroit Negroes, or New York Jews. How would you feel about the Los Angeles Mexicans?" He squinted at Mundo, who looked back at Hoey with a trace of a smile.

"I guess you're right," Mundo said finally. "How about the Wasco Wetbacks, or the Guadalupe Gringos?"

Hoey grinned back. "Right, or the Pismo Palefaces."

"How about you just laying back and letting me take care of what happened to Attis?"

Hoey frowned. "You ought not say his name like that, Mundo."

141

"Why not?"

Hoey looked directly at Mundo and, after a pause, said, "Let's say it's a question of respect."

"I'm sorry. He was my best friend, you know."

"I know. But he was my first son."

"It was just a dream, Hoey. You can't kill somebody because you saw something in a dream."

Hoey stood and walked to the window, lifting the fringe of curtain to look out at the pickup and river beyond. "You know, Mundo. One time not too long after you both came back from over there, I found him down in the river bottom. I was out after rabbits, and I heard a funny sound in some bushes. It was him. He was inside there, laying on the ground all curled up, and he was crying. He never saw me, and I just walked away. I figured if my son had wanted someone to see that, he wouldn't have crawled into them bushes. Now I think I should've crawled in there with him."

Hoey glanced at Mundo and then back out the window. "I better get that head back on before dark," he said softly, as if to himself. Then, turning, he said, "You ain't white, Mundo, so you ought to understand. It don't matter how you feel about it, or how that old grandfather of yours felt about it, you and me both know you got Indian blood in you from way back. You're a mixed-blood just like me. So you ought to know about dreams."

Mundo sighed and stood up. "I know about dreams. And maybe you're right, but you have to let me take care of this."

Hoey continued looking out the window. "My boy never really came back from that war. They killed him and gutted him over there. What came back was just part of him, but the only part we still had. I read that there used to be ceremonies for warriors coming back home, ceremonies that would take all the evil out. Maybe something like that would have put him back together again. But we don't know those ceremonies anymore. Now it's like he was

142

killed twice."

Mundo crushed the beer can in his fist. "I'll do everything I can to stop you. I'll haul your ass in if I have to."

Hoey turned from the window and held out a hand. When Mundo returned the light pressure in the Indian fashion he'd learned from Attis, Hoey said, "That river's dropping fast. I'd say a man could walk it already."

Mundo went to the porch and slipped his shoes on. Outside, the stars were as sharp as razor blades, and he felt sorry for Hoey McCurtain who would be tightening head bolts in the cold night. He knew the truck would have to be running to get Hoey to work in the morning. For a moment he considered staying to help get the motor back together, and then he spoke aloud to the stars, saying, "To hell with it." If he left now he'd get home before dinner was too cold and Gloria was mad again. Walking to the car he looked up at the darkening sky. He tried to remember a story Attis had told about the stars of the Big Dipper, but he hadn't paid enough attention at the time. The stars of that story weren't these stars. This was a different story. It seemed like some people had stories for everything, like the viejo. It occurred to him that he should talk again to the Mondragon sisters, ask them about the threads that linked him to them somehow in a past that was as distant and ambiguous as the winter sky. The nights were already growing shorter, the days longer. That time when the year hung in balance between light and dark had passed.

"I'll hit the river in the morning," he said aloud as he eased into the car.

He drove slowly, wishing the police car had an a.m./f.m. radio. He wanted to hear Hank Williams sing about people so lonesome they could die or cheatin' hearts, or Buck Owens with his Bakersfield rockytonk. He passed houses with lighted windows and saw the flickering gray of televisions. It saddened him. A newspaper boy pedaled by with bags of papers over his shoulders, flinging the flattened rolls disconsolately toward porches and doors. He remem-

143

bered how the old women would snap open their change purses and fish for quarters at collection time, how it felt to approach such a door. All the lonely people. *Yo soy un hombre sincero,* and on and on and on.

A block from the Memorial Building, Angel Turkus's car sat at an angle across one side of the two-lane road, with lights flashing a thin red in the cold evening.

"Puta!" Mundo muttered as he pulled to a stop behind the other car.

Angel had someone spread-eagled against the door of a Chevy pickup, Angel's stumplike body hunched strangely at the culprit's back. The spotlight of Angel's patrol car cut the two figures in half, one side glaring white and the other a black outline, reminding Mundo of an old movie.

He got out of his car and approached the scene slowly. A dozen feet away, he saw why Angel looked so odd. The other north county deputy had his gun drawn and pointed, with both fat hands, at the back of the man spread against the truck.

Angel looked around at Mundo, the eyes wild in his flaring face.

"I'm going to kill him!" Angel shouted. "I'm going to blow his fucking brains out!"

Mundo stepped close to Angel's side, studying the two men. The one against the truck turned his head to look at Mundo.

"Don't you move," Angel shouted. "Don't you fucking move!"

"Easy, Angel," Mundo said. "Take it easy." He turned his attention to the other. "What'd you do, Bucky?"

"I ain't done hardly nothing, Mundo," Bucky Travis said, turning his head nervously. "And this tub of guts says he's gonna kill me."

"Nothing!" Angel yelled. "I'm going to kill him, Morales. I'm going to blow his fucking head off."

144   "What's he done?"

"What's he done?" Angel jerked his head toward the front of the truck. "Look."

Mundo stepped around Angel and stopped. A corpse was draped across the hood of the pickup, clots of white hair clinging to the decaying skull, rotting white cloth punctured by putrid flesh and tangled bone. Then he noticed the stench.

"It's his fucking grandmother. His own fucking grandmother."

Mundo walked backwards, to the other side of Angel Turkus. He covered his face with his hands.

"He dug up his own grandmother, Morales. He's been driving around town with her like that."

Mundo looked at the teenager between his spread fingers. Bucky had his head half turned and was smiling pleasantly at Mundo.

Mundo leaned an arm on the top of his car and studied the sharp-pointed stars. After a moment he said, "Put him in my car, Angel. I'll take him to San Luis."

"Fuck that," Angel replied, jerking his face sideways toward Mundo. "You ain't leaving me here with that thing."

Mundo lifted his arm off the car and rubbed a hand over his cheek, noticing the words "Just Buried" soaped on the back window of Bucky's pickup. He shook his head. "Angel, you just told me you were going to blow Bucky's brains out. If I let you take him in, after you said that, I'll be neglecting my duty. If you really did that, I'd be responsible. Remember, Amarga is my territory."

"I ain't touching that thing," Angel said.

Mundo sighed again. "You just sit in your car, Angel, and make sure nobody bothers it. I'll call Dave Johnson at the funeral home and have him take care of everything." He stepped closer to Angel and the boy. "Now put your gun away, Angel, before you do blow somebody's head off."

As Angel stepped back and reluctantly holstered the pistol, Mundo gestured with his thumb toward the patrol car. "Come on, Bucky."

Once they were headed out of town, Mundo radioed San Luis to tell them he was coming, and then they settled back in silence. After a few minutes, Mundo looked in the rearview mirror and was almost startled to see not his grandfather but the pimply-faced boy. He realized that it had been months since he'd had a criminal in the back seat of the patrol car.

Watching the boy's friendly face, Mundo said, "Why'd you do it, Bucky?"

Bucky's expression became incredulous. "Didn't you ever want to do that, Mundo?"

Shaking his head slowly, Mundo said, "No, Bucky. The dead are special. Your grandmother deserves her rest."

"My grandmother," Bucky replied flatly, "was a cunt."

Mundo let out a deep breath. "What's wrong with kids today, Bucky? We never used to do things like this."

"You know what I say, Mundo? Fuck the world. That's what I say. Fuck the world."

Twenty-four

Diana held her long hair in one hand and brushed it where it hung over her naked shoulder and breast. The candles flicked slivers of light in the mirror of her dresser, and the single small electric lamp on the table near the bed brought a soft glow into the room. The aroma of sweet grass laced the room from the incense holder on the chest.

Running her hand down the smooth strands of hair,

Diana thought of the river. All of her life she had lived on its edge, rising in the morning to see it from her bedroom window. In the summer it would seem, like a great mother, shaken with life, as if the myriad movements of all the small life down there caused a vibration in the very air. In the fall she'd watch the broad leaves spin down from sycamore and cottonwood, catching on the thick brush and falling further, down to the sand she couldn't see. Then she'd feel the river in her blood as it slowed, feeling as though it pooled behind some kind of thickening obstruction until one day the big rains would come and the water would respond, erupting into life.

Once they'd found a wonderful spring in the heart of the river, she and Jenna. They'd slipped beneath their father's barbed-wire fence and gone into the riverbed to play. The July sun burned the white sand until it seemed molten to their bare feet, and insects chattered in the brush. And they'd found it in a little clearing between walls of brittle growth, a spring of clear, cold water bubbling up from the shining sand, water so pure that each grain of sand shone like a jewel. They'd dug a basin for the wonderful water, making a pool that filled and grew with absolute clarity. They'd rushed to one of their father's cow troughs and netted the goldfish that lived there, releasing the fish into water so pure that it didn't seem to exist. When dark approached they went home explosive with joy, determined to return at daylight.

But they'd had to help their mother at home, and it was midday before they got back. When they burst through the brush to the magical spring, a man stood there, his shadow slanting across the white sand. Where the water had been there was a hole dug down to darker rock. At the bottom of the hole was a black pipe.

"Got her fixed," the man said. "You girls put these fish here?" He looked at them sharply, the three-day bristle on his chiseled face black and hostile. From the open chest of his overalls thick black hair protruded, and the backs of his   147 hands, heavy and scarred, were covered with the same dark hair.

Around the man the goldfish lay dead and drying on the sand. "Sorry about the fish," he said as he picked up a shovel and toolbox and stalked away toward the other side of the river.

A face had appeared in the mirror, watching her. The eyes were deep and almost black, the hair longer than her own, silvery and shining. The thin mouth was set in a line close to a smile.

"It is all right now," the face said. "But you must stop it, granddaughter, or else it will go on and on forever."

"Stop what?" she asked the mirror, but the old man's face was gone. She turned toward the room and she was alone there. She reached to crush out the sweet grass and then she stood and blew out the candles. Once in bed she turned off the lamp and drew the comforter close around her, feeling the soft cotton sheets on her skin. She touched her stomach, drawing her hand up to her breasts and then down to trace a line along the inner curve of her thigh. There was an empty feeling, a vague ache, and she thought of Attis McCurtain. She'd been fourteen when she'd come home early and rushed to her sister's room to gossip the way they always did. Attis and Jenna had been on the bed, Jenna's legs spread and Attis naked on top of her. She'd stood in the doorway, frozen, watching Attis shoving himself into her sister, while Jenna made sounds midway between laughing and crying. She'd backed away before they saw her, gone to her room and crawled into bed, pulling the covers over her head.

She slid into a light sleep, and in her dreams Mundo stalked the riverbed, walking more and more rapidly over the pale sand until he was skimming the sand and then rising over the river and soaring. He became a dark bird, sending calls out over the river, waiting for an answer that didn't come. Attis threw back the comforter and lay heavily upon her so that she could not move. His lips sought her throat and shoulder, kissing and then biting. His body weighted and terrified her, growing so heavy that she could not breathe. She tried to scream, but he had taken her breath. And then the voice came again, saying, "It is all right now, granddaughter. Let it go."

In the ancient white oak outside the house, a great horned owl sat in a fork of the tree and called. Unmoving, it sent a call out into the dark and then waited. When there was no answer, the owl called again, but this time it was not a question but a declaration. The yellow eyes divided the night and the wings reached, sending the bulking shadow of the bird soaring up over the house and barns in a wide curve toward the dark river. Helen Nemi shivered and touched the body of her husband. Diana soared over the river, searching the tangled shadows alongside the dwindling stream.

Twenty-five

Jessard Deal was wrecking his house with a sledge hammer. It had begun with his fist, a few holes through the drywall, then the sixteen-pound sledge. "I am not drunk," he told himself as he paused and tilted the bottle of Johnny Walker Red to his lips again. "We begin with the world around us, and we gradually move inward, centripetally, toward the center. When we get there, we smash that, too. But that's always last."

The walls crumbled with ridiculous ease, the two-by-four studs clipped off their moorings and the inner walls splattering shrapnel and white dust on furniture and floor.

Lifting the sledge to the level of his chest, he spun and swung it around and around and flush against the side of the fireplace, smashing brick and dropping the mantle six inches. Then he walked outside, placed the ladder against a rain gutter, and mounted the roof. He teed off on the wooden ridge, bashed holes through, strewing cedar shingles, sheared the chimney off with six quick strokes, splintered joists, and leveled the gabled roof. Then he descended and moved to the outer stud walls, marauding out the toenailed spikes, letting the plaster cascade upon his head and shoulders, until a snake's tongue of sparks spat toward him and one end of the house began to sag and crumple like a dying elephant. Seeing the house kneel, Jessard unleashed havoc upon the frail structure. In three hours he destroyed his home. Then he burrowed into the rubble for books.

His arms full, he looked at the flimsy wreckage, breathing roughly and loudly. "Most men," he said aloud, "lead lives of quiet respiration." Laughing, he dumped the books on the passenger seat of the pickup and went back for another load. Finally, he set the sledge hammer on the floorboard, picked up the bottle of Johnny Walker, and slammed the truck's door. Then he walked to the shed and corral where the horse stood watching him. "One must have a mind of fucking winter, you old fart-bag," he said as, with one hand, he tore a flake from a hay bale and tossed it at the animal's feet. "Common household pets will gnaw your bones yet, Bucephalus." The horse ripped strands from the flake and tossed its head, eyeing its master hatefully.

Twenty-six

The old man heard the crying first, a hollow lamentation like the sound of a Mexican flute. "So, even the dead have dreams," he said to himself. He thought of blood and found himself on a tiny wedge-shaped island in the middle of a stream. Mist obscured the trail ahead, and wings beat the air around him. "The dead do not sing," he told himself, wondering what new path this was as he stepped into the blood-red current and watched it lap over his black shoes. "Angel wings make no sound and trouble not the earth," he hummed to himself.

And then he saw the form of her crouched against the stream bank, her bare feet bathed in the liquid and her hands shielding her eyes. Behind her stood a forest of trees like cardboard cutouts, each propped on a tri-form base, their branches painted on an undulating curtain. The stars above them were sharp-pointed cutouts in a black ceiling.

Her back and head were curved toward the current, and her long hair blocked his vision of her face and trailed in the red stream. Blood patterned her naked thighs and arms and shoulders, and she sang her hollow cries to the water. He waded close and reached to touch her shoulder through the weighted hair. When she looked up at him he felt for the first time the immense, unfathomable despair of the young dead.

"He passed by in the night," she said. "And now it seems to be day, but there are those stars. It's all blood, old man. Where has he left me?"

Because there was nothing else he could do, he squatted beside her in the river of blood, his back to what seemed to be a curtain.

"Your voice, Jenna, is like wind through the bones of

birds."

"It's blood. Why did he leave me here?"

He took her hand and helped her rise, and they began to walk through the shallow stream, her naked body traced with images of blood and his suit pants darkening where they touched his shoes.

"There are others," he said. "Though sometimes the faces of others become our own, and it is difficult to tell. But I am an old man and I can show you some things. I have a fine suit, don't I?"

Twenty-seven

Mundo moved inside his wife, hard and fast, arcing against her as she raised herself toward him, her knees and hands on the bed and her dangling breasts swaying with the movement. "Oh god," she said. "Fuck me, Mundo. I want you to fuck me." He fucked her, hearing himself slapping against her, reaching to touch her nipples, bending to kiss her back, bite her shoulder and neck as he moved rhythmically inside her. And he thought of the long stretch of the river between Amarga and the sea, a black line in the night along which, somewhere, Attis was lying and waiting. "Yes," Gloria moaned. "Oh yes, fuck me." And he thought of Diana Nemi, her green eyes and the way she had smiled in the doorway, the tight sweep of her thighs and her breasts. He held Gloria's waist tightly in both hands and thrust into her, and abruptly she pulled away and turned, swinging her legs around him so that now she lay on her back and pulled him down and into her again. They clutched one another and rocked, their mouths together, Gloria's tongue searching as he felt her body stiffening and beginning to convulse. Then they were coming together in a single outpouring. "Te quiero," he whispered. "Para siempre." In his mind he saw Diana Nemi as she stood with one arm raised, nipples hard through the black leotard, thigh lifted inside the skirt. Diana smiled and winked. "Fuck me, Mundo."

When Gloria went into the bathroom and closed the door, Mundo lay back in the bed and tried to shut the girl from his mind. "I love my wife," he said, seeing Diana's face and body.

"Of course you do, hijo." The viejo sat in the oak chair in a corner of the room, one leg over the other. Even in the dark Mundo could see that the suit was more disheveled than ever, looking more outsized than before, as if the old man was growing smaller in death.

"What are you doing here?" Mundo hissed. "Have you no respect for a man's privacy?"

"You might say I was drawn by the joy of life spilling from this room." The viejo seemed to smile beneath the moustache that looked blue in the darkness.

"Sex, you mean."

"The joy of life."

"You have to go away, old man. Gloria will be out of the bathroom in a few seconds. You'll scare her to death."

The viejo smiled broadly beneath the moustache. "Quite a woman, Gloria. A wonderful woman, and one, I might add, who does not scare easily. You don't deserve such a woman, but you could learn much from her."

"What do you want, grandfather?"

The old man stopped smiling. "I'm disappointed niño. I came to help you because I felt the bruja in this room. I think you need my help with that one."

"I appreciate your concern, but I can take care of myself, old man. Now you have to go."

The grandfather shrugged expansively, the suit wrinkling as he did so. He held out both hands, palms up. "I had a dream of the sister. She is troubled and doesn't understand her death yet. It is easy for an old man, but the young ones are lost in death. Has the indio come yet, grandson?"

Mundo shook his head. "I don't know what you're talking about."

"Who are you talking to?" The bathroom door opened and Gloria stood there beautifully naked in the light, her creamy brown skin glowing golden.

Mundo looked from his wife to his grandfather, but the chair was empty.

"No one. I was just thinking out loud," he said.

Gloria plucked a nightgown from the foot of the bed and slipped it on, the thick, pink cotton reaching from her neck all the way to the floor. She slid into bed. "That was nice, Mundo. But I think maybe you're under too much pressure. This thing with Attis may be too much for you. Why don't you just let San Luis and that federal guy handle it?"

Mundo went into the bathroom and shut the door. He urinated and wiped off the residue of lovemaking and looked wonderingly down at his flaccid cock and scrotum. Then he went back into the bedroom. As he pulled on a pair of boxer shorts he said, "Because they won't handle it. They'll just let it go. Attis will just be a missing patient forever. That's the way they want it."

"Maybe that's best, Mundo. Even if Dan Nemi killed him, will you make things better by proving that? Attis did a terrible thing, Mundo; maybe now you should just let it alone."

Mundo crawled into bed and pulled the blankets up to his chin, staring at the ceiling. "It's beyond Attis, now," he said. "I don't know how to explain it, but it just feels like it's huge, like it has to do with the whole damned world somehow." He folded his hands across his chest under the blankets and felt his wife's thigh alongside his own.

154

"Besides, Hoey McCurtain's going to make it all a lot worse if I don't fix things."

"What?"

"Hoey's going to revenge Attis's murder. He told me as much, and there's nothing that can stop him except me. I have to stop Hoey from doing that, and I have to find out who did it, all at the same time. And I have to find Attis to prove what Hoey and I already know."

"Could you talk to Cole and get him to stop his father?"

Mundo sighed. "Cole's gone, disappeared. Probably hiding out from the draft. Besides, I don't think Cole McCurtain has the balls to do it."

It was Gloria's turn to sigh. "He always looked to me like he had plenty of cojones."

"Don't start getting ideas, chiquita. I might have to cut those huevos off."

Gloria giggled faintly. "Gosh, what a man my husband is."

They lay in silence for several minutes, and Mundo heard his wife's breathing become deep and regular. Diana Nemi came into his mind again, and he felt himself becoming aroused once more.

"Pendejo," he said under his breath. "Fool."

Twenty-eight

Dan Nemi stopped the pickup and reached across to roll down the passenger-side window. "How about a ride?"

Cole looked up in surprise. Burrowing into his own thoughts, he hadn't heard the El Camino pull up. Now, as the half-car, half-truck idled, he couldn't hear the engine. He nodded, "Sure."

Nemi pushed the door open and leaned back to the steering wheel. The pickup cruised toward the river, passing gray, winter houses and dead lawns.

"Haven't seen you around lately," Nemi said.

Cole looked through the wide expanse of windshield. It was one of those winter days when the sun seemed to shine from an infinite distance, its light pale and washed. In the Greyhound coming up from L.A., he hadn't been aware of the day through the tinted windows, but walking from the bus station in town he had breathed the cool air deeply, thinking of the moist swampland around the old uncle's cabin, wondering what Onatima and Uncle Luther were doing at that moment. By his watch, they were in a different time now, but, of course, there was only a single time. He rolled down the car's window and smelled the air. It held a faint promise of rain, but only a few tatters of cloud hung over the coast range. He considered the rancher, wondering what had made him stop to offer a ride and what had caused him, Cole, to accept. It was an odd merger of motives, maybe just curiosity.

"I was visiting my father's uncle," he replied. "Down in Mississippi."

"Mississippi? I've never been in the South. They still pretty racist down there?"

Cole thought about the question. "I don't know," he said, thinking of Uncle Luther and the white whale. "It depends."

"I heard a rumor you'd been drafted."

Cole turned to look at Nemi for the first time, wondering how the rancher would have heard that. Mundo wouldn't have told him, not after he'd shown Cole the letter.

"I was."

"When you going in?"

Nemi's hands divided the steering wheel neatly in half. The Stetson hat sat square on his head and he looked straight toward the railroad trestle they were about to go under.

"I failed the physical," Cole replied. "They won't take me."

Nemi glanced at him and then looked back at the road. "You look healthy as a horse to me."

"They say I have a heart problem." Until the crew-cut doctor asked him about childhood illnesses and told him he had a heart murmur, he hadn't remembered the rheumatic fever that had kept him in bed for two months when he was eight years old. "Romantic fever," Attis had called it, making a singsong chant out of it to get Cole's weakened heart pumping faster. Until he was in high school, Cole, too, had thought of it as romantic fever.

"Well, I guess that's either good or bad, depending how you look at it," Dan Nemi said. "I hope it's not serious."

Cole was impressed by the absolute clarity of the windshield. There was virtually no distortion. He imagined how the wipers would move across the glass, smoothly and easily. He thought of the rancher's daughter, Diana, and then he thought of Attis. What had happened to his brother had started long before. Dan Nemi was caught up in it just like they all were, and he had suffered. Now there was only the river and the bundle he had to find down there.

"I stopped because I wanted to tell you something," the rancher said without looking at Cole. "I didn't kill your brother. Of course, we don't even know that he's dead. He may be hiding out somewhere. But I want you to know that I didn't do that. I don't care what anybody else thinks, but I don't want you to think that."

Cole watched the trees along the creek for a moment before replying. "I believe you," he said finally. But then, if not Jenna's father, who? he thought to himself.

Nemi drove a half-mile out of his way and dropped Cole off at home before he turned the El Camino around and headed toward the bridge. Cole watched the pickup vanish, and then he walked around to the back door of the house, 157 knowing by the feel of the air that no one was home.

He went into the kitchen and saw the carburetor parts on the table. The house was cold and stale. When he opened the refrigerator, he discovered that two of the shelves had been removed and a haunch of venison filled the remaining space. Stuffed around the deer were cans of beer. He pulled one of the black and gold cans out and levered the tab open just as someone began to knock at the back door.

When he opened the door, Diana Nemi stood there, staring from the depths of a hooded parka. Her eyes were wide and shining, and her hands were stuffed into the pockets of the red jacket. From the knees down her Levi's were dark with water, and her western boots had left heart-shaped watermarks on the cement of the porch steps.

"May I come in?"

When Cole hesitated, she added, "Don't worry, I'll take my boots off."

He held the door open and stepped back, and balancing impressively on one foot at a time, Diana reached down and slipped the wet boots and socks off, setting them on the porch before following him inside.

"Gosh, it's cold in here," she said. "Don't you have a heater?"

Cole walked to the wall and turned the thermostat up. The gas furnace kicked in with a loud whoosh.

"I waded the river. It's almost dry already." Diana smiled at him and then nodded toward the beer. "I'll take one of those if you have more."

"Oh, sure," he said.

When he returned with the beer, Diana was standing over the floor vent for the furnace. She had taken off the parka and hung it on a chair by the table. Already, the room had begun to warm.

"How come?"

She reached for the beer and took a drink before responding. "What?"

"How come you waded the river?"

"To see you, of course. I live on the other side. Remember?"

"I just got home. How did you know?" He set his beer on the table and slipped Attis's jacket off, tossing it onto a chair seat.

"Just a hunch," she said.

"Why'd you want to see me?"

She sipped the beer and looked at him over the top of the can. "Let's just say that I was lonely. You know, neither you nor I ever had too many friends in this town. We're a lot alike in that way. Maybe people are afraid of both of us."

Cole snorted. "You maybe. I doubt that people are afraid of me."

Diana nodded. "I'm very sorry, Cole. I wanted to tell you how badly I feel." She took two steps toward him and reached to touch his cheek. "We've both lost somebody. I know how you feel. It's like we're part of the same thing."

Cole looked at her eyes, where tears were just beginning to well at the corners. Her fingers were wonderfully warm.

Diana stepped back close to the heater grate. "These wet jeans are freezing. Do you mind if I take them off?"

He wondered for a moment if he'd understood her. Then he said, "I don't know. If my father. . . ."

"Don't worry, he won't be home for hours."

"How do you know?" he asked, watching her eyes.

"He's working over in Creston today. I heard one of our hands say that."

Diana set the beer on the floor and began unbuttoning the Levis. As she slipped them down over her hips, she used one hand to carefully hold her red bikini panties in place.

She walked to the table and hung the pants over a chair. Then she returned to stand, with feet slightly apart, by the heater. She picked up the beer and took a long pull and set it down again. "You ought to stand closer to the heater, 159

Cole. It feels wonderful."

Cole tried not to look at the smooth muscles of her legs, or at the fine pubic hairs that curled at the edges of the panties. He fixed his eyes on her face. The tears had disappeared, but her gray eyes were shining.

"You're beautiful," he said.

"Thank you." She smiled perfectly. "You know, Cole, I feel funny here like this. Do you mind if I take off this shirt?" Before he could respond, she raised her arms and pulled the black turtleneck off, tossing it toward the table. The cold had made her nipples taut, and she looked down and then back at Cole with a smile.

"You're a very attractive man," she said.

Wordlessly, she led Cole to his bedroom and took off his clothes. She turned the bed sheets down and slid between the covers, still holding to his hand and pulling him after her. She kissed him, touching his body everywhere, until finally, she very carefully guided him into her. Then she pulled the covers over both of them and she began to make love to him, slowly and precisely, moving beneath him like water.

"I've wanted you for so long, Cole. You're a beautiful boy."

He kept his eyes closed and felt himself drawn into her currents, surging and ebbing with her, her arms tight around his back and hips so that it seemed they were one. Delicately she kissed his chest and neck and lips, whispering comforting sounds as though she were afraid he would panic and flee like a wild animal. When he came, he felt the flood surge out of him, as if the dam of his life had broken.

"Virgins are so sweet," Diana said as she leaned on one elbow and looked down at him. She reached to touch his penis and then trailed her fingers up his flat belly until she reached his face. She pushed her fingers across his cheek and into his long hair and then caressed his shoulder and arm. Then her mouth moved down across his belly again

160

and she took him in her mouth. When he hardened again, she straddled him and guided him inside. With her eyes staring intently into his, she fucked him until she stiffened and came with a strange meowing. Then she thrust harder and faster upon him until he, too, came with a soft cry.

"Why are you here?" Cole asked her when he felt able to speak once more.

"I'm here for you, Cole. Can't you tell?" She was quiet for a moment, as he lay there with his eyes closed.

When he heard her leave the room, he opened his eyes. He lay on his back for a few moments, listening to her moving softly beyond the room and thinking of what she'd said. Her words had reminded him of badly read lines in a high-school play. Finally, he got up and pulled his pants on.

When he went to the kitchen, Diana stood in the porch doorway, fully dressed. "If you don't call me, I'll call you," she said. Her smile faded as she turned and went out the screen door of the porch, walking quickly toward the river.

Cole sat in a chair and felt the flare of heat from the furnace. When he went to the thermostat, he saw that it was set at ninety. He pushed it back to sixty-five and returned to his room. He reached for the pouch where it had hung from the bedpost, but it was gone. He searched the floor and then the shelf over the other bed, but the pouch wasn't in the room. Finally, he sat on the edge of the bed with his head in his hands, feeling as though he had nearly drowned. In his stomach was a hollow throb he associated with loss, a feeling he'd known before.

Barefoot, with just his Levi's on, he went to the refrigerator and sliced a chunk off the haunch of venison. He spooned Crisco into a cast-iron skillet and lit the gas stove. When the oil had melted, he laid the meat in the skillet and went to stand by the floor grate again, listening to the sizzle of the frying deer and trying to remember where he might have put the pouch. He felt weak, frightened, not the way he thought he was supposed to feel. And then she had waded the river on a cold day with a part of him inside of her, taking it home.

He wanted to run after her, splash across the thin, clear stream of the river and grab her. But he was afraid.

Twenty-nine

"Does he know who he is, old man?"

Onatima sat on one of the log rounds in Uncle Luther's cabin, combing her beautiful hair. Holding a long strand of silver hair in one hand, she ran the porcupine-quill comb carefully down its length. As she combed, her eyes would occasionally close with pleasure. Her white nightgown rose high on her neck and fell all the way to the deerskin moccasins on her feet.

"He is learning now," Uncle Luther said. "Such things take time, especially when a child grows up so far from home."

"Has he begun the hunt yet?"

The old man brushed glue around a hole in the rubber boot he was holding and then laid a patch over the hole. "I'm going to need me some new boots pretty soon," he said.

"Luther?"

He looked up from the boot.

"That river I told you about, old lady, it has only just begun to go back to sleep. Now it is beautiful, a little stream at the river's heart. There are strange, wonderful fish that come from the sea, with the colors of the rainbow. They are quick and beautiful, these fish, but they make me sad, because they are just memory-fish. They believe that they

162

swim in the other, older river, the one that never ceased. Now they will die when this one goes back underground. The young they leave behind will dry in the sun. Each year these fish come and die. The river has been broken only a few years, the time of a person's life, and to the fish this is less than one of the specks of sand in the river. Naturally, the fish cannot acknowledge what has happened. So they will continue to die until their circle, too, is broken."

"And the nephew?"

"Look," he said. He lifted a dipper of water from the bucket and poured it into a clear glass. Onatima rose from the chair and bent over the glass on the table. Within the water a form began to take shape. Cole McCurtain was there, peering about himself as if lost.

"He hasn't begun his search yet, but he's ready."

The form in the glass dissipated.

"What about the other, darker one?"

"He, too, is ready. And I think he will help us."

"I've seen the birds, old man."

Uncle Luther nodded and set the boot behind the wood stove, holding a hand at the small of his back as he straightened. "Yes. It's happening the way it's supposed to. There is a tree, and the *sheki* has come. The cleansing begins. It's not quite time for the younger nephew to find what he searches for."

"These people make me mad," Onatima said. "They work against themselves. They never understand."

"They don't know shit from shinola." Uncle Luther grinned at the old lady, who had completed the combing and was patiently braiding her hair. "They don't know their asses from holes in the ground."

"Don't be vulgar, old man. You're lucky you don't read the newspapers. It's everywhere, all over the world."

"What do you think about God, Old Lady Blue Wood?" Uncle Luther looked at her with one eye squinted.

"What kind of foolishness is this?" she answered.

"Well, listen. In this book you gave me they say some   163 interesting things about these people called Choctaws." He took the glasses and green book from the shelf and set the glasses on his nose, carefully arranging the wire hooks behind his ears. Then he turned the pages slowly until he came to the place he wanted. He began to read, "At the time of their formation from the earth, their Maker prescribed no form of worship, nor did he require any homage to be paid to him. The Choctaws appear to have been emphatically without God in the world. When the inquiry has been made, 'Did you ever think of God?' They answer, 'How can we think of him, of whom we know nothing?' " He looked up at her and winked as she continued braiding. Placing his finger on the page, he began to read again. "They have no idea of the moral turpitude of sin; indeed their sense of moral obligation is extremely feeble. Not regarding the Superior Being in the light of a lawgiver, and of course having nothing to expect from his favor, and nothing to fear from his displeasure, they are not influenced in their conduct by a desire to obtain the one, or avoid the other. Being thus deplorably ignorant of God, they have no higher motives to excite to a virtuous course of conduct, than the approbation of their own hearts, and nothing more powerful to deter from sin, than the disapprobation of their uninstructed and torpid consciences."

"Deplorably ignorant?" She stared at the book indignantly.

Uncle Luther held up a palm. "There's better stuff, old lady. Listen." He pushed the glasses up on his nose. "Having had no knowledge of the law of God as a rule of conduct, they have no word that signifies sin. From this barrenness of their language in relation to moral subjects, and from their extreme ignorance, it is very difficult to give them any correct notions of sin."

"Wonders never cease, do they, Old Lady Blue Wood?"
Onatima scowled.

"They been working hard to teach us, ain't they?" he said.

"I've never thought you needed much teaching, old goat."

Luther set the book back on the shelf and took off the glasses, folding them carefully atop the book. He turned to the old lady and lifted a braid in one hand.

"How about teaching me about moral turnipitude, Miz Blue Wood?"

She slapped the hand away and turned her shoulder to him. "Some goats are all beard and hog talk."

The old man stepped close and lifted the shining hair. Softly he kissed her neck. "*Anushkunna*. You know that word, old lady?"

"You butcher the tongue, old man. You don't speak the language." She turned and touched his cheek with the palm of her hand, raising the hand to brush it across his eyes.

Thirty

Mundo Morales had borrowed a horse, a huge, raw-boned buckskin that from a distance seemed to move without bending its knees. Against the pale sand and dark skeletons of brush, the animal loomed like something prehistoric, the man on its back a puny afterthought. From the bridge, Lee Scott watched the deputy sheriff coax the animal awkwardly down the thin stream of the river, sometimes wading the shallow current to get around stranded logs or brush piles. In the binoculars man and horse were somewhat hazy, slightly out of focus.

"It's shit creek pretty soon," Scott said aloud as he moved the binoculars downstream to where the trees and brush gathered into what looked like an impenetrable wall. As he swept the glasses back toward the horseman, a figure appeared at the edge of his vision on the far bank, and he swung the glasses in that direction. Cole McCurtain stood on the riverbank behind his house, and by the slant of his shoulders and head Scott could tell that the McCurtain kid was also watching Mundo Morales.

For a few minutes he shifted the glasses between Cole McCurtain and the deputy, until Mundo and the horse disappeared into a mess of tall cottonwoods piled high with torn brush and flotsom. Scott let the binoculars hang against his chest and walked toward the car at the end of the bridge. Across the river, Cole McCurtain turned back toward his house.

When the federal investigator pulled into the McCurtain driveway, Cole was stepping out the back door, wearing a fatigue jacket and carrying a twenty-two rifle in one hand. He stood with the rifle cradled in the crook of one arm, watching Lee Scott walk toward him. Beneath the roll of his black stocking cap, the boy's brown hair hung straight past his shoulders. His eyes stared directly at the approaching investigator.

"Going hunting?" Lee Scott's words came out much too loudly, and he flinched at his own voice. More quietly, he added, "I didn't think anything was in season this time of year."

Cole waited.

"I heard you had a stroke of bad luck," Scott grinned weakly. "Poor choice of words, I guess." A spaniel-type dog came up and shoved its nose into his hand and he reached down to ruffle the fur of the dog's head. The dog sat back on its haunches and grinned up at him.

"With the military, I mean. I heard you didn't pass the physical."

"Hoyo," Cole said softly, and the spaniel bounced to Cole's side, wriggling and eyeing the rifle happily.

"They said I have a bad heart."

166   "So I heard."

They stood watching each other. After a minute, Hoyo wandered over to piss on the trunk of a black walnut and sniff the weeds.

"Tough break." Scott shook his head and eyed Cole with sympathy. "I was over there, you know. Long-range recon. Scared the shit out of me, but I loved it. Had a pet praying mantis, carried it with me everywhere in a little wicker cage. Everybody said I was nuts, but it was like a totem, you know—a helper like you Indians used to have. I think it saved my life."

"Who are you?"

Lee Scott cocked his head and looked at Cole slyly. "It was like my animal helper, you know? Assistance from the transcendent beyond."

"I was about to go for a walk," Cole said. "Is there something I can do for you?"

Scott held out his hand and Cole looked at the hand and then back at the man's eyes. The hand retreated slowly and came to rest on Scott's chin, where it rubbed the day's stubble. "My name's Lee Scott, I'm with the Federal Bureau of Investigation." He pulled a billfold from the inside of his coat and let it fall open, displaying a badge. "I've been assigned to your brother's case. He kidnapped that girl he killed, and that's a federal offense. Now that he's escaped, he's a federal fugitive. They want to know where he is."

Scott's expression became shrewd. He narrowed his eyes. When Cole didn't respond, he went on. "But I'm sympathetic. I was over there. A lot of us came back just walking wounded, like Attis. Confused and mad as hell. Innocent people suffered. Out of the six of us who came back from the lurps together, everyone but me is dead or in prison for murder. I guess you could say I'm the only one who got it together. And it was especially bad for your people."

"My people?" Cole thought the man must be talking about his brother or the other boys from Amarga who went, like Mundo Morales.

"Native Americans, you know, the red brothers. Soon as somebody found out a boy was Indian, whisko-chango and he went out on point. Dead meat. We had us a Navajo boy who grew up in the desert and they stuck him out in the jungle on point, thinking he could see at night and smell charley. Kind of ironic, isn't it, after Sand Creek and Wounded Knee and smallpox-infested blankets and all the stuff white people did to Indians? Of course, some of the Indians got off on that, asked for that job. You see, I've always been fascinated by Indians. Made a hobby of Indians when I was a boy. Collected arrowheads and stuff. It was like I was trying to find out who I was, and those things could tell me. Back then I didn't know there were any Indians left alive. I thought you'd all vanished like dinosaurs. But you don't look like a real Indian, and you don't have an Indian name. That Navajo's name was Garcia. One night I asked him why he didn't have a real Indian name, and you know what he said? He grinned as wide as he could and said, "Cause I ain't real." I always thought Indians had names like Afraid-of-his-Horses or Ten Bears, or Lake Trout. You speak Indian?"

Cole looked up at the FBI agent and then glanced to where Hoyo crouched staring impatiently at the river bottom.

"Mundo Morales is down in the river right now looking for your brother. Is that where you think your brother is?"

"I don't know where my brother is. Why don't you ask those two agents who brought me back to California? Maybe they know something."

Lee Scott threw his head back. "Those two? One of 'em's in a D.C. hospital right now. Nervous breakdown. The other one claims an old medicine man turned you over to him and says he doesn't know anything about Attis McCurtain."

"He's lying."

The agent grinned. "Of course he is. It's what we're trained to do. You want Mundo to find your brother?"

"Do you think my brother's in the river?" Cole rested the barrel of the twenty-two upon the toe of his boot.

Lee Scott shook his head emphatically. "No, no, no. I don't. I believe Attis ran away. Everybody'd expect him to run south, down to those Chickasaw relatives. But he's too smart for that. I figure he went north. Probably turn up as a lumberjack. Lot of Indians are lumberjacks."

"Choctaw."

"What?"

"We're Choctaw, not Chickasaw," Cole said, deciding not to try to explain the Cherokee and Irish.

"I thought Choctaws were in Oklahoma," Scott said, looking confused. "Say, I heard a joke you might like. What did the Navajo say when dinner was over?" He grinned at Cole, who waited. "Doggone," Scott sputtered. "Get it?"

"Navajos don't eat dogs," Cole replied. "Only a few Indians, like some of the Sioux, ever ate dogs."

"Okay, here's another one, then. What's a Sioux picnic?" He looked at Cole expectantly. "A puppy and a six-pack."

Cole let the gun fall and took a step forward. When he swung his fist caught the agent square on the flat jaw muscle. Lee Scott landed on his back with a look of astonishment. Immediately he sat up, holding a hand against his cheek.

"Why'd you do that? Was that a joke Indians don't like? It didn't hurt."

When Cole didn't answer, the agent got to his feet, still staring incredulously. "You shouldn't have done that. I was trying to make friends."

Cole bent to pick up the twenty-two. "Get out of here."

"You Indians have always been paranoid. Even mixed-breeds. That's why you're always fighting among yourselves. Indians killed Crazy Horse. It's a felony to strike a federal officer."

When Cole didn't answer, Scott said, "Mundo Morales has a strange idea that Dan Nemi killed your brother. He thinks he saw Attis in the river that night, you know. Poor 169

Morales was in Nam, too, and if you ask me he's just a quarter-inch from going over the edge himself."

"If I run into Mundo, I'll tell him you think he's crazy," Cole said. He turned and walked to the edge of the yard and disappeared down the bank.

"I won't file a report on that attack," Scott shouted after him. "You were just upset, and it wasn't much of a punch at all. I barely felt it." After a few seconds, he added, "I'm a vegetarian. Nobody died to make my dinner."

He turned and headed to his car. "We've never had a cowboy in heaven before," the agent said to himself as he rubbed a hand across his jaw. It was the punch line to an Indian joke he'd forgotten. Somehow, it reminded him of Mundo Morales on horseback. One night in the jungle it had snowed. He'd awakened to it coming down in fat, heavy flakes, layering the air and coating everything in white silence. He'd tried to sit up, remembering what it was like to play in snow, but it had rested on him like steel, pressing him to the rotting humus as it piled up around him and over him, blotting out the jungle and his patrol and eventually the whole war. Three, five, ten, twenty feet it drifted down, muffling his heartbeat, and he stared up at the whiteness with frozen eyeballs, imagining how surprised they were in the rice paddies and out in the delta, the lurps who were miles and miles out like his patrol facing now an unbreachable world of white between them and home. It had been the only quiet night in a war of loud terror, and the next morning there was no sign of it. When he'd tried to explain the wonder and beauty of the snow, the others had just looked at him. One guy, a little Puerto Rican from New York, had sighed and walked away shaking his head. Afterward, Lee Scott had waited and hoped and yearned for the snow to come again, but it never did.

As he wheeled the gray Plymouth four-door toward the Nemi ranch he began to sing.

If I was a dead man hanging in a tree,
The coyotes would come and they'd gather round me.

They'd gather in a circle round the hangin' tree,
And they'd howl at the dead man—
The dead man, me.

As the agent sang he tapped the steering wheel in time and nodded his head while the heel of his left foot danced on the floorboard.

Oh, if I was a dead man in the sea,
I'd float to the bottom so peacefully,
I'd float to the bottom so peacefully,
If I was a dead man in the sea.

And if I was a dead man on the ground,
The buzzards would come and they'd gather around.
They'd say hello in their friendly way,
And the flesh and the bones wouldn't last a day.

In a baritone he added the refrain:

And the flesh and the bones wouldn't last a day.

If I was a dead man in the fire,
Stretched right out on the funeral pyre,
The flames would leap, and they'd keep leaping higher,
If I was a dead man in the fire.

He slammed the steering wheel with the palm of his right hand and chanted in a louder, deeper voice,

Oh, earth air water and fire, too,
They're going to make their mark on you.
They'll say hello in their friendly way.
And the flesh and the bones won't last a day.
And the flesh and the bones won't last a day.

He closed his eyes and nodded with pleasure. It was a song he'd made up one night near the Cambodian border on a long patrol. For a while he'd thought about being a songwriter when he got back from Nam. "They'll say hello in their friendly way, and the flesh and the bones won't last a day." He boomed the final refrain again. "And the flesh and the bones won't last a day. Yeeha!"

A steelhead flashed through shallow water, its rainbow sides brilliant with red and green and silver, its dorsal fin and tail cutting the air and sending a spray into the sunlight. The horse shied sideways, tossing its head and rolling its eyes. Then it began to buck, curving its broad back reluctantly and snapping it straight again like an arthritic octogenarian. Mundo dug his heels into the stirrups and gripped the saddle horn, feeling each convulsion building in the buckskin like an earth tremor until the animal arced unconvincingly and came down with all four massive feet braced. After the fourth buck, Mundo slammed the heels of his boots hard into the animal's ribs. The horse seemed to deflate. It sagged with a loud sigh and slowly settled to its knees and then, as Mundo jerked his feet from the stirrups and leaped, the horse heaved over and lay on its side.

Mundo spun in the air and came down on his back in a foot of water. He sat up quickly, staring around him in amazement. Through the clear water the rocks formed patterns of bright colors against the sand, the ripples blurring and rearranging edges. Then he stood, feeling the water like ice between his toes and in the crotch of his pants. Currents ran down his legs. He watched the steelhead fight its way across a gravel bar and into two feet of water. Then it became a shadow in the bright water, a dark arrow racing toward a memory in the blood.

In a cottonwood close by a crow began to bark, and Mundo glared at the bird. Precariously, Jessard Deal's horse began to rise, rolling to its knees with a shudder and bracing the forefeet before trusting weight on the rear legs. Then the animal unfolded upward, water streaming down its flanks, straightening each leg as though it were ancient parchment. Once erect, the buckskin stood spread-legged and swung its great hammer head to the side toward Mundo. Hatred burned in the brown eyes, and Mundo took a step backward. The crow laughed and flapped skyward, craning its head sideways to study the scene. The horse shivered like a dog, shaking a halo of water from its coat and causing the stirrups to flap wildly. Then it turned and began to run upstream, loping through the stream with a fluid and lovely stride, each hoofbeat sending an explosion of water into the air.

Cole McCurtain sat on a sycamore log close by and watched Mundo watch the horse splash smoothly toward the upstream bridge. Hunched in the fatigue jacket with wool pants and wool shirt and gloves, Cole felt the cold in his bones and pitied Mundo.

"A beautiful animal, isn't it?"

Mundo kept staring at the loping buckskin. "Hijo de la puta," he said to the river and sky. He wiped water from his forehead with the palm of his hand, and then turned toward Cole.

"You been spying on me? It's just like its owner," Mundo said. "Jessard Deal won that piece of dog shit in a poker game. What are you doing here?"

"Hunting. You better come up to the house and dry out, Mundo."

"Nothing's in season. You got any beer?" Mundo was looking toward the bridge again. The horse had run beneath the bridge and vanished.

"You're on duty, Mundo."

"Fuck duty. Your old man has beer. Let's go."

Cole stood up and turned back toward the far bank. Mundo walked after him, listening to the squish of his boots. A flock of crows had joined the solitary original now at roost in a cottonwood, and the whole murder of birds shouted and jeered at the men below. A rabbit squirted from the brush and danced up the sand alongside the water. Cole glanced at the cottontail and then up at the crows. A pair of buzzards sailed by high overhead, following the river to the south with unusual directness. Then a red-tailed hawk made the mistake of coasting out over the river from an alfalfa field, and the crows rose in a single impulse to loudly assault the bigger bird.

Thirty-one

Luther knelt to examine the track. The panther was ahead of him now. A few minutes before, just after he'd left the trot line, he'd felt it behind him. He peered at the thick trees and brush at both sides, and he chuckled. A catfish croaked in the wet gunnysack he'd set beside the trail, and the old man stood up and picked up the sack.

"Painter don't walk in daytime," he said aloud. One of the fish croaked in agreement. Overhead, the sun was visible in broken points of light through the trees. The cold smell of winter woods hovered over everything.

"Keeping track of things, ain't you?" the old man said to the trees. "Well, you just gotta wait like the rest of us."

He moved up the trail toward home, holding the gunnysack away from his thin leg to avoid the spiked whiskers that protruded through the burlap. "Soul-eater don't know a danged thing about moral turpitude," he said to the dripping sack. "He's got a uninstructed and torpid conscience sure as hell."

The trail broke from the woods into the cabin clearing, and he walked to the shed and dumped the half-dozen mud-cats on the ground. The two hounds came scooting from beneath the cabin and slunk close to sniff the gasping fish. When one of the foot-long fish gaped its mouth open, the dog called Yvonne jumped backwards and growled.

"Oh, them bones, them bones," the old man sang softly as he prepared to clean the fish. He was satisfied with the way the story was going. The only uneasiness he felt was from the other one who had somehow become involved. He had a disquieting feeling that he was being watched and evaluated by the old dark one, as though that one was outside the story but intensely interested. Occasionally he caught glimpses of the old man in the baggy suit and blue moustache, but in his dreams the man was never entirely clear, never quite in focus. At times he thought the old one was a shadow, but it was neither inside nor outside shadow, as if perhaps there was no separation between the two. That was what bothered him most. The one with the shining eyes wasn't among the living, but he was still whole, just one thing, and he seemed to be enjoying the story immensely. He wasn't an Indian, but there was an oddly familiar feel to him, and he seemed to understand things. If he was outside the story, could he make a difference, change the outcome in some way? The possibility worried the old man.

"I better tell Onatima about that one," Luther said to the hounds. "Onatima knows about stories." The dogs wriggled their bodies in affirmation.

Thirty-two

Hoey McCurtain watched the federal investigator park beneath the biggest white oak and approach the door of the ranch house. From the scrub oak and elderberry thicket near the river, he could watch the house easily. He shifted his back into a more comfortable position against a scrawny live-oak trunk and raised the thirty-forty Krag, waiting for Helen Nemi to cross in front of the big window. When the woman appeared, the long barrel of the rifle followed her across the room. He'd waited there all morning, patiently watching the house, comfortable with the wait. It was something Uncle Luther had taught him, the art of waiting.

When he was ten years old, they had gone into the woods before daylight, to a place the uncle knew, and they had waited. Eventually, the cougar had come to the exact spot where Uncle Luther had said he would, a golden brown male with the soft and gentle face of a kitten. "Watch how the hunter waits," Uncle Luther had said before they left the cabin. "Be the *koi*." So they had lain in wait, each breath rationed, the very heartbeat calmed, watching the place where the cat had become a rock, a log, a spot of earth. Until the little wild pig came to the river to drink and the big cat killed it simply and quickly. After the cougar had dragged the pig away into the brush, Uncle Luther had explained more. "You got to remember that cat. Be that cat. Dream it. And then you can be more. You got to be the dirt and rocks, the grass, the way the water sounds when it goes by, the smell of the air, the woods when there ain't no noise anywhere, the sound of everything breathing everywhere in the woods."

He wondered where the rancher was. For four hours he had watched the house. Helen Nemi had driven away and returned an hour later. The daughter had walked down to the river far below the bridge and disappeared. Later she had returned, her legs dark with water from the knees down. One of the ranch hands had knocked at the door, said something to Helen Nemi, and gone back to the big barn. But the rancher had not shown.

Hoey worked the plug tobacco in his cheek and settled closer to the tree, knowing that sooner or later a man must come home. Near his feet, a bluebelly lizard crept across the brittle leaves, its head jerking nervously. At the crossed boots the lizard stopped and raised its head. The stream of tobacco juice caught the bluebelly on the tail, and it sprang miraculously away into the mess of fallen branches. Hoey lifted his head and sniffed. He'd caught a whiff of frying fish, and he looked all around. The smell had to come from the Nemi house, but he couldn't imagine Helen Nemi frying catfish in cornmeal and lard, which was what he smelled.

As he was breathing very slowly, trying to find the fragrance again, the El Camino pulled into the driveway and Dan Nemi got out. Hoey raised the rifle again, swinging the barrel to a point between the tall man's shoulders. And suddenly Diana Nemi appeared from the side of the house. Running toward her father, she leaped up and flung her arms around his neck, knocking the Stetson from his head. He bent to pick up the hat and then walked toward the front door with Diana beside him.

Hoey steadied the rifle once again between the rancher's shoulders, the notch of the sight exactly centered. He took a breath and held it and, just as Nemi reached for the front door, he let the breath out in a whispered, "Bang!"

Hoey lowered the rifle and watched the father and daughter disappear into the house. The fragrance of frying catfish was stronger now, and he looked about him with his eyes narrowed to slits. He stood and slapped the oak leaves off his pants and then slipped backwards through the brush. As he broke from the trees into the sand of the riverbed, he heard the pounding splash of hoofbeats and saw the buckskin galloping toward him. Propping the rifle against a log, he waded into the river and spread his hands. The big horse raced at him, plunging toward the side at the last second, when Hoey grabbed the dangling reins and braced his feet. The horse stopped instantly, stumbling and spashing water all the way up his captor's chest.

"Whoa," Hoey said softly. "Easy there you old bucket of wormshit."

The buckskin stood spraddle legged, shivering and looking at the man out of the corner of one eye.

"What'd you do, throw Jessard Deal in the river?"

When the horse didn't answer, Hoey led it to the edge of the stream and, holding the reins in one hand, picked up the rifle. He looped the reins together over the saddle horn and climbed into the saddle, holding the rifle across his lap. Then he turned the animal back in the direction from which it had fled and began walking it downstream.

When he reached the trail to his backyard, he kicked the horse hard and it leaped up the steep bank in a surge that nearly sent him backwards out of the saddle. A few feet from the back door he dismounted. He leaned the gun against the door and tied the horse to a tree with a length of electrical wire hooked through the bridle.

Inside the house, Mundo Morales was sprawled in the big chair in his underwear, his feet propped on the footrest and a can of beer resting on the belly of his white tee shirt. Cole lay on the couch, his head against one arm and his feet crossed. He held a beer balanced on his belt buckle.

The two looked up in surprise when Hoey appeared in the doorway.

Mundo was the first to speak. "You're wet, Hoey."

Hoey looked at the green and brown sheriff's uniform hung on chairbacks around the floor furnace and then back at Mundo. He turned his attention to Cole. "I don't suppose you two know something about Jessard Deal's horse."

"That nag threw me. You seen it?" Mundo asked.

"I tied him up outside."

"Muchas gracias, Hoey. You just saved me a lot of trouble."

Hoey went into one of the bedrooms and shut the door.

Mundo looked at Cole. "Where's your old man been?"

Cole shrugged. "I don't know. I thought he was working out in Creston today. I've been waiting to talk to him." He stood up. "Let's shoot some hoops, Mundo, while your clothes dry."

Mundo raised his eyebrows. "Hoops? How can I shoot hoops while my pants are drying in here?"

"You can wear your boxer shorts. Nobody can see behind the house. We'll do a little one-on-one."

"Naw, I don't think so, Cole. It wouldn't look good, the deputy sheriff bouncing a ball around in his choners."

"You're afraid I'll beat your ass, aren't you? Remember all those times you and me and my brother'd play cutthroat and you guys would kill me? Well, Mundo, you're old and I grew up, so you don't stand a chance."

Mundo stood up and chugged the last of the beer. "Let me put my boots on, bro, and you got yourself a game."

Cole went into the bedroom and came out with a basketball in one hand and a pair of Converse hightops in the other.

"Hey, man. You can't wear basketball shoes if I got to play in my boots."

Cole looked at Mundo's pale legs, with his socks protruding an inch above the boots, and the blue paisley shorts.

"Okay. I'd probably better wear boots anyway to keep you from smashing my toes to pulp."

Cole laced his boots up on the porch and followed Mundo to the cement slab and backboard behind the house.

Behind Mundo, Cole dribbled once and launched a sixteen-foot jump shot that went through with nothing but net.

"Chingada." Mundo grabbed the rebound, dribbled in a short circle and turned for a short hook shot that came off the rim straight into his face. He grabbed the ball and dribbled closer to put in a reverse lay-up, his boots coming down with a dead thud.

"Let's go, bro. Shoot for outs."

Cole shot from eighteen feet and again hit nothing but net.

"Your ball. You been out here practicing, niño."

Cole brought the ball in, dribbling with his back to the basket, switching hands and faking a drive. Mundo stepped back to block the drive and Cole spun and went up for a jump shot. Suddenly Mundo was there, swatting the ball back over Cole's head. The ball bounced off the shed wall near Jessard's horse, and the horse bucked twice and snorted at them.

"You talk to your dad. I'm going to have to stop him," Mundo said as Cole brought the ball back onto the cement.

Cole dribbled toward the basket, spun, gave a head fake,

179

and ducked under Mundo's arms for a lay-up.

Mundo collected the ball and dribbled back to the imaginary in-bounds line. He began a methodical dribble toward the basket, keeping the ball to one side and shielding it with a long arm. "Not bad. You find anything down there in the river, you tell me, okay compadre? By the way, you ought to trim those fingernails."

Cole shoved his knee into Mundo's hip, forcing Mundo to sidestep with the dribble. "Man, you almost got my cojones there," Mundo said as he worked toward the basket from the other side. "I'm scared my dick's gonna get broken anyway with no jockstrap." Suddenly he pivoted and spun to the basket, going up for a stuff. But instead of the stuff, the ball wedged into the angle between the metal rim and backboard and remained there. Mundo came down with a grunt and looked up at the ball in disgust.

"Can you believe that shit?" he said, shaking is head.

Cole backed off and ran at the basket. Effortlessly he jumped and knocked the ball loose.

"What will you do if you find my brother?"

"That's basket interference. It should be my ball out of bounds," Mundo said. When Cole bounced the ball to him, he added, "What I have to do. Turn it over to the coroner so they can do an autopsy. It's the only way we can prove anything."

Cole bent his knees to anticipate another drive, his hands spread chest-high. "That's what I thought. You know, Mundo, my father's trying to think like an old-time Choctaw."

With a grunt, Mundo rose into the air, the tips of his boots soaring an inch off the pavement as he let the ball arc off his fingertips. Hitting the back of the rim, the ball came back to him in a high arch.

"It's these boots. I can't play ball in boots with my dick flopping around like this." He dribbled sideways closer toward the basket. He spun to his right and, with a head fake, turned to drive to his left. But Cole was there and

180

easily flipped the ball away.

Cole stood twelve feet back, dribbling the ball and watching Mundo. "My father doesn't understand that the whole world's so messed up that none of that applies any more. He thinks things are more simple than they are. Uncle Luther, my father's uncle, explained some things to me. I tried to explain those things to Hoey, but he wouldn't listen."

"You better try again, bro," Mundo replied, stepping close and slapping at the ball.

Cole drove past Mundo's outstretched hand and laid the ball into the basket. He tossed the ball to Mundo.

"I will. But what about you, Mundo? You think you have to solve this murder. But maybe you don't understand what's going on either."

Mundo held the ball over his stomach. "I don't get it, Cole. You and me both know Dan Nemi killed him. You want him to get away with it? That ain't right. You can't let somebody do something like that and get away with it. It's not fucking right." Standing flat-footed, he launched a fifteen-foot shot that banked off the backboard and through the basket. "We ought to play winner's outs," he said.

"We never play winner's outs," Cole replied as he took the ball back to the in-bounds spot and turned to dribble slowly toward Mundo. "You're wrong, Mundo. Dan Nemi didn't kill my brother. He told me that, and I believe him. Somebody else did. Maybe he paid somebody. I don't know. Besides, think about everything. Your family used to be rich. They used to own everything you can see around here for miles and miles, didn't they?" He stopped and held the ball on his hip. "But the whites came and took it. That's not right. Are you going to let them get away with it? Your family got it from the king of Spain, but where'd he get it? How about the Indians who used to live here? This land never was your family's or the king's. And there are still a few Salinan Indians left, you know, up near King City. Maybe they shouldn't let you get away with what you did, but I guess they just want to live now. They know that you can't solve everything."

As Cole talked, Mundo edged closer. Suddenly his hand shot out and knocked the ball free. They both jumped for it, and Cole grabbed it, spun, and put up a jump shot that swished the net.

Mundo glared and bounced the ball to the back of the court. He turned to face Cole, holding the ball over the small ridge of his stomach. "You've heard me bitch about that stuff myself, but that doesn't have anything to do with what I'm talking about. And I think Nemi did it, somehow. He as much as told me he did." He started a methodical dribble, using his hip to push Cole closer and closer to the basket. Three feet away, he turned slowly and put up a hook shot that banked in.

Cole caught the ball as it fell from the net. "You can't do that Mundo. You can't just shove me out of the way with your ass."

Breathing hard, Mundo said, "That's just hoops, man. It's a contact sport." He faced Cole, who was dribbling slowly and looking at the basket. "Listen, Cole. I'm talking about your brother and my best friend being murdered. If you don't have the cojones to do anything about it, I do. Besides, it's more than that. It's not just Nemi and your brother anymore."

"It's all the same, Mundo. You think those Indians are all gone from here? They're not. You go out in the hills at night some time and listen." Cole head faked and drove for the basket, Mundo spinning and moving with him. Under the basket, Cole shifted the ball from his right hand to his left and used the right to shove Mundo away. The left hand laid the ball neatly into the basket.

"Puta maggie. What you call that move?"

"A lay-up," Cole said, grinning.

"You better watch those flagrant violations when you're playing against the law."

182   Mundo held the ball against his chest near where the

free-throw line would have been. "I'm out of shape, man. But you know, I'm talking about right now. You're talking ancient history. Yesterday ain't today, man. You know, those fat asses in San Luis would like to let this drop. They could just put your brother down as escaped and never have to think about it again. That federal douche bag who's been poking around wants the same thing. They don't want it solved, man, because to them Attis just doesn't matter. He didn't matter when they sent him to Nam, none of us did, and he doesn't matter now. Only thing is, he came back and fucked up their neat little picture, showing everybody just what they did to him in that war. They don't like it when their sloppy work shows." He tried to spin the ball on his index finger, but it rolled off. He caught it and held it behind his back. "So now that he ain't around to embarrass nobody they want to just forget the whole thing. It's like what they've been doing to your people for a hell of a long time, you know. Hiding them out on reservations somewhere so they won't embarrass rich white folks by looking poor and hungry. It's like all those braceros they stick in shacks way off the road so nobody will see how shit-ass poor and hungry they are."

Mundo tucked his undershirt into his boxer shorts and patted the small curve of his belly. "Now you're telling me you agree with them. He was your brother, man. It was Attis, remember? It's not right, Cole."

"You're sounding like my father," Cole said, glancing toward the house. "And you shouldn't say his name out loud."

Mundo drove, slicing past Cole and going up for a successful stuff. Cole collected the ball and dribbled slowly back from the basket. "I wasn't ready," he said.

Mundo followed him, saying to Cole's back, "Well, in a way Hoey's right. He doesn't want to let them get away with it again. But it has to be done according to the law. I can't let your father commit another murder. We have to have rules, values. People can't just be killed, goddamn it. 183

You know, Cole, it was me your brother called. I was the one who found him and the first one who saw what he'd done to Jenna. And I was the one who took your brother in. There's too much bad shit going on in this county, too much in the whole goddamned world. What Hoey has in mind is just more of it. You or your dad get in my way, I'll arrest your asses for obstructing justice. If Hoey shoots Dan Nemi, I'll be the one who comes for him."

Cole stepped back and launched a fifteen-foot hook shot above Mundo's outstretched hands. Mundo spun for the rebound and the ball caromed off the front of the rim into his groin. He doubled up for a moment and then straightened, breathing deeply.

"I think I better get dressed and get that nag back to Jessard," Mundo said.

"Sorry about that." Cole stood beside Mundo holding the ball against his flat stomach.

As they walked back to the house, Mundo said softly, "You know, sometimes I have this fantasy about being way the hell and gone out in some wilderness, Alaska maybe. I'm in a little plane flying over this huge wilderness, and the plane crashes. I'm the only survivor, and I have to live out there all by myself for months and months. It's just me, no family, no job, no name, no nothing. Just me and what I can do to survive. I rip things out of the plane to use, make snowshoes out of tubing and seat covers, a stove out of sheet metal from the plane. I use electrical wire to make snares for rabbits and deer, make an axe out of a sharp piece of busted metal. I make a shelter two-day's hike away from the corpses in the plane because I'm afraid if I'm too close I'll get desperate and turn cannibal. And I live there in the snow all winter and spring, in a place where I'm the only one that knows I exist, the only thing that knows who I am. There, I'm not a Morales or a deputy sheriff, not even Mexican. Just nothing, you know?"

Cole nodded. "You've got a tough job, Mundo. You know how to set snares?"

When Mundo shook his head, Cole said, "I could teach you sometime. Box traps, too. And deadfalls. My dad showed us. I could teach you how to catch fish with your hands. Things that might come in handy."

"You never can tell," Mundo replied, rubbing his crotch.

Thirty-three

Onatima was scattering corn to her chickens when the old man appeared.

"So you already cooked those fish," she said without looking up.

Holding a tin plate with a piece of burlap over it, Luther stopped beside the chicken wire and looked in at the old lady and the dozen Plymouth Rocks and Rhode Islands. Onatima's hair hung straight from the red turban and a brown calico dress showed beneath her wool overcoat. She shuffled in rubber boots several sizes too large for her. As she clucked and cast the last of the corn to the hens, a big red rooster flared its wings and threatened her legs. She pointed a finger at it, and the rooster danced backwards toward a corner and began to scratch with intense interest at a spot on the ground.

"I baked some corn bread to go with the fish," Onatima added as she finally glanced toward the old man. Her smile was bright and cheerful.

"It's getting harder and harder to surprise you, old lady."

She came out of the coop and shut the wire door, clapping the dust from her hands. "We'll talk about the thing that's troubling you when we eat," she said as she walked toward

185

a silver Airstream trailer that gleamed in the middle of the clearing. Beside the trailer leaned a heavy-looking bicycle with balloon tires and a basket on the handlebars.

Inside the warm trailer, the old man sat back on a deep couch with a sigh.

"Civilization isn't so bad sometimes, is it, Luther?" Onatima set the plate of fish on a gas stove and lighted a burner beneath it, turning the fire down to a flicker. From the oven she pulled a cast-iron skillet of corn bread. She turned the bread out onto a wooden plate and took a pitcher of buttermilk from a little refrigerator.

"All this with butane?" Uncle Luther said, looking around the little trailer.

"Electricity too. You always pretend you don't know about that. You could have them run wires to your cabin, too, old man, if you weren't so backwards."

He set his hat on the end of the couch. "Seems to me that backwards these days is forwards."

She poured milk into two wooden mugs and moved the tin plate of fish from the stove to the center of the little Formica table, setting it on a hot pad.

"Sometimes you make sense," she said. "Now tell me about that other one that's been worrying you."

As she forked pieces of fried fish and wedges of corn bread onto plates, Luther rose from the couch and lowered himself cautiously onto a chair. He described the old man. "He's watching the story. I've seen him there, right on the edge of it, and he's very interested. He dresses well." He lifted a piece of fish with his fork and looked beneath it suspiciously.

"You're the one who cooked this fish, so don't be looking at it like you think I fried up some skunk for you."

At the old lady's words, he withdrew the fork and reflected for a moment. "I think he's a shadow, but he ain't Choctaw. He ain't waiting to go somewheres else, and he ain't two different shadows neither. It's unnatural. It's like this old man just goes and comes when he wants to."

Onatima snorted and broke corn bread into the mug of milk. "Some of these Indians say it's poisonous to drink milk and eat fish at the same time. You ever hear that?"

The old man nodded in the affirmative and began to crumble corn bread into his mug. "What I come to ask you is whether you think this old man might be able to change the story somehow. I thought he was outside the story, but it seems like he's ready to jump in." He described the old man in more detail, how he looked and the way his face would sometimes come into focus in the middle of the story being dreamed, rising right through.

She broke a piece of catfish with her hands and nibbled on it thoughtfully. "This old man wasn't part of things to begin with?" When he shook his head, she added, "And one day he just showed up?"

"That's right, old lady."

"And you're sure he's interested in the story?"

He nodded again, and she spooned corn bread out of the mug and mulled it over for a moment. "Then he's part of it and you've got to take him into consideration."

"But maybe it's like a man reading a book," Uncle Luther said. "Maybe he's just going to sit back and watch what happens."

Onatima snorted again. "Nobody reads like that, old man. You'd better reckon with this one."

"Hmm." He chewed the fish thoughtfully. "What really troubles me about this one is he's got some antiquated notions. He believes in witches."

Onatima grinned widely at Luther, and then the two of them began to laugh. When the hilarity had passed, she wiped her eyes and said, "A man in this day and age believing in witches? Can you imagine?"

"Strikes me as a kind of moral turniptude," Luther said.

"Turpitude, old man."

"That's what I said."

"Well, you'd better divide and reckon with this one, Luther Cole."

187

He stared at the corn bread and milk in his spoon. "Where you think folks ever got the idea it was poison to eat fish and drink milk at the same time? Must have come over with white people."

"White people don't have a monopoly on ignorance, you old fool. Neither do red people or black people."

Thirty-four

Cole walked the river. Bare-limbed sycamores and cottonwoods bent to him. Brush reached for him with spiny fingers. The silver stream flowed darkly into mats of broken and rotted vegetation. Fragments of styrofoam ice chests and cups and faded aluminum cans dotted the river's refuse. Doves flushed from alfalfa fields at the end of the day, their wings whistling in the cooling air as bats came out to hunt. All around him the diminished river quickened with small life-forms. The sky ended on the points of fence posts and barbed wire. He thought of *nalusachito*, the soul-eater.

Mundo Morales watched the evening news, Gloria beside him and their daughter snuggled in his lap. They were giving body counts. Cameramen had produced dramatic footage to go with the numbers. Mundo closed his eyes and listened to helicopter blades hammering the air. Walter Cronkite was speaking numbers through gritted teeth.

Hoey ran a cleaning rod down the barrel of his old rifle and listened to Buck Owens on the radio. The house was cold and becoming dark. He missed his wife with a deep ache. He thought about his uncle in Mississippi, and he wondered when Cole would really talk about what happened back there. He knew the old man had done something for the boy, because Cole was different. He was quieter and more certain of himself. His hair was getting longer, and until recently he'd been wearing the leather pouch from his belt wherever he went. But so far, he'd only tried to talk about Dan Nemi, and there wasn't any use in talking about that.

Buck Owens made way for Hank Williams, and Hoey thought about his other son. There was a sick and empty place right below his heart, a feeling that had been there even before Attis had come back from the war. He imagined the river by night, most of its water gone back into the ground. What was down there now? He'd been feeling something in the river since Attis had disappeared, but it wasn't his son. It was something desperate, something that was impatient and angry. He remembered the night Attis had been born back in Mississippi. They'd tried to banish him according to custom, to send him away like they always did, but he'd refused, standing spread-legged beside the bed and catching his son when he came. His hands had touched Attis first, in violation of all the laws, and the thought that other hands had touched his son last alternately sorrowed and enraged him. He thought of Dan Nemi, and he ran an oiled rag along the barrel of the gun.

Diana Nemi held a mask to her face and looked in the mirror. Mardi Gras feathers and cat's-eyes looked back at her. In the hinged and angled sides of the mirror, other masks looked on with the same eyes. She felt the hayfields and fenced hillsides rising up around the house with unbearable weight, felt the huge barns leaning toward the little house. The whole ranch had become monstrous to her. She thought of Berkeley and escape, and then she thought of all the water behind the dam upstream. If she could release it, it would cleanse the earth of her father's foul constructions, of all the works of men, of her own bloody sinew and bone. "Can it be," she whispered, "that we have walked the earth for eighteen years and come to this?" She smiled ironically at her reflection. Up on Pine Mountain in the lengthening shadows was Jenna's grave. They had buried her beneath a live oak. In the early summer Diana had gone there to pluck the sprouted acorns from the grave, hating the little curling roots that split each shell and twisted into the earth like the tails of pigs. She thought of Mundo Morales. They were all doing what was necessary, what they had to.

Behind his bar, Jessard Deal polished a glass and set it in front of Lee Scott. He set a second glass in front of Dan Nemi. Beside each glass he set an opened bottle of Mexican beer. From beneath the bar he brought a remarkably long, thin knife that gleamed in the tavern light. With exquisite care he quartered a lime on the scarred bar, dropping two quarters into each glass. He smiled and behind him the barroom swarmed in the mirror, the blue, rippling boatman struggling for control, the green pool tables tilting, customers moving about awkwardly, as if losing grasp of motor reflexes.

"I am innocent," Dan Nemi said. "I have suffered loss, but in all of my life, Mr. Scott, I have never broken a law."

"Then it's my job to protect you," the FBI agent replied. "That's how our great nation began. Protect the innocent and cut the fucking nuts right off the guilty." He poured the beer carefully against the side of his glass. "The servants of Satan in the howling desert. That's Indians from the word go."

"Looney fucking toons," Jessard Deal said with a smile. "Not worth a warm bucket of spit, either one of you. What a piece of work is a man. How express and admirable."

"I beg your pardon?" the rancher said, looking at the bartender through his beer glass.

"Not worth the powder it'd take to blow you to hell. You're my kind of people." Jessard leaned his head back and laughed. The pale assistant hurried across the room. One of the blonde barmaids came and leaned against the bar, smoking bitterly. She watched herself blow smoke rings in the mirror. The rings drifted across the reflected beer sign, blending with the ripple reflections. Jessard's laugh froze the barroom.

Out over the river an owl's wings rose and fell, the blunt tips nearly touching on the downbeat as the bird followed the twisting stream. Now and then the owl sent a call through the air, designed to stir small things into panicked flight. Not far away, the owl's mate echoed his warnings. In her bed, Helen Nemi rolled onto her side and pulled the comforter up to her chin. Soundlessly, she mourned the loss of her firstborn child. She remembered the infant and child, the first feel of a baby's mouth at her breast and the first tumbling attempts at steps. The hollow place inside her was immense and echoing. She considered going to her other daughter, just to touch her, but the owl's call reminded her of all the evil that washed the earth, touching everyone. The only hope any of them had was to pretend they did not see it or feel it. To imagine themselves untouched. It was a story she told herself.

Thirty-five

Cole walked the river. As the early winter evening came on, shadows were flushed from the trees and strangling brush that clumped and spread beside the little stream. Fish in the darkened water made sudden eruptions and whipped out of sight. He had searched only three or four miles that day, moving slowly, switchbacking from one bank to the other across the wide riverbed so that he could

191

probe every clot of debris caught in the broken river growth. He found shredded plastic and globules of styrofoam, old boots and milk cartons, the half-buried bones of an ancient automobile, corrugated tin siding torn from barns, tires, buckets, boards with rusty nails, a bloated white dog, wooden fence posts with strands of barbed wire attached. He looked for a glint of bone, a texture that would mean straight, black hair, a difference in the shadows that might be wool or cotton, an angle suggesting flesh instead of brittle wood.

He had traced the buzzards' flight, prowling his way through the thickets toward the heart of the river where the birds stood in tall trees and plunged periodically downward. He had felt himself followed and had taken precautions, doubling back, thinning himself behind tree trunks to watch his trail, listening with the skill learned from hunting. He'd heard and seen nothing, but he'd felt something there, just out of eyesight, almost audible, as if it held its breath when he held his, stood still when he stopped. Wading the river, he'd stopped in midstream to look suddenly back, expecting something to be there surprised in midstride. But it remained a feeling and, as the afternoon wore on, it became familiar. He knew what it was and he ceased turning around.

When he'd breached the buzzards' clearing, he had held his breath and steeled his muscles, fearing his own panic and flight. The birds shrouded a form on the ground, and when he approached, they retreated resentfully, hopping sideways and backwards, their black eyes as timeless as obsidian. The birds had shuffled away from the remains of a cow, a black and white Holstein half-devoured already by the river and the carrion eaters. One of the buzzards flapped upwards with ragged wings, vomiting a stream of bile, and Cole backed away, retreating into the brush to skirt the corpse, beginning once more his zigzag search.

Now, in the near-dark, his feet ached with cold and he turned for the walk homeward. Along the edges of the small stream, animals started from him and scrambled noisily into the brush. Twice he recognized the humped backs of raccoons scurrying away from their night fishing. Four times he heard the owls calling across the water. Seven herons flapped away in the night. Always he listened to the sounds of the rippling water, cool and delicate in the dark. And he thought of Diana Nemi wading the river home. The thought of her caused an ache that was new to him, and he examined the feeling wonderingly. His fingers became spines of pain and he shoved them into the jacket pockets, cradling the rifle in the crook of his arm.

As he walked homeward, he felt the two behind him, downstream. One prowled the river bottom, sniffing, peering easily into the darkness, knowing precisely where its prey hid but unable yet to close. The other was restive, nervous, anxious to be gone but held to a single place in anticipation.

He thought of the panther outside Uncle Luther's cabin. He imagined himself the cat. His stride changed and he felt the torsion in his blood, the smooth wrap of tendon and muscle. His step became effortless, silent, his vision penetrating and certain. Sounds were myriad on the still air, the ripple of water as sharp as breaking glass, the snap of a branch under a deer hoof as definite as a gunshot. He knew what it was to have a single purpose, to have a concentration as sharp edged and exact as a flint point. "Be a warrior, nephew." The old man's voice came from the air, and brought Cole tumbling out of his vision. His boots were suddenly heavy and stumbling, his eyes weak and fearful of the tangled shadows. He heard his pulse pounding in the night. What was a warrior? If Hoey had been there, he would have asked him. He walked silently through the dark, considering. Had Attis been a warrior? He had gone to war, and he had probably killed in the war. But old-time warriors had been respected more for counting coup than for killing. So what did it mean? It must be the act not of killing but of accepting death that made one a

193

warrior. And what was death but the unknown. Sure, the people had stories about the world after death, but in the end it was still the impenetrable unknown. It was darkness. Had Attis recognized death when it came to him? Had he stood up in the dark to be reckoned with? To be a warrior was to give oneself over to the unknown. To go out into the invisible world and announce one's presence. Thus a warrior must have a name. A large animal crashed clumsily away in the brush, startling Cole. Just ahead was the trail that lead to his house. As he started up the trail, he thought of his father, wondering what his father's name was. Had Uncle Luther named him as well, or had Hoey's real name come from somewhere or someone else?

Thirty-six

Mundo Morales watched the evening news. The war was still going on. It had seemed to him that it must end when they came home. It had been inconceivable that it would go on and on, churning out the dead. General Westmoreland was on the television screen, talking numbers. The screen changed, and there were students dancing at night in front of a burning building. They waved their arms and cheered. The students had sacked the Bank of America and set fire to it. Now they were dancing as Walter Cronkite described the busloads of national guardsmen enroute to Santa Barbara to restore order. It had something to do with the Cambodian invasion, and Mundo had not even been aware that the U.S. had invaded Cambodia. He had tried to obliterate such consciousness. Had tried *not to think about it*. Would there be a massacre in Santa Barbara, he wondered, like there had been over there? Would the national guardsmen open fire like they had at Kent State? Should he, Mundo Morales, do something to stop it? A number of the dancing students wore green fatigue jackets and had the faces he'd come to recognize in Vietnam vets. Their dance was jerky and erratic. Warriors returned to sack the villages that had sent them to war. Seeking the enemy that must, at long last, stand and be reckoned with. Better this than Attis's way.

"Can you believe they did that?" Gloria asked as she handed him a bowl of popcorn. "It's the biggest bank in the world."

A bank official was on the screen, talking about the bank's determination. The bank would be rebuilt as soon as possible, on the exact spot. They would have a temporary structure set up on the site within a week. The hooligans responsible would be prosecuted. Walter Cronkite came on the screen to announce that a student had been shot through the heart earlier in the evening. A group of fraternity brothers had gathered in front of the bank to protect it from rioters. A police sharpshooter's rifle had accidentally discharged and killed one of the frat boys. Cronkite offered the explanation with no sense of belief. The fraternity boys joined the rioters. The police had been chased out of the student community by Molotov cocktails but were returning with national guardsmen in force. The situation was chaotic, anarchic.

Mundo stared. It had come to this country, first in the damaged ones like Attis and now this. It was everywhere. He bounced Maria on his knee and crushed the unpopped kernels of corn between his molars. The little girl began to cry, and he handed her to Gloria without taking his eyes from the screen where an automobile commercial had replaced the news. A young girl drove a Mustang convertible along a road that wound above a rocky cliff that fell to a blue ocean. It looked like Big Sur. The girl seemed unaware

195

of the disaster that had befallen the Bank of America. If she knew of the boy with a bullet through his heart, the news had not fazed her. She sat at the wheel of the sleek car as though she would drive forever, a joyous, eternal rocket to nowhere. Mundo imagined the car exploding, cartwheeling off the cliff and into the broken sea. He thought of how big the lingcod must get at the base of the rocks. He remembered diving for abalone, prying muscles from the black stone, the spiny sea urchins and the otters that surfed the waves. He imagined the infinity of waves rolling shoreward. He thought of the bodies taken out to sea and dropped from helicopters, living bodies with unpronounceable names. The intrusive line where river met ocean, and all that lay in wait at such a point.

"When will this horrible war be over?" Gloria said, more to Cronkite than to her husband. Maria waved her hands in the popcorn bowl, scattering popcorn onto the floor and laughing.

Mundo imagined what it must have been like to burn the bank. It was an urge that went back to the beginning of time. The Indians must have felt that way when the caballeros came to raise cattle and leave the carcasses rotting skinless across California valleys. The Indians had tried to burn the ranchos, but, like the students, they were outgunned. And his own ancestors must have felt the same when the gringos came and, with guns and paperwork, took the ranchos for their own. Joaquin Murieta had been like these students. He'd joined with Three-Fingered Jack to pillage and murder the length of California. Or so the cheap novel said—a novel, he remembered, that had been written by a half-breed Indian. And now these students would dispossess their elders of their right to dictate who would kill and be killed. But like the Indians and Mexicans, the students would lose.

Somehow it all seemed related, tangled up together like a ball of used baling wire. He and Attis and Jenna and all of them were caught up now in whatever this story happened to be. Indians, Mexicans, gringos, mixed-bloods. He, Mundo, was part Indian, though no one in the family had ever liked to admit it. Pure Castillian, they had always pretended, holding out their underarms to show the whiteness. And the McCurtains were white and Indian both. Tangled, mixed, interrelated. He thought of the Mondragon sisters and vowed, again, to speak with them. The sisters might be able to sort something out of the mess.

Thirty-seven

Diana looked in the mirror. Water was rising over everything, rushing from the bowels of the earth in a fountain until it covered all, cleansing the earth in a whirling flood. Diana dreamed of looking through the mirror into the brown eyes of Mundo Morales. She shut her eyes against the mirror, and Attis came and lay with her, easing his cold shadow down alongside her and lifting away the shroud of her nightgown with delicate fingers. The shadow's cold mouth was on her breasts, her stomach, her thighs, and she dreamed that she began to scream. And then the old man with long hair appeared, and the shadow was gone. The old man placed a palm against her forehead and said, "Shush." She could feel the warm, pulsing blood in the hand. "You have to let it go, granddaughter," the old man said once again. "All the way back, to the beginning."

She sat up in the bed, feeling her young body, her tingling breasts. She reached a hand to touch the wrinkled face and raised her mouth toward the old man's lips.

"Ha!" The laugh came from the far corner of the room,

197

where an ancient, thin man stood spread-legged in a wrinkled suit, his arms behind his back and his brown face grinning beneath a moustache like a dove's wing. "Bruja!"

"No," she began, but then she was alone in front of the mirror. She started to cry, holding the feathered mask in her hands.

Thirty-eight

"Jesus fucking christ, Morales, how many times do you have to hear it? McCurtain ain't in that goddamned river. We have reports he's been seen in Texas, Oklahoma, Mississippi. Official, typed reports. The story is he's hightailed it for injun country, Mundo. Can't you get that through your ridiculously thick skull?"

Carl Carlton leaned back in a swivel chair and belched. "I ain't going to assign any men to search that motherfucking river for you. Give it up. Just do your job."

Mundo stood in front of the sheriff's desk, his arms folded across his chest. "I know what I saw, Carlton. I don't give a damn how many false reports you have from hell and back."

Carlton let out a long breath. "Mundo, you want to search that goddamned riverbed, go right ahead. But you better do it on your own time. I find out you're wandering around in the brush on county time, and I'll have your ass back cleaning toilets."

"I thought it was my job to solve crimes."

"Ha! That's a great one, Morales. You've been watching too much television. Your job's to keep punks from stealing chickens and fucking somebody else's sheep. Your job don't have nothing to do with solving jack shit." Carlton took a wad of gum out of his mouth and wrapped it in a scrap of paper before tossing it in the wastebasket. "Solving crimes is the responsibility of pencil-heads like that FB-fucking-I moron who's on this case. And just between you and me, the feds don't seem any too eager to find our runaway redskin."

Mundo put his hands in his pockets and waited.

"You keep hunting for a corpse, you do it on your own time, Morales, understand?" The sheriff wadded up a wanted poster and tossed it at the wastebasket, banking the paper off the wall into the basket. "You wanted to solve something, why didn't you solve that hobo killing? Seems to me you didn't do diddly squat about that. Maybe if that 'bo had been a friend of yours you'd taken more interest, no?"

Mundo looked out the dirty window of the sheriff's office, wondering whether he was seeing storm clouds or just the filth of the window. "You've lived here long enough, Carl. You know what happened to that hobo."

Carlton pulled open a desk drawer with the pointed toe of his cowboy boot. He leaned forward in the chair and came up with two beers. He shoved one of the cans toward Mundo and jerked his head in the direction of a chair. "Sit down and have a beer, Mundo. Take a load off your mind."

Mundo started to speak and then, instead, sank into the chair reserved for those who sat across the desk from Carlton. He levered the warm beer open and held it in his hands.

Carlton took a long drink. "I know this rancher over near Bakersfield," he said slowly. "He likes to shoot things. But he smoked so much he got emphysema and now he can't go anywhere without his oxygen bottle, and can't walk much either. It just killed him not to go hunting, but he figured it out. He got himself one of those little airplanes they call an ultralight. He rigged up an attachment for his

199

oxygen bottle. Now he goes flying over his ranch in that little thing with a two-twenty-two rifle, shooting at coyotes and squirrels and just about any damned thing that moves. You should see that scrawny old sonofabitch hanging up there in the sky with his gun and his oxygen bottle and tubes coming out of his nose. It's one of the goddamnedest scariest things I ever saw. It looks like death. That old man just couldn't stop killing things.

"Truth is, Mundo, that dead hobo just don't matter. And the same goes for your buddy. Wherever he is, he's saving the taxpayers a lot of money for room and board. You know, we could send a man to college for the same money it costs to keep him at the funny farm." Carlton took a long drink. "Nothing like the first beer of the day." He grinned. "Or the fourth or fifth. Now if we thought this half-breed buddy of yours might be out there about to commit another one of those sex crimes, we'd be all over this state like ticks on a bloodhound's balls. But we got a powerful feeling he ain't going to do none of that stuff ever again. So everything's kind of hunky-dory just like it is, if you savvy. Let's just all stick to the official story and stop worrying about Attis McCurtain."

"You think Nemi killed him, don't you?" Mundo asked.

"What I think, Mundo, is that there's catfish big as my leg out in the reservoir, and they're just bustin' to get at a juicy night crawler. So I'm going to finish this beer and go home and then do a little winter night-fishing. I'll build me a good fire, take along some baloney sandwiches and a six-pack, toss my line out, and think about fish." He took a long pull on the beer and looked at Mundo over the top of the can. "My wife," he said. "My wife's been picking food out of the dumpsters behind Safeway again. She won't admit it, but our fucking kitchen's full of dented-up cans of the weirdest shit. She started doing that a couple years ago. Until I figured it out, she was dragging in all kinds of goddamned crap, cases of dog food and rotten fruit and shit like that. She'd check the dates on fucking dairy products and go to the stores the day they expired. Said she was saving money. I put a stop to it, but now she's doing it again. Cottage cheese and shit like that. Now how the hell can you live that way?"

Mundo imagined Carlton's plump wife bent over the edge of a dumpster, her stumpy legs in the air. He shrugged. "I thought you were as anxious to find Attis as I was."

Carlton tilted the can and drained it. He crushed the can between his palms and banked it into the wastebasket. "That was before and this is now, Mundo. And right now I'm going fishing. I'd invite you along, but I got a feeling you might just talk so much you'd put all them fish to sleep."

The sheriff got up and lifted his jacket off the rack by the door. He held the door open and motioned for Mundo to go out first. Mundo set his untouched beer on the desk and went out. In a nearby office a young deputy looked up from his desk and waved. Mundo waved back, though he didn't recognize the deputy.

"New man," Carlton said as they left the building together. "College boy." He snorted. As they parted at the foot of the steps to the county building, the sheriff put a hand on Mundo's shoulder. "Just let it go, Mundo. They got their story all worked out. Don't try to read between the lines. There ain't nothing there."

Mundo got into his patrol car and sat still for several minutes. He thought of Lee Scott. If they had their story all worked out, why was the federal investigator still in Amarga? If he wasn't looking for Attis, what was he there for?

"Go see the bruja, niño."

Mundo jumped and then turned to look through the screen at the back seat. The viejo was there, sitting cross-legged. The suit rose up around him now so that he seemed ready to disappear into its dark interior.

"It would be better to go to her, grandson, than wait for 201 the bruja to come to you. If she comes, she will have all of her strength ready. But if you go first, perhaps you can surprise her."

"Diana Nemi is no witch, grandfather. She's a girl whose sister was murdered in a terrible way. She's young and troubled."

The viejo shrugged. "As you will, grandson, but sometime you must venture forth to this confrontation. And keep one thing in mind. She is not so young."

Mundo started the car and pulled out into the tunnel of the headlights, watching his grandfather in the mirror. The old man, looking like an ancient and wizened mafia don through the dividing screen, smiled and smoothed his drooping moustache with a forefinger. "You know, grandson, from the back like this it is apparent that your hair is thinning. I'm afraid you may suffer from the baldness on your grandmother's side. A tragedy. But you must be careful, Mundo, for you also have too much of your grandfather in you. This bruja is a lovely one, and very smart. She dreams of you, grandson."

The car left the town and began to climb the long grade between San Luis and Amarga. Mundo looked out the side window for stars but found that the sky was sealed. "Okay, old man, so tell me what I should do." He watched his grandfather in the mirror.

The old man toyed with his moustache, saying nothing.

"I need advice, grandfather. Why should I go see Diana? What can she tell me?"

The viejo shook his head. "What's in the river is not Attis, grandson. What you saw beneath that bridge was something far more interesting than your dead friend. That's an intriguing story. To go in search of that requires more knowledge than you possess. Go see the sorceress. The *indio* I told you about is watching her, and I think he will help you. But keep in mind that the old man is himself a brujo, and he likes the girl."

"Forgive me, grandfather, but I'm afraid you're as crazy

in death as you were in life. I mean no disrespect, but you don't make sense."

The viejo's face was no longer in the mirror, and Mundo turned around to search for his grandfather. There was no one in the back seat.

As the car topped the grade and began the long, curving road down toward Amarga, Mundo saw the first fine points of rain coming through the headlights.

"Great," he said aloud. "All I need is another flood." But the rain remained a fine drizzle, stippling the windshield and creating a silver fringe in the lights. After a few minutes he stopped considering the possibility of the river rising again, and he began to think instead of Diana. What did the viejo mean when he said she wasn't so young? She was eighteen, almost nineteen. That was young. A little more than a year before, her sister had been killed brutally by his best friend. At the funeral services Diana had stared unblinking at the coffin. At no time had he seen her cry, not even when the casket had been lowered into the earth, when her mother had thrown herself on the grass with great wails, and her father had turned away, his shoulders shaking. Diana had seemed to grow more rigid with each moment, so that he'd found himself wondering if she would be able to walk away from the grave in the end.

He remembered a summer a few years before. Could it have been only four years? They were about to enlist on the buddy system, he and Attis, and they had gone for a last swim in the sandpit in the river. Attis had brought Jenna and Diana had pleaded to come along. She'd been, how old then? Fourteen. And already a disturbing beauty who seemed balanced at a maddening point between child and woman. He remembered that he hadn't wanted Diana to come with them. She made him nervous in a way that Jenna never had.

The sandpit was an enormous hole dug out of the river-bed by the sand and gravel company, fifty yards in diameter and twenty or thirty feet deep. In the late spring and early summer, the underground river ran through the pit, sifting in on the upstream side and filling the hole with cold, incredibly clear water. Within the unnatural pool, a few lucky steelhead and other fish flashed colors across the white sand. It was a private place near the Nemi ranch, almost hidden by trees.

They'd gone skinny-dipping, Jenna racing to the edge of the water and throwing her clothes off on the sand. He remembered the arc of her body as she'd dove into the pool. Attis had followed Jenna, and then Mundo had found himself slowly fumbling at the buttons of his own shirt, conscious of Diana behind him. He had removed his shirt and was slipping his tennis shoes off when Diana walked by him, slowly. As she passed, she turned to smile, and he stopped breathing. The taut curve of her belly from pubic hair to breasts stunned him. Then she turned and walked into the water, her body so perfectly brown and hard that it might have been cast from bronze. With agonizing slowness, he'd taken off his clothes and then rushed toward the water, cannonballing into the pool so that he sank deep toward the bottom, letting himself fall until the sky seemed a thousand miles away.

The memory hurt. Jenna had been alive then, laughing as the water ran off her long, dark hair and down her back to her bare legs. Attis had been alive. Attis and Jenna had been in love. Even across time and experience, Mundo knew they had been in love. And Diana? She had been close to childhood still. There had been a newness about her, a tentativeness beneath the growing determination that had come more and more to mark her. He thought of the small, adolescent ass she had turned toward him as she walked to the water, the hard shoulders and long sweep of brown back. It was a girl's body, not a woman's, and the memory of it caused a deep welling of sadness in him. And he, Mundo, what had he been as he fell, curled head to foot, toward the bottom of the pool? He had been the viejo's favorite grandson, the spoiled one, the one who sat at the grandfather's knee and accepted candy and stories with the same greediness. A basketball star, he had not yet been to the war in a little, remote country on the other side of the earth, and he had not met Gloria. He had not yet been even a high-school janitor, much less the deputy sheriff for the tight-strung little town. He did not have a daughter, and he had not yet divided and weighed the world. The sand had been hot and the water as cold as an ice pick.

When he got home Gloria was dancing alone in the living room, bopping to "Runaway." There was no light on in the kitchen or the hallway leading to the bedrooms. Except for one ceiling lamp, the only light came from the dials of the record player. Gloria wore a white sweater and black, pleated skirt that swirled as she spun and revealed her hard, brown legs. When he stepped through the doorway she spun toward him, grabbing his hands and lifting them to duck beneath and twirl away and back again.

"Care to dance, deputy?" Gloria said as she bopped in front of him. She took each of his hands and did a two-step, looking into his eyes.

Mundo smiled. "Momentito, chiquita."

He stepped away from her and took off his coat. He unbuckled the gun belt and laid it on a chair on top of the coat. Gloria whirled up to him, and he caught her and spun her under his hand. They both turned and caught hands behind their backs and spun again.

When they were facing each other, Mundo said, "Where is Maria?"

Gloria grinned. "At Loraine's for the night. I thought we needed a night out, and since tonight is one of Officer Morales's only free evenings, I pawned our daughter off on the neighbors."

Finding himself in front of the overstuffed chair, Mundo collapsed backwards, falling with his hands on the arms of the chair. Gloria danced in front of him.

"Dinner and dancing. How about a date?"

He smiled up at her. His feet ached. His head hurt from listening to Carlton and then thinking of the past. He wanted a glass of red wine and a bed.

"Why not?" he said. "You decide where we eat while I change." He shoved himself out of the chair and joined hands with her. They danced to the other side of the room as the record ended and he slipped away toward the bedroom.

As he took off the uniform and folded the pants and shirt carefully over the foot of the bed, he heard a song called "Poison Ivy" start up on the record player. Turning on the shower, he tried to imagine Gloria bopping all alone to that frenetic tune. "At night while you're sleeping, poison ivy comes a creeping around," he sang softly to himself. "Dinner and dancing," he said aloud. "Ah, cabrón." As he stood in the shower it occurred to him that the water falling on his head had come from the river. All the town's water came from wells located at the edge of the riverbed. He wondered how deep the wells were.

When he walked into the bedroom with a towel around his waist, Gloria was there. She had his good clothes laid out on the bed. The uniform had disappeared. At the side of the bed were his wing tips with socks laid across them. A red tie lay next to his belt between black slacks and white shirt.

"Ah, no, querida," he moaned. "Not the tie. Have mercy."

Chuck Berry was shouting from the living room. Mundo felt dizzy.

Gloria stood with her hands on her hips, looking him up and down. "Qué hombre," she said. "Okay, no tie. You can wear the gray sport coat over the blue sweater."

Mundo sighed and searched a drawer for clean underwear. Since Gloria had thrown out his army boxer shorts, it took longer to sort the multi-colored shorts from the confusion of socks.

"Hong's Cafe," Gloria said, as if a stroke of genius had come upon her.

"A brilliant idea," Mundo said, pulling on the slacks and realizing with a shock that the pants were tighter around the middle than they had been the last time he'd put them on. "You have picked the only restaurant in town."

"No. We could go to Virgil's."

"No burgers and fries tonight, my love. Only the best for you. We'll have Hong's freshest mountain oysters, on the half-shell."

Gloria made a face and picked the wet towel off the floor, carrying it to the bathroom.

Two and a half hours later Jessard Deal was bending toward their table in the Tiptoe Inn. Jessard smiled broadly. "Well, Mr. Morales, this is a first. I'm deeply honored that at last you have brought your lovely wife to my establishment."

Mundo glared at Jessard. When he noticed Gloria smiling back at the tavern owner, he glared harder.

"What may I bring you, Mrs. Morales?" Jessard intoned, with a nod that looked suspiciously like a bow. "It's on the house."

"Why, how nice." Gloria turned to Mundo. "You see, Mundo, I told you the Tiptoe Inn couldn't be half as bad as you make out."

Mundo looked at the beer sign. It was the first time he had not sat at the bar, and from the new angle the man in the boat looked more confident and in control of his situation.

"Mundo hasn't been telling tall tales about my place of business, has he?" Jessard's smile was directed at Mundo.

"How about a couple of beers?" Mundo said, looking from the sign to the face leaning toward him.

"My pleasure." Jessard leaned closer to Gloria. "You don't know how proud it makes me to have Amarga's symbol of law and order patronize my inn. Especially when he brings such a lovely companion."

Before Gloria could respond, Jessard had returned to the bar.

"This place doesn't seem so bad, Mundo," Gloria said, touching her husband's arm. "Besides, no place else was open."

One of the waitresses brought their beers and set them down. Before Gloria could complete her "thank you," the blonde had slipped away.

"Look around, querida. How many women like yourself do you see in here?" Mundo's expression was sober.

Gloria looked around at the ranch hands and truck drivers and national guardsmen and mechanics. The only other women were the two waitresses.

"I guess you're right. I guess we'd better not dance. But I'm glad we came. It's time I saw this famous den of iniquity." She grinned and took a deep drink.

"One beer and then we go, okay, Gloria?" Sensing a large number of eyes on them, he sat up straighter in his chair and glared around him. A tall, skinny cowboy's eyes locked on his and the cowboy grinned and stood up.

"Chingada," Mundo muttered beneath his breath. More loudly he said, "Listen, Gloria. If there's trouble I want you to run for the door. I don't care what happens, just get out. I can take care of myself."

"What are you talking about?"

"That." Mundo jerked a thumb at the tall cowboy, who now stood at Gloria's shoulder.

"I was wondering if the lady might like to dance," the cowboy said. The jukebox played a song about not smoking marijuana in an Oklahoma town, and in the suddenly quiet bar the singer's twang was sharp.

"I don't think so," Mundo said, looking up at the man's hatchet face.

"Cain't the little lady speak for herself?" The cowboy was grinning at Gloria now. "Or does she need a spic to talk for her."

"I can speak for myself," Gloria said, reaching a hand out to keep Mundo in his chair. "And I don't dance with shit-for-brains redneck assholes."

The cowboy's face darkened and suddenly he seemed to go into convulsions. Only then did Mundo see Jessard Deal's immense torso behind the cowboy. With the fingers of one hand clamped on the back of the cowboy's throat, Jessard caused the man to crumple. Jessard held the cowboy with his knees buckled on the floor as indifferently as a hunter might hold a just-shot pheasant.

"I apologize for this fool's rude behavior, Mrs. Morales. As your husband knows, I don't tolerate rude behavior in my tavern."

Jessard carried the body to the door and threw it out into the night. The bar's silence turned to a hum and the hum rose to a clatter that framed a song about hobos on the jukebox. According to the song, they were kings of the road. Mundo thought about the dead hobo.

"You were right, Mundo. Let's go home," Gloria said. But before they could stand, Jessard was back at the table. He had a bottle of brandy tucked into one fist and he set it on the table between them.

"Mind if I join you for a moment?" He hooked a chair close with his foot and sat down. "I thought Mrs. Morales might like something a little finer than watered-down draft beer. This is very old brandy. Very special. You might appreciate this, too, Mundo. You see, I bought this from your grandfather a couple of years ago, just before he passed away. He'd had it a long time then. It is aguardiente de los muertos."

From the palm of his hand he produced three brandy glasses and arranged them on the table. When he uncorked the bottle he held the cork to his nose and breathed deeply. "The musty fragrance of Spain. Deep and dark and full of hidden knowledge," he said as he poured the liquor.

"We are honored," Mundo said, looking skeptically at the bottle. "I will mention it to the viejo."

209

"What?" Jessard was looking at him peculiarly.

"Salud." Mundo held his glass up so that the amber fluid caught red and blue and gold tints from the lighted advertisements.

They raised their glasses.

"How does an evil town deserve a woman of such obvious distinction?" Jessard smiled at Gloria and then Mundo.

"An evil town?" Gloria responded. "I never thought of Amarga that way."

"Gloria is from Santa Fe," Mundo said. "New Mexico."

"Santa Fe?" Jessard laid the words out carefully on his tongue. "From Santa Fe to Amarga. An interesting pilgrimage. Can a person go the other way?"

"I came here to be with Mundo," Gloria said simply, sipping the brandy with pleasure.

"So, let me see now. A woman comes from Santa Fe to Amarga to be with Mundo Morales. A dull brain like mine is too easily muddled. This is not a half-bad brandy, no?"

"It's delicious," Gloria said, touching the edge of the glass with the tip of her tongue.

Mundo drank half the brandy in one gulp and felt it burn into his stomach, leaving a bitter-sweet aftertaste. He finished his beer and returned his attention to the remaining brandy. Suddenly he realized what was different. Jessard Deal was speaking in a voice Mundo had never heard before. He looked more closely at the big man. Jessard's face had changed. The lines of the face were more definite, the eyes more open. Beneath the beard, there was a certain delicacy about the mouth. Mundo sat up straighter.

"So, do you think your husband will find Attis McCurtain?" Jessard stopped smiling and looked intently at her.

Gloria sipped the brandy and appeared to roll it around on her tongue for a moment. She glanced at Mundo with a smile and looked back at Jessard Deal. "I think Mundo will find whatever he searches for."

"Perhaps more than he searches for," Jessard replied,

looking at Mundo now.

Mundo slung the remaining brandy down his throat and considered what he might say in response, feeling the bottle of red wine they had split at dinner blending with the beer and brandy. He began to feel somewhat dizzy again.

"I believe, Mr. Deal, that my husband will find exactly what he searches for. It is my experience that he always has." Gloria turned the brandy glass and watched the liquor spin. "You see, I think most men don't have the slightest idea what they're looking for. Ever. That's why women are almost always a long step ahead of you, and why you men are always trying to keep women from having power. Women know what they're after the moment they're born. It takes men a long, long time to figure it out and usually by the time they do a woman has already been there. Imagine what would happen if you men didn't have brute strength on your side. My husband is an exception. He likes women and he knows what he wants to do with the world. When I met him, he wasn't quite sure. You could say he hadn't quite woken up. But Mundo Morales is awake now. He will find whatever it is he looks for."

Jessard finished his brandy and poured another drink for Mundo and then himself. Mundo watched his wife with fascination, while Jessard sipped the brandy and seemed to reflect.

"If you'll pardon me, Mrs. Morales, it's been my experience that most people—women and men both—don't know shit. Look at my barmaids. I found them both in a Juarez whorehouse, turning tricks and waiting until it was their turn for the donkey show. I didn't ask these ladies if they wanted to come to work for me. I stole them and brought them here. Now they're relatively happy. Would you say my two blondes knew what they wanted, or know what they want now?"

Gloria looked at one of the barmaids at the next table, then she turned her head to consider the other one at the rear of the room. "Some women start at a disadvantage,

Mr. Deal. And because they know what they want but can't get it, they can get broken early. Men don't usually break like that, because they don't know what they want, so they don't know they can't have it."

"How did such a young woman become so wise, Mundo?" Jessard focused upon Mundo's face, and Mundo looked back into the nearly black eyes. Jessard's face had begun to change again, becoming more familiar, with blurred lines and heavy, animal jaw evident through the beard.

"I'm not wise," Gloria said. "But my grandmother was wise. She came from Chimayo in New Mexico. I listened to her stories."

"You see, I read stories differently," Jessard said. "I believe that we are all essentially and fundamentally evil. But we are born innocent of our full potential. We must grow into our evil, you see. My two blondes didn't break. They were just in the process of becoming their real selves down there in Juarez. I saw that and I wanted to have them here. In Amarga we're all in the process of becoming our real selves. We need role models." Jessard laughed loudly.

When he stopped laughing, his face and voice were the ones Mundo had always known. Gloria held the brandy halfway to her mouth and edged her chair back from the table.

"I'm counting on Mundo here to teach us all about our real selves." Jessard chuckled softly. "You see, I think your husband's a kind of touchstone. When he finds what he's looking for everybody's going to understand it but him."

Jessard stood up and pushed the chair back with his foot. He picked up the brandy bottle in one hand and raised his glass in a toast with the other. "Do you know Jonathan Edwards, Mrs. Morales? No? A pity."

"Does he live in Amarga?" Gloria asked.

Jessard shook his head. "I never had the luck of a good education, but there was a period in my life when I had a great deal of time on my hands, Mrs. Morales. In a small room with a very small window, in a hard, desert place. Outside the window was a stone wall, and above the wall was a sky that never changed. I had access to a library, and thus it was that I came upon the solace of words." He swallowed the brandy. "To poetry," he said. "And to the moral world." He took a step away and then stopped and turned back with a perplexed expression. "Somebody," he said, "has destroyed my home. I think the police should investigate." He began to laugh again.

As Mundo and Gloria and everyone in the bar watched him, Jessard, still laughing, went behind the bar and disappeared into a back room.

They got up and left the bar. As he tried to fit the key into the ignition switch, Mundo felt a desperate desire to hold his daughter. More than anything in the world he wanted to bounce Maria on his knee, to hold her and feel her entire weight in his arms.

Thirty-nine

"It's worse than we thought." Onatima stirred sugar into two cups of tea and carried them to the little table in front of the couch.

Luther bent to pick up the tea. He settled his back more deeply into the soft upholstery of the couch. In the chair the old lady curled her feet beneath her.

When he tasted the tea, the old man made a face and drew back. "What kind of stuff are you feeding me, Old Lady Blue Wood?"

Onatima laughed. "It's called red zinger. I bought it because that name reminded me of myself."

Uncle Luther took a second sip and smiled. "You're right. It's got the same kind of sting to it. Wakes you up, don't it?

"It is not difficult to understand the evil that afflicted the son that died," he continued. "It makes me admire Hoey. He's off the track a little bit now, but you know, I think I taught him pretty good. He has managed to keep himself free of the worst evil by thinking in the oldest ways he knows. He don't really understand, and those ways don't always work anymore anyway, but they've helped him. Perhaps if it had not been for that war, both of Hoey's sons would have been warriors, not just the young one." He gazed at one of the oddly shaped trailer windows. "This trailer reminds me of a fish bowl, with me inside. Sometimes I miss Hoey. You know, when we was children living over the river there, I used to tell my sister that when we grew up she would have a son and I would teach him everything. I learned so much then just so's I could teach my sister's son. And when Hoey was born, you know, I watched and waited till he was old enough. Then I brung him away to the woods and I taught him. And when my sister and her husband died of that pneumonia that went around, I raised Hoey up."

Luther smiled at Onatima. "I remember once when I was showing Hoey how to grapple for catfish. We was going along the river reaching under the cutbank the way you do, feeling for fish, when Hoey says, 'I got a big one, Uncle Luther.' And then Hoey took off toward the middle of the river like he had a outboard motor on his feet. He'd got hold of a cat big as hisself, and that fish was swimming away with him." The old man grinned. "I got to laughing so hard I couldn't hardly move, and then Hoey disappeared. That fish dove with him. So I skinned my clothes off and jumped in, but by the time I'd taken a few strokes after them, Hoey come to the surface sputtering and yelling." He grinned. "He was mad because that fish got away."

"Maybe he will come back, too," Onatima replied. "This is one of the best trailers made."

"Maybe he will. It's a shame that Hoey's sons didn't have no uncle out there in California who could teach them. Such things were never left to fathers before."

"It's lucky those boys had a good mother," Onatima said. "Don't forget Ida. She was the one who told her sons stories when they lived across the river. She was a strong woman." Onatima seemed to contemplate the dead mother for a moment before she went on. "But I guess it's a mess out there now, Luther. There are too many stories going on. It's time you confronted that old man. He's already helped you once."

The old man snorted loudly. "Helped me! I ain't needed no help yet."

"That's what you say. The one in your cabin's getting impatient for its bones. And that one," she nodded toward the woods outside the trailer. "Have you noticed the same thing I have?"

He shook his head up and down and looked keenly at the red tea. "You mean soul-eater's been following an old man around instead of prowling after that shadow?"

"That's precisely the point I was going to make, Luther Cole." She sipped the tea and eyed him across the cup. "There's something going haywire with this story."

"You read too much, old lady. Reading all them books makes you think everything's supposed to always come out the same because the writing never changes. This here soul-eater's just stirring thing's up a little. Thinks it has a chance for better meat than a scrawny old shadow." He winked. "And that's just part of it. You know there's always got to be room for things like that."

"Those people are stirring up a mess if you ask me. I think you'd better get the boy back here with the bones pretty quickly, if you know what's good for all of us."

"Chief Doom," Uncle Luther replied in a voice that suggested deep thought. "He was in one of them other books you brung me. I think he was supposed to be a Choctaw or a Chickasaw, but to me he was a kind of devil. It was like that white writer took all the death that ever happened to us Indian people and put it in one devil character. Like he was going to write all us people away." He sipped the tea and Onatima waited.

"They do that, try to write us to death. And that's the reason, old lady, that we got to make room for soul-eater to change things. When that cat can't come sniffing around a dried-up old turd like me, why that's when that white writer'll have what he wants. Chief Doom couldn't face death the way a Choctaw does. Instead, he was death, was dyin' in every word that white man wrote."

Onatima nodded. "Don't be vulgar, Luther. But I see what you mean. That white writer thought change only meant death. And you could tell he loved death better than life. That's what they've all been writing about for a long time. Even that boy in the novel I gave you, the one about the boy and the slave. Remember how the boy kept making up stories and they were always about death? They have a romance going with death, they love it, and they want Indians to die for them."

Luther nodded. "Lucky thing most of us Indians wasn't reading their stories."

"Lucky thing some of us were. But don't change the subject. It's a mess, old man. You'd better do something."

He swirled the red tea and watched it with fascination. "Maybe that Hoss Cartwright show is on tv," he said. "I like that medicine man they got, that Hop Sing."

"You'd better deal with it, Luther," Onatima said as she got up to turn on the small gray television. "Hop Sing isn't going to help you."

Uncle Luther sighed and settled back into the couch, waiting for the picture to resolve on the tv screen.

216

Forty

Mundo drove the country roads beyond the river. Owls flew up, and fence posts bracketed the car in frantic shadows. He listened to the rip of the tires on the wet blacktop and leaned into the corners, accelerating, urging the car to higher speeds, feeling the wind-driven rain on his face through the windshield. At greater and greater speeds, the car smashed through corners on the narrow roads, moon-silvered rain angling sharp across the ripe grain. A buck leaped onto the road, with antlers flaming off into the stars in a hundred points. In the rearview mirror the great cat sprang in immense, sinewy strides behind the vehicle, stretching low and bunching to hurl itself after him. The yellow eyes of the cat burned in the mirror, and Mundo drove the car into the corners. An owl flared in the headlights, rising from the road with spreading wings that blotted out everything.

Forty-one

Mundo drove the patrol car slowly across the bridge, looking downstream to where the ribbon of clear water vanished in the brush and trees. He held the steering wheel carefully, still disturbed by last night's dream and wondering what he might say to Diana Nemi. The face and voice of the viejo urged him on. "M'ijo, you know you have to deal with the bruja." His grandfather had not smiled, nor had there been the mocking edge that seemed to always mark the old man's voice. So he had telephoned. Diana had picked up the phone. She would answer his questions. She wanted him to come. Afterwards, he could search the river again.

The house and barns were still. On a far rise a group of black angus were bunched like brushstrokes. In a corral near the smaller barn a spotted stallion stood motionless as a statue, head lifted toward a distant hillside. In front of the larger barn a tractor idled, symmetrical puffs of gray smoke rising in a perfectly straight line from its exhaust stack. The scene had a feeling of abandonment, as if someone had set the stage, arranged the props, and then gone away.

Diana met him at the door, holding it open and leaning against the doorframe in a sweater and white miniskirt. Seeing her bare feet and legs, he thought she must be cold, but her face made him think of sunshine and distant, warm places.

"How nice to see you, Officer Morales." She smiled sweetly.

"Good morning, Diana. I'm glad you could talk to me." Hearing his own voice, he was incredulous at the wooden words and flat tone. He reminded himself of an actor in a foreign film, when the wrong voice came out of a face and mouth at odds with the dubbed words.

"Won't you come in, Mundo?" Diana stepped to the side, still holding the door open, so that when he stepped through he felt the tips of her breasts brush against his arm.

She closed the door and he blinked in the dark room. All of the shades were drawn against the winter day, and a single small table lamp illuminated the living room. From the back of the house came music he tentatively identified as something by the Beach Boys, the shrill harmonies cutting into the still air of the house like a bone saw.

"Please sit down. Would you like some tea? I just made some." When he nodded, she glided toward the kitchen. When she returned immediately with two cups of oriental-smelling tea, he realized she must have had the tea poured even as he drove up to the house.

"I'll bet you've never had tea like this." She smiled brightly and brushed hair back from her eyes. "It's a secret blend from far, far away."

He touched his lips to the cup and the musty fragrance of the tea surrounded him. The tea had an odd taste that reminded him of earth and grasses, with a faint suggestion of pine. He recoiled from the taste and then found himself taking a second sip at once.

"It's good," he said. "It kind of reminds me of a tea-medicine my grandmother used to give us."

"I'm sorry I never met your grandmother," Diana replied.

Mundo nodded. "She never got over to Amarga much. She loved La Luz and hated to travel. She died in the same room she was born in, the same room her mother was born in."

Diana looked acutely interested. "I think the land my father's ranch is on used to be part of the Morales Grant, didn't it? I think I heard my mother say that my father owns most of what used to be your family's land."

He shrugged and drank more of the tea, feeling it warm him. "I don't know. The viejo, my grandfather, knows—knew—every foot of it, but I never paid much attention. You can't bring back the past, and you can't live on what your great-grandfathers had."

Diana cupped the tea in front of her face and seemed to inhale the fragrance. "You don't resent what happened? That's something I love about you, Mundo. You live in the present. You're a realist.

"Speaking of the present, you said you wanted to talk to me about something. I hope you don't need to speak to my parents also—they went to Santa Barbara for a while. I'm here all alone."

219

The music stopped and he found his eyes on the smooth angles of her legs as she sat with them folded to the side in the armchair. The skirt came down just far enough to make a dark triangle in the conjunction of her thighs. When she shook her hair back he looked up at her face, knowing from her smile that she had been watching him.

He looked at the murky brown tea. The air in the room seemed palpable, like a dark film. "I did," he said. "But I'm not sure what I wanted to ask you. Something about Attis."

"He's dead," she said flatly, setting the teacup on the table beside her chair and shifting so that the skirt rode higher.

Mundo nodded. "I know. I saw him. And I want to find him and find out who did it."

They were both quiet for a moment and then Mundo added, "I want to bring his killer to justice."

When he saw Diana's smile, he realized how ridiculous his phrase seemed. Again he felt as though he'd been given the wrong script. "I guess most of all I want to find Attis. You know, I can't stand the idea of him either somewhere down there in the brush and trash or floating all the way to the ocean. I suppose I'm here because I thought you could help me find him."

She shook her head slowly, keeping him fixed in her gaze. "I'm sorry, Mundo. I can't help you find him. No one can. Attis is gone. Think about it. He's become part of all of those things in the river, disintegrated, lost." She unfolded her long legs and stood up, walking toward him. She moved behind his chair and placed her hands on either side of his neck, sliding them inside the collar of his shirt and beginning to massage his shoulders.

"Officer Morales, you're too tense. I'm afraid this has been a very stressful experience for you. You need someone to help you relax."

He felt his muscles calming, his thoughts dissipating into pure feeling as her fingers probed the back of his neck and shoulders. She reached around his head to release the top two buttons of his shirt and he felt her breasts against him. Her hands went inside his shirt and spread over his chest, massaging upward till they rose to his cheeks and then descended again. Her hair brushed his neck as she bent, and he felt her breasts more sharply and then her lips. His body stiffened with desire, and he set the cup to the side and stood up. Diana moved around the chair and pressed herself to him and kissed him, her mouth hungry and her body hard and electric.

Attis floated out from beneath the bridge, and Mundo saw his face clearly. The eyes were alive and yearning for something. Mundo pushed Diana away and stepped back. He ran a hand across his face and shook his head.

"I can't do that, Diana."

She stood panting, staring at him in amazement.

"I want you, Diana, but I guess we all want a lot of things we can't have." He took another step backwards and began to button his shirt.

She stepped toward him. "But we can have this, Mundo. It's life. We won't hurt anyone if we make love. We'll just be more alive together for a little while. No one will know. You're worried about your wife, but it doesn't have anything to do with her. You can still love your wife and make love to me. It won't change anything. Nothing at all." She stepped close enough to put her head against his chest, and he was overwhelmed with the warm smell of her.

He put a hand on each of her arms and pushed her away, shaking his head. "No, hija. I can't do it."

Diana stepped back and looked at him with an expression that hardened as he watched. "Then you're a fool. Every man wants me. I can have any man I want. You're not a man, you're just a joke that walks around playing cowboys and Indians. You think you know what's right and wrong when you don't even know how to be alive when you have the chance. You're as dead as he is. As dead as my father and all of them."

She glared at him, gauging her words. "He didn't miss

his chance. Attis made wonderful, incredible love to me." She smiled and her eyes were like gray ocean water. "Right in my sister's bed. We fucked right in Jenna's bed." She brushed her hair back with both hands and laughed. "He was so crazy he thought I was her, my sister. Then he called me a witch, as if that would make it all my fault and he weren't responsible for fucking his true love's little sister. That's what all you men want to think, isn't it? That we're witches, and you're all poor little innocent boys. Well, it wasn't my fault."

She moved toward him and he retreated another step. "When he left he still thought I was her. He was babbling. And you should have seen Jenna when I told her the truth about her great warrior. She acted like I was to blame, like the fool didn't know what he was doing. I tried to tell her I'd done it for her, to show her what he was really like, what all men are like, but she was too brainwashed. She'd seen our father do that to our mother all these years, and she still didn't believe it. And then he killed her."

Mundo backed out of the house, closing the door carefully so that he could hear the click of the latch. He started the car and drove delicately onto the gravel and then onto the asphalt and concrete of the bridge. The tea burned in his stomach, and he stopped the car suddenly and threw open the door. Hanging his head over the railing of the bridge, he vomited until there was nothing left. Then he remained folded over the railing, feeling empty and watching the little stream that spun transparently over sand and rock below him. In the shallow edges he saw tiny minnows arrowing into the shadows of pebbles, waiting for the fulfillment of an ancient promise.

"So that was it," he said to the river. "Attis, you poor, fucked up bastard." He hung over the railing and for the first time since childhood he began to cry, sobbing in loud, wrenching wails that came from his center, mourning for Attis and Diana and all of them. On and on it went until he became aware of tears pouring from his chin to the river below. He buried his face in his hands and then wiped his eyes on his shirt sleeves. When he could breathe evenly again, he opened his eyes. On the white sand a hundred feet upstream Hoey McCurtain stood at the edge of the water, his deer rifle held in one hand and his face turned toward Mundo. For a moment they watched each other, and then Hoey turned and walked away into the brush on the east side of the river.

When Mundo got into the car, his grandfather was in the back with his legs stretched the length of the seat.

"I'm proud of you, m'ito," the old man said. "I would embrace you if I could."

Mundo clenched his jaws and looked into his grandfather's dark eyes in the mirror. "It was her, wasn't it, grandfather? She did it."

The viejo stared unblinking into the mirror, his white hair disheveled, his brown skin translucent and fragile looking. "I'm sorry, m'ito, but it was necessary. One must know what one is looking for. This girl is just part of it." He sighed and, suddenly, the grandfather seemed infinitely old to Mundo. It was as if now, in death, the viejo was finally growing old.

"You must think about what this young woman has said, grandson. She is not entirely wrong. I am sorry for her now."

The face vanished from the mirror, and when Mundo turned around the back seat was empty once again.

Forty-two

Luther was ready when the stick struck his door. "Come in, old lady," he shouted as he began to pour the coffee.

Onatima pushed the door closed behind her and said, "Good morning, Luther. I'm cold enough to even drink this concoction you call coffee."

As she laid her overcoat across one of the beds and rearranged her turban, he poured condensed milk from a can into both cups and then spooned sugar in and stirred it.

"A man would think you couldn't stay away from him, Miz Blue Wood, coming so early in the morning." He set a cup on the table in front of her.

"I have some information for you," Onatima said triumphantly. She looked him in the eye and contemplated the coffee suspiciously.

"This here's a new kind," he said, pointing at her cup with his chin. "It's grown in high mountains. Says so on the can."

She tasted the coffee and kept her expression on him. "From your description of that other one, I'd say he was Spanish."

She stopped and while he waited for her to continue, he picked a piece of red yarn from the table and reached behind him to tie his hair back.

When he made no objection, Onatima said, "He's not Indian and he's dark and he's in California, so he's probably Spanish. Spanish people are Catholics, we all know that." She paused for dramatic effect. "That old man is a Catholic ghost."

When he continued to drink his coffee in silence, she went on in an irritated voice. "I went to the university and read up on Catholic ghosts, Luther. It's the big problem in

Hamlet. The prince can't decide if his father's ghost is Catholic or Protestant, you see. If it's Protestant it may be a devil. But Catholic ghosts are different. They're sort of allowed to come back to try to fix things that are wrong, to balance things you might say. Do you see?"

Luther watched her in silence for a moment. Finally he said, "That's one book you ain't never made me read."

"It's a play, old man, probably the most famous play in the world."

"You mean like a ceremony?"

"Don't give me that, Luther. You know what I mean."

He nodded. "So this old man's got a plan, you think?"

Onatima shrugged. "I don't know if he has a plan, but I'm trying to explain to you why he ain't like one of our shadows. Why he's a different kind of spirit."

"Your grammar's slipping, Onatima, but you're right. This here story's getting kind of messy."

"You'd better talk to that one."

The old man shook his head. "Can't. I done tried and it don't work. I can see him there plain as day now—even hear what he says, but it's like he can't hear me. There's a world between us, old lady. All I know is, that old man don't care about the bones. He's got something else in mind."

"What do you think he has in mind?"

He shook his head again. "Beats me. But it must have something to do with his grandson, the one with the right name."

"What about the girl?"

Luther sighed. "He's learning a little more about the girl, but he still don't understand. Neither does she. She's going deeper into this thing, and I think it may be too late to help her."

Onatima shook her head. "Poor little thing."

Forty-three

Attis McCurtain soared on the night wind over the river, swooping and diving and settling only to lift again toward the clouds. He spoke in the voices of night birds as he rode the currents of dark air.

Forty-four

Mundo sat on the elaborate paisley couch, sinking into the ancient cushions and deep springs. On a little table in front of him was a china cup so fragile he could see the tea through the cup's sides. Next to the cup was a china saucer with very small cookies.

"There, Ramon, you enjoy Evelina's cookies while I get the tree." The old lady smiled radiantly and glided from the room.

He picked up one of the cookies between thumb and forefinger and pushed it into his mouth, wondering if he was expected to nibble at it instead. He took a drink of tea to wash down the dust-dry cookie.

"We're so happy you came to visit, Ramon." Evelina Mondragon pulled her wing-back chair closer to the couch and beamed. "We've been waiting and planning for this day, you know. We've even dreamed about it. We often have the same dreams, though I have to say that Alicia's dreams are a bit too loud, you know." She winked at him and he nodded, picking up another quarter-sized cookie.

The room was draped in ancient and expensive-looking materials of deep green and magenta. Glass and china figurines stood on tables and shelves, prancing deer and tiny dancers. An elaborately painted fan was pinioned against one wall, and richly colored rugs lay on the hardwood floor. In the close air, with its heavy smell of age and time, surrounded by a whirlpool of textures and deep colors, he felt dizzy and slightly confused.

"I'd like to know our relation," he'd said after Alicia had ushered him into the apartment.

"Ramon has come to find out who he is," was the way Alicia put it to her sister. Evelina's face had lit up at the thought.

"The bearded ones still come at night," Evelina whispered to him, glancing at the doorway through which her sister had disappeared. "The language they speak, Ramon Morales." She rolled her eyes.

"Here we are," Alicia whisked back into the room. "I have the family tree."

She knelt on the rug and began to unfold a brittle paper so yellowed and timeworn that Mundo thought it must be the parchment he'd heard of but never seen.

"It is so complex," Evelina said as she, too, knelt on the rug.

Mundo rose from the couch and went around the little tea table, falling to his knees beside the old women. As the squares of paper unfolded, a smell of dust and mice ascended. When she had the large sheet laid out, he bent closer to look at the upside-down flowering of elaborately scrolled names. In vain he tried to read the florid lettering.

"This is you, Ramon." Alicia pointed to a name near the bottom of the paper. "And Gloria and Maria." Across the bottom of the paper were scores of other names like his and his family's.

Seeing his surprise, Evelina said, "We keep track of ev-

227

eryone, Ramon. That is essential. If we were to miss anyone, the whole thing would fall apart."

"Now, you can trace your identity from your name." Alicia's bony finger moved from Mundo's name a quarter inch to a pair of names that signified his parents. The finger climbed to a name he recognized as that of his grandfather. Next to that was the name of his grandmother. Above them were names of people he had known only through family stories, his great-grandparents, and their parents. And then the lines began converging on the center of the paper, climbing toward a pair of names in heavy black lettering at the very top.

Mundo stared at three names that rested alone above the tangle of descending roots.

"This one was a slave," Alicia whispered, fingering a single name that had been written in pencil between the two names at the top. "A young Indian woman the patrón took from the mission." She looked sharply at Mundo. "They tried to hide it, you know. Moraleses sired by the old patrón on a slave girl. Oh, they didn't call them slaves. They baptized them into the mission and made them work till they died. That one—they called her Adelita—was one of your grandmothers." She gripped his wrist with a hand that had no weight to it. "They lied about her for years, for generations. They thought it was a disgrace. They made her an outcast, wandering between the worlds of dead because no one would claim her."

Evelina leaned close between them over the paper. "It was Antonio who told us the truth," she whispered.

He looked blankly at her.

"Antonio Morales, your grandfather."

"But how did he know? If they kept it a secret."

Evelina placed two fingers to her sharp-pointed chin and looked curiously at him. "The dead told him."

"The dead—?"

"Nothing is secret from the dead," Alicia added. "Antonio has been an invaluable resource."

"Adelita couldn't go to her people when she died because she had become a Catholic. But the Morales dead wouldn't recognize her."

"It is a sad truth, hijo."

Mundo spun toward the voice. The viejo was sitting at the far end of the couch, with one leg crossed over the other and an arm along the back of the couch, his head almost disappearing into the folds of the suit. He swung the top leg and nodded.

"I had to straighten it all out. You should have seen those Castilians. One would have thought their necks would crack if they had to look down at the poor girl, and their dead tongues might fall out should they claim her."

"Antonio made them take her in," Alicia said proudly, looking with admiration toward the old man.

Mundo looked from his grandfather to the sisters.

"Old man, I thought—"

"Calm yourself, grandson." The viejo waved a hand in the air. "Alicia and Evelina and I are good friends."

"An invaluable resource," Evelina said.

"The rest of that family tree is of dubious accuracy," the old man said. "The woods are full of bastards, grandson, just as the world is full of secret joy." He smiled broadly.

"Antonio!" Evelina bowed her head modestly, but Alicia looked at the old man affectionately.

"Yes, the world is full of joy," Alicia said. "Just look." She gestured toward the paper.

Bending closer, Mundo saw that the spaces between names were filled with faint, penciled notes, questions, corrections, and additions. Arrows had been drawn in from one descending line across to another, between brother and sister-in-law, uncle and nephew and niece. Upon close examination, the paper became a spider's web of crossing and connecting lines. At the top and center sat the heavy black name of the patrón, flanked on one side by his Castilian wife and on the other by the interpolated name of Adelita. From the trio the lines spread in an inextricably

229

tangled weave. Near the bottom, a filament in a distant corner connected the names of Alicia and Evelina Mondragon and Antonio Morales. Suspended by a faint thread beneath the triad was the name of Rudolfo Mondragon.

"Over here there's a whole new tree," Evelina said, motioning toward the edge of the paper. "Adelita's Indian people are over there, off the paper. We've started that one on a new chart, and it's just as confused as this one, but it goes backwards instead of forwards."

"That's a can of worms," the old man said with a sigh. "There's no tracking them down."

"Antonio tried so hard," Alicia said. "But it was no use."

"You can't get there from here," the viejo said. "And the girl was no help. She would not direct me."

"Grandfather," Mundo said. "Why—"

"Why did I never tell you these things? Well, m'ito, how can one explain such things? Alive, even I did not understand, and now, just look. How can one explain that?" He held a palm out toward the paper. "Look at that mess. There are Irishmen and Italians in there. You should hear them all talking. One fine evening, when the stars shone like diamonds, a Chinese gentleman from Canton planted the seed of future Moraleses with interesting eyes in one of your great grandmothers. And look. There is Luis Morales, the one who sold his birthright for a bottle of whiskey. Poor Luis is ashamed to show his face among the dead."

"So, Ramon, do you know who you are now?" Evelina beamed at him, and he straightened from the paper and sat back.

"How can you talk to my grandfather?" he asked the sisters.

"Why, Ramon, what a question. How can we not, when we are such near neighbors?"

Mundo rubbed his hands over his eyes, imagining the young Chumash girl, one of his grandmothers, taken by the brutal patrón. Or had it been love? Maybe the great man had rescued her from pain and taken her to his heart?

Maybe she had ruled the heart of the man, and his relations had ostracized her in death for that reason. He opened his eyes. A stooped shadow was creeping across the far wall of the room, slipping behind the tapestry and out again. He started to his feet and there was no shadow. His grandfather was gone from the couch, and the sisters were looking up at him with concern.

"Ramon, do you feel well?"

"Perhaps some more tea?"

"No, thank you, ladies. I think I'd better go. Gloria will be keeping dinner for me."

Extricating himself from the sisters' solicitations, he backed out of the apartment, descending the stairs two at a time. In the abandoned lobby of the hotel, he brushed at spiderwebs and kicked through ancient litter as he rushed for the outer door. A single, unshaded bulb illuminated the deserted registration desk where a rat sat back on its haunches to study him. Heavy dust motes hung in the lighted air above the desk.

When he was outside, he flung the door closed and took a deep breath. The early evening had a crisp edge to it, and he savored the taste of it. But when he turned toward his office door a body stood in his way, blocking entry to the substation.

"Checking an empty hotel for burglars, Morales?"

Lee Scott stood with his arms folded, the hood of the parka thrown back so that his scalp shone dully in the streetlight.

"I was visiting," Mundo began, but he cut himself off. "What's it to you, Scott. You're blocking my doorway." He stepped close and looked down at the investigator.

Scott edged out of the doorway and stood sideways to Mundo. "Visiting ghosts, Mundo? Nobody lives in that hotel. I checked it out."

"What?" Mundo stopped and turned back. He shook his head. "You're nuts. Go to hell, or back to Washington, or wherever it is you came from."

231

"Sounds like you're under stress, Officer Morales. I saw a lot of that in Nam. Guys like you. Guys who didn't have what it takes to deal with the real ugly shit in life, the gut-puking bile that it all comes down to eventually. Like the guy who just walked off in the jungle one day. Threw his shit down and walked away playing with his pecker. Told his buddy he was going to Greece. You ever hear of shit like that? You ever think of walking off to Greece? It was within the realm of possibility back then."

When Mundo didn't reply, Scott said, "We found him a couple days later, impaled like a pig on some pungi sticks."

Mundo unlocked the office door, saying over his shoulder, "Everybody got sick of bullshit war stories a long time ago."

"I thought you might like to know that Jessard Deal has the Nemi girl."

Mundo turned and stared back through the door.

"What do you mean, 'has' her?"

"Just that, Mundo. Right now. Down there in his place. He's got the door locked and she's in there."

"You think—"

"I don't think anything at all. Small-town corruption isn't in my contract. I thought snatch was your line." He put his hands in his coat pockets. "You know Jessard Deal's history? You know why he did time in Leavenworth? Technically, he shouldn't be allowed to own a tavern, but what the hell? There are bigger fish to fry. Know what I mean?"

The FBI agent turned and walked across the street, pausing at the edge to let a pickup jolt past. On the other side he got into his car and drove away.

Mundo went into the office and touched his palm to the cold coffeepot. He let out a long breath and went to sit with his elbows on his desk, staring at the door.

"She knows what she's doing," he said aloud. "But she's eighteen, not old enough to be in a bar. And I am the law." He was silent for a moment. "Jessard Deal," he said. "Fuck it." He got up and left the office, getting into the patrol car and driving south, toward the Tiptoe Inn.

He tried the door handle and then he knocked and then he kicked the door in. The barroom was nearly dark and empty, the beer sign unlit. A soft glow radiated from the back of the bar, where the mirror seemed to collect all the minute lights of the room and hold them.

"Jessard!" he shouted. His voice died in the cold air.

He walked around the bar and through the door to the back room. Jessard's desk was there, neat stacks of papers arranged geometrically across the top. Above the desk, a wallet-sized photo of Louise Vogler was tacked to the wall. Wearing a miniskirt and tight sweater, the coach's wife leaned against the trunk of a tree, smiling at the camera. Beside the desk, a small bookshelf held two dozen leather-bound volumes. On top of the bookshelf more books spilled in a pile onto the desk. On the floor beside the desk a tumble of books sprawled, covers bent open and turned under, as if book after book had been hastily opened, thumbed through, and left open to certain pages.

A safe stood at the other end of the desk, with a beer mug and coffeepot on top of the safe. Against the far wall was a folding cot with blankets piled on it and a nightstand beside it holding a student's lamp. A sledge hammer and a pair of gray boxer shorts lay on the floor beside the cot.

Mundo went to the door that led out the back of the office. He pushed the door open and stepped into the alley. Empty cardboard boxes were stacked neatly along the cinder-block wall.

He was turning to go back into the office when he noticed a movement at the far end of the boxes. Slowly, Bobby Bart raised himself from the dirt, using his bent legs as a fulcrum to swing his upper body erect against the wall.

"J-j-j-j-jes," he stuttered almost inaudibly. "J-jessard t-took her." He pointed out the alley toward the road. "In his t-t-t-truck." The shriveled arm waved as he pointed, and his head bobbed.

233

Mundo came close to Bobby. "Jessard took Diana Nemi? In his truck?" he said slowly.

When Bobby nodded rapidly, Mundo put a hand on his shoulder. "Thanks, Bobby. You're a big help to me. Now why don't you go on home and rest."

Mundo ran around the building to his car and, reaching through the window, grabbed the radio before he remembered. It had gone out again. He cursed and ran back inside the bar to the telephone.

Forty-five

"See, Diana. Stars, ocean breeze. Very isolated. Now, we'll talk about how infinitesimally small and lost we all are, about the evil that engulfs the frail world. Saddened by enormous drafts of time that waft about us, we'll discuss your potential in this dark world. Listen, coyotes howl. See, Diana, the grass is a thin coat on the bare bones of the mountains, and the mountains stretch infinitely north and south. Loneliness is the essential human condition. Connection is made through pain. Only through pain is someone truly reached, touched. As I'm touching you now. Look at the stars, at the incredible distances. Unnamed seas surrounding us."

Diana twisted away from him, and he jerked her backwards so that she lost her balance and fell against him. He lifted and held her with one hand by the hemp rope that bound her wrists behind her back. He traced her cheek with an enormous, blunt finger, letting the finger trail downward and across one breast.

"See the clouds below, to the west, Diana? That's the ocean. La mar amarga. It goes on forever, unlike you and me. Ever read Tennyson? Far folded mists and gleaming halls of morn? Me only immortality consumes? Tithonus wanted to die, you see, just like we all do. Only first he wanted to live and he wanted that too badly, just like we all do. And so he made a mistake. He trusted a woman."

Jessard's mouth was bent close to her ear, and when he laughed she felt his beard and his spittle on her neck. Far below she could make out the lights of a car on the winding road between Amarga and the coast. She shivered and whimpered at the pain of her wrists.

"Did Attis want to live so badly? What do you think?" He laughed again. "Let's sit down, Diana." He dropped to a sitting position on the ridgetop, dragging her down with him.

"You're hurting me!" she cried as she fell against him.

"See?" he said. "We're not bored now, are we? You know you're alive. We're connecting. Pain and poetry make up the real language of truth. You're too young to know that, Diana, but eventually you'll come to understand. The woods really *are* lovely, dark and deep, and full of constant, uncounted deaths. It really *is* design of darkness to appall, for you see, design does govern even in things as small and inconsequential as you and me."

They sat in silence for several minutes. On one side was the steep ridge up which Jessard Deal had dragged her from the road. On the other side the ridge seemed to plunge straight toward the ocean. Clots of darkness suggested clumps of trees surrounding the large clearing in which they sat. The air was damp and cold, rising from the ocean and carrying scents of the wild coastal mountains. She could smell the dead, damp grasses and musty oaks.

"Your potential, Diana, is unlimited. You're growing into your evil, learning who you are. Aren't you?"

When she didn't answer, he gently brushed a strand of hair from her face and went on in a soft, musing voice. "I don't know what to do with you. Perhaps you can advise me. After all, you knew what to do with Attis, didn't you?"

"You're insane," she muttered between clenched teeth. "My father will have you in prison the rest of your life for this. This is kidnapping."

"Kidnapping? Inviting my soul mate out for a walk and philosophical exchange? Merely intimating that I knew certain things that were best kept secret. I wouldn't call that kidnapping."

"That's what they'll call it when I tell them you tied my hands behind my back and forced me into your truck."

He grabbed her shoulders with both hands and turned her carefully until they faced one another. "But won't they want to know why you were in my bar all by yourself, with a 'closed' sign on the door? Won't they be interested in how, with a simple phone call, I got you to come there? How do you think I learned your secret, Diana? Perhaps they'll want to know why you withdrew an unusually large sum of money from your college account? Remember that pudgy intern at the hospital, the one somebody paid to make certain things possible? He feels guilty, poor boy." He stopped and held up a hand. "Listen."

In the silence she heard a faint tangle of cries from somewhere down the dark ocean side of the ridge.

"Death," he said. "Down in one of those little creases in the mountains, a drama has unfolded and something has died. From the sounds of it, it was a little creature of small consequence. A rabbit, perhaps. They can scream, you know."

He brushed a hand down the length of her hair and then gripped the hair tightly close to her skull. "Can you imagine how much that inconsequential little creature wanted not to die? Silly, isn't it?"

"I want to go home," Diana said. "I'm cold and my arms hurt."

Jessard pulled a knife out of his boot and the blade jumped open in his hand. Diana heard the sound and stiffened. She let out a low sob.

"I apologize for the discomfort," he said as he cut through the rope that bound her wrists. "But I'm sure you'll agree that you wouldn't have come otherwise. Unfettered, you might have resisted and hurt yourself." He raised the knife and, for a few seconds, held its cold, flat edge against her cheek before he folded it and put it away.

Diana turned to face him in the dark. She felt the upslope breeze from the ocean. "What do you want?"

"Communion." He laughed. "A sacred commitment of kindred souls. The awful daring of a moment's surrender. Ecstatic violence. Ah, love, let us be true to one another. For the world that seems to lie there like a bag of dreams hath really neither hope, nor joy, nor diddlysquat. We lie alone, you and I, upon the naked shingles of the world. We seek the nothing that is not there and the nothing that is. You see, I know your secret."

He stood again and, gripping her arm above the elbow, lifted her easily to her feet. He released her arm and looked off toward the cloud-covered night sea. "The sea of faith was once, too, at the full," he said. "But now we hear its melancholy, long, withdrawing roar. Let me be cruel, not unnatural. Do you like poetry, Diana, here on the vast edges drear of the whole goddamned show?"

"You're crazy." She edged slightly away from him.

"Yes, but madness in great ones must not unwatched go. Why did you come to me? Would you play upon me like the others?"

Suddenly she spun and plunged down the ridge toward the road, her hands held out to break the dark. Behind her she heard Jessard laugh again, and then her foot caught on a fallen branch and she was thrown to the ground.

Jessard reached down and drew her up with the back of her sweater. Once again he turned her and she could smell him. Abruptly, he slapped her hard with the back of his hand, snapping her head back and releasing a salt taste in her mouth.

237

"Bitch!" he hissed. He threw her down and knelt beside her. "What a wonderful pussy you are, you are, you are," he chanted. She felt his hands at her belly and then heard the sound of her jeans being ripped open at the crotch.

"No," she gasped, tasting more blood.

"Shut up!" Grunting with each word, he whispered, "And there in a wood a piggywig stood, with a ring in the end of its nose, its nose."

She felt the cold air on her belly and thighs. He tore the tennis shoes from her feet and threw them, and then he dragged the torn pants off, lifting her legs in the process. She closed her eyes and tried to crawl backwards on her elbows but then his weight descended upon her and his hands were at her, probing, finding her opening and spreading it. "Move and I'll cut your throat," he said, and she felt the point of the knife in the soft place below her chin.

"Please," she said, and she felt the knife point penetrate her flesh. And then he was shoving his cock inside her, tearing at her so that she cried out and he pinioned her head to the earth with a hand in her hair.

"I'll kill you," she whispered as his body pounded down upon hers. "I'll kill you."

"You well may," he grunted. "But you won't tell anyone, will you?"

Then he was coming inside her, and she began to scream. She felt him withdraw and then he was over her face, the knife blade flat against her throat, and he was forcing his cock into her mouth. "He has to kill me now," she thought. And she imagined her mother at home in the big house. And she hated Dan Nemi with all of her soul.

Forty-six

Hoey McCurtain watched from the shadow of the great oak as the door opened and Diana stumbled out of Jessard Deal's pickup. He saw the pickup go back across the bridge and Diana move like a sleepwalker to the front door of the house. He watched her fumble with the keys, drop them, kneel, and then sprawl on the steps of the porch. When her crying grew loud and uncontrolled, he stepped out from behind the oak and went to her.

When he touched her, she screamed, but the sound was lost between the river and the hills.

"It's okay, girl, I won't hurt you," he said, touching her shoulder again. "It's me, Hoey McCurtain."

She turned to look up at him and made a sound that was midway between a laugh and a sob. He found the keys and the third one he tried opened the lock on the door.

"Come," he said, lifting her with one hand on her elbow and the other beneath her shoulder. Inside the house, he felt for the switch beside the door and turned the lights on. When he saw Diana, he shook his head and led her to the couch.

"Jessard?"

She nodded.

"Do you want a doctor? Should I call Mundo?"

She shook her head. "No. Please. I want to take a bath."

"Wait," he said. "I'll help you."

She sank more deeply into the corner of the couch, not looking at him.

He left the house and went inside the hay barn. A moment later, he came out of the barn carrying a large, folded tarp and a shovel, leaving the big barn doors open so that the space in front of the doors was flooded with light. He

239

went back into the barn and a moment later came out carrying an armful of long two-by-fours. He dropped the boards and went to the woodpile beside the house. When he had piled two armfuls of wood near the boards, he went to the walkway at the side of the house. One by one, he carried half a dozen big rocks from beside the walk, dropping the rocks near the pile of firewood.

Working quickly, he dug a pit in front of the barn and placed the rocks in the pit. He piled the firewood over the rocks and went back into the barn, returning with a gas can. He splashed the gas over the wood and then tossed a lighted match into the pit. The wood exploded into flame and he watched for a moment, until he was satisfied that the fire would not go out. Then he returned to the house.

Diana lay on the couch, her knees drawn up to her chest, staring across the room. Her breathing was rapid and deep, the kind of breathing he'd seen often in wounded animals, the kind of breath that bided time.

"Wait just a little longer," he said. "I'll help you."

He went back outside and returned to the barn. He came out once more with a bundle of baling wire. In a few minutes he had the two-by-fours lashed into a low teepee. Over the teepee he threw the canvas tarp, tying it shut at the top with baling wire and weighting the edges with more rocks. Then he went into the house, walking past Diana to the kitchen. He found a large pot and filled it with water. As he passed back through the living room, he picked up the Navajo rug that lay in front of the couch. He went outside with the pot and rug.

When he entered the house once more, Diana had curled into herself so completely that her face was hidden in her knees. He bent over her and took her up in his arms and carried her out the front door, kicking the door open and then shut again with his foot.

He bent to carry her through the opening in the canvas and set her on the rug.

"What are you going to do?" When she spoke, her voice

was a distant whisper.

"I am going to help you," he said before he went out of the teepee.

In a few minutes he returned with a pitchfork. On the tines of the fork he carried one of the rocks from the fire, which he placed in the middle of the teepee. One by one, he carried in seven rocks, arranging them precisely in the center of the little shelter. Then he carried the pitchfork back outside and returned with the pot of water, closing the flap of canvas behind him so that only a little light penetrated from the barn.

"Take off your clothes," he said.

Diana drew in a sharp breath. "I can't."

He crawled counterclockwise around the stones to where she was huddled and he undressed her, lifting the sweater over her arms very carefully and removing her blouse and bra with delicate motions. Last of all he laid her on the rug and gently drew the torn jeans off of her. When his hands touched her bloodstained panties, she reached to push him away.

"No," she said. "Please."

"It's okay," he said, and very gently he drew the underwear off and then he lifted her so that she once more sat upright, her head and arms resting on her knees.

He moved back close to the water and removed his own jacket and shirt. "Now," he said. He threw a handful of water on the hot stones and, with a loud hissing, steam rose into the canvas enclosure. He repeated the action several times until the little space began to fill with steam. "Breathe the steam in deeply," he said. "Let it come into you. Open yourself up to it."

From a pocket of the shirt beside him he withdrew something which he tossed onto the stones. A pungent aroma began to arise with the steam. He threw more water onto the stones and the steam thickened. Diana drew in a deep breath and choked. "It's too hot. I can't breathe."

"It's okay, daughter," he said. "You can breathe. You

must let go of the things that prevent you from breathing."

Diana began to cry once more, her sobs choked and broken. The sobbing diminished and she began to breathe more carefully, drawing the steamed air in with a fearful precision. Then her breaths began to soften and become more regular.

He threw more water onto the rocks and the little room became tight with the steam and the aroma of cedar. "I don't remember enough," he said. "Sometimes we have to just guess."

Diana breathed slowly and deeply, feeling the steam deep in her lungs and in the open pores of her skin.

"I don't know how to pray," he said, "so we have to do it without words."

For a long time they sat in silence. Twice more Hoey threw water on the rocks and replenished the steam. Diana's breathing grew more smooth and regular, until she was breathing in unison with Attis's father. Finally he moved, crawling counterclockwise around the stones once more. When he reached the entrance to the structure, he threw the canvas flap back and the cold night air came rushing in.

"Oh!" Diana exclaimed. "I'm cold."

Hoey came back into the sweat lodge and picked her up, stooping with her back through the doorway to the outside. He carried her to the house and swung the door open with his foot.

"Where is your room?" he asked when they were inside.

"At the back of that hallway," she said in a voice close to a whisper.

He carried her down the hallway and pushed a door open with his foot, clicking the light switch on with his elbow.

"What are you going to do?" she said.

He held her with one arm and turned the blankets and white sheet of her bed down with the other, then he laid her on the bed and lifted the covers over her, tucking them carefully around her shoulders.

"You can sleep now," he said. "No one will bother you."
Diana closed her eyes and seemed to be asleep at once.

Back outside, Hoey retrieved his shirt and coat from the sweat lodge and put them on. They were damp and cold. He carried Diana's bloodied clothes into the house and folded them outside the door to her room. Then he went back outside and dismantled the sweat lodge. When he had returned the folded canvas and boards to the barn, with the pitchfork he carried the stones back to their places along the walkway. He used the shovel to cover the fire pit and then placed the shovel and gas can inside the barn and turned out the barn lights. Returning to the house, he replaced the rug and kitchen pot, then he went outside to the oak tree and sat on the ground beside his rifle. Cross-legged, he leaned against the tree and watched the approach to the house. Across the road, a coyote slinked out of the brush and hesitated at the edge of the gravel, eyeing the house. It walked slowly to the middle of the narrow road and raised its head, looking straight at the big oak. For a long time the animal studied the base of the tree, and then it started at a trot up the center of the gravel road toward the higher reaches of the river canyon. In the branches of the tree a great horned owl began to call in a deep, cautious voice.

Hoey glanced upward and shifted his position slightly, with the rifle cradled across his lap. He pulled a plug of tobacco out of his coat pocket and bit off a chew. Then he sat watching the road and working the tobacco in his cheek, occasionally spitting into the dark.

When the El Camino pulled into the driveway, Hoey disappeared behind the oak. From the tree's shadow, he contemplated Dan Nemi's back as Diana's parents got out of the pickup and approached the house. He was still watching the door when Dan Nemi came out twenty minutes later, got into the pickup, and drove away, skidding through the turn onto the bridge and accelerating when he came out of the first curve on the river road.

Forty-seven

"You'd better do something, Luther Cole."

Luther rubbed mink oil into a boot with the fingers of one hand and watched Onatima.

"Perhaps you're right," he said. "The dark one isn't helping the way I thought he would. He's very confused right now. But that's not so bad. Maybe he'll come out of this better than he was." He reflected for a moment. "But Hoey and the young nephew are getting stronger. The boy is learning who he is, and the father is remembering."

"The bones, old man. This one is too anxious." She nodded toward the corner where the shadow had moved several feet further toward the center of the room. "And the soul-eater."

He nodded. "As usual, you are right, Onatima. But things aren't very simple. It seems that we must be careful. I think this *shilup* is only a small part of something much bigger now, and it's all tangled up. The girl was making her own story, but now she is part of another, more powerful one's story, and it is painful for her. The dark one who bears the name of the world is becoming aware now that his own story is very, very old and complicated. And he is caught up in the others' stories as well. Hoey is beginning to remember, but he is still in danger. Only the boy, now, is on a straight path. Right now he is walking on the top of that river, and his brother's bones are calling to him. He is learning how to hear such things. He is beginning to dream. He has begun to know who he is."

There was a heavy thud that rattled the cabin's shake roof. A sound like wind-borne grief came from outside. The couple looked up at the roof, and Onatima moved close to the old man and placed a hand on his shoulder.

"Don't worry," he said. "It can't come in. That's what makes it so mad."

They listened to the big cat walking back and forth on the roof. There was a loud snarl, and they heard it leap to the ground. Suddenly the door shook with a great blow, and the old couple moved closer together.

"It can't come in," he repeated, watching the door.

When there was silence outside, Onatima turned away from the door and gave a sudden start. The shadow had moved out of the corner and close to the table where they stood.

"Luther!" Onatima cried.

The old man turned from the door and saw the shadow. For several minutes he considered it in silence. Finally, he waved a hand at it the way he might shoo a fly. "Go back, you," he said. "There ain't nothing for you to get concerned about. It can't get in."

When the shadow remained in the center of the room, the old man shook his head. "It's stubborn," he said to Onatima.

"The poor thing is just scared," she replied. "It's okay," she said. "Luther won't let it in."

Luther held two fingers to his chin and considered the tabletop. After a moment, he sighed. "It ain't practical for you to be out here in the middle," he said. "Look how little my house is. I can't have no haunt right smack in the middle. You got to be more considerate of an old man." He waved his hand upward again. "Now go on back to your corner."

The shadow remained unmoving. "Okay, old lady," Luther said. "You can get that cedar out now."

At once the shadow glided backwards, stopping a couple of feet from the corner.

"You scared the poor thing," Onatima said.

Luther grinned at her. "Kinda hard to scare a ghost, ain't it?"

Forty-eight

W hen he saw Jessard Deal's pickup, Mundo stomped on the brake and clutched the wheel around, throwing the patrol car into a one-hundred-and-eighty-degree spin on Amarga's main street. He flipped the flashing red light on and accelerated up close behind the truck.

The pickup pulled to the side of the street near Hong's Cafe. The door opened and Jessard Deal rose out of the truck's cab, stepping into the flashing red and the glare of the patrol-car lights.

"You'd better have a goddamned good reason for this, Morales," Jessard said in a flat, quiet voice when Mundo approached. The red light strobed on Jessard's face, and his eyes burned with a red flame.

Mundo walked around the big man and looked through the truck's window. The interior pulsed with the red light. He walked back to where Jessard stood. In the lights of the two vehicles, the trees above the cafe seemed to burn.

"Where's Diana?"

He stared up at Jessard with a hand on the butt of his gun.

"Where is she, cabrón?"

Jessard folded his arms inside his Levi jacket and looked down at Mundo.

"How the hell should I know?"

"Lee Scott told me she was with you. What'd you do to her?"

Jessard took a step closer. "You must be confusing me with your breed buddy, Mundo. I don't do things *to* women."

"If you did anything to that girl, I'll kill you," Mundo said.

Jessard laughed. "So many people have made that same promise, Mundo. And they have all disappointed me. As you see, I seem to be alive. All my life, it seems, I've been waiting for the one who could live up to such responsibility. But always I am disappointed." Jessard threw back his head and laughed again, a loud, booming laugh that echoed out over the empty street.

"Maybe you should talk to Diana. I think you'll find her at home and very much alive. I believe, however, that young Diana may be a little less confident of her ability to toy with the world. And now, if I may be excused." Jessard turned and got back into the pickup. He started the motor, and Mundo jumped backwards from the shrieking tires as the truck fishtailed on the blacktop.

When the taillights of the truck had disappeared, Mundo got into the patrol car and drove out of town toward the Nemi ranch. As he angled beneath the railroad trestle on the river road, Dan Nemi's El Camino shot past, skidding into and out of the tight corner. Even going away, he could hear the scream of the geared-down V-8. He punched the accelerator on the patrol car and raced toward the river bridge. A few minutes later, he pulled into the driveway and jumped from the car. He was reaching for the doorbell when Hoey McCurtain spoke from behind.

"Jessard raped her. She asked me not to tell you."

Mundo spun around.

"Goddamnit, Hoey," he said, keeping his voice as quiet as he could. "You scared the shit out of me."

Hoey stood with the rifle cradled, saying nothing.

"Is she okay?"

Hoey nodded. "She's okay."

Mundo looked at Hoey more sharply. "What the hell are you doing here?"

When there was no answer, Mundo said, "I'm going to have to haul you in, Hoey. You're sitting out here waiting to blow Dan Nemi's head off."

"I just went for a little walk, Mundo, and I happened to

notice that Diana Nemi needed some help. You can't arrest me for that, can you?" He spat onto the gravel and watched Mundo calmly.

Mundo sighed. Looking back toward the house, he said, "Are you sure she's all right?"

"I put her to bed," Hoey answered. "She was sleeping before they come home." There was a thud from the horse barn and they both looked in that direction.

"Did Jessard hurt her?"

Hoey looked away toward the river.

"Goddamn!"

"What're you going to do?" Hoey asked. "She ain't going to talk about it."

Mundo sank to a sitting position on the porch step. Hoey squatted in front of him, holding the rifle upright.

The door opened behind them, and Helen Nemi stood framed in the rectangle of light.

"It's happening again," she said. "Oh, my god, it's happening again."

Mundo stood up and put a hand on her arm. "I need to see Diana," he said.

Helen Nemi stepped aside and followed the two men as Hoey led the way to the back of the house. The door to Diana's room was open, and the full glare of the overhead light filled the room.

"I found those," Helen said, pointing at the torn and bloody clothes.

Diana lay in bed, clutching the covers tightly below her chin and staring at the door.

"He made me tell him," she said, her voice hollow. "He's going to kill him."

"Who?" Mundo said.

"My father. He's going to kill Jessard."

"He's got his pistol," Helen said behind them. "Please stop him. I can't stand any more of this. Please."

Mundo headed for the front door, saying, "I need you, Hoey. Pretend you're deputized."

They drove with siren and lights and encountered no traffic between the Nemi ranch and town. Hoey sat with the rifle between his knees, staring out the side window at the houses that flashed by.

The El Camino was parked next to Jessard Deal's Ford in front of the bar. They climbed slowly out of the patrol car, and Hoey followed Mundo to the front door of the Tiptoe Inn.

When Mundo pushed, the door swung open. He pulled his gun out of its holster and eased into the room, hearing Hoey slip the safety on the rifle and step in behind him. The only light in the room came from the beer signs on the walls. In the long mirror behind the bar, the blue light of the Hamm's sign rippled, the boatman only a dim fluorescence.

"Jessard!" Mundo said as he slipped sideways toward the corner of the room that had no hiding place. His voice echoed, and then Hoey spoke.

"There."

He followed Hoey's nod and saw Dan Nemi. The body was stretched the length of the pool table, on its back, the arms hanging over the sides of the table. The pistol lay near the feet, and the head was turned sideways. The throat was cut, and from the wide gash blood had pooled and run in a heavy stream into a corner pocket of the table.

Watching the recesses of the dark room, Mundo felt beneath the jaw for the pulse he knew wasn't there. His eyes probed the corners of the room, and he heard his heart hammering in his chest. Then he realized that Hoey McCurtain had disappeared.

He backed away from the pool table toward a wall. "Jessard!" he shouted, his voice obscenely loud in the still room.

Jessard Deal rose above the bar with the knife in his hand. As Jessard rose, Mundo could see the blue ripple of the sign through the huge man, and he could see the black stain that ran from the knife down over Jessard's hand. He could make out the white of a smile through the thick beard, and the blue and twinkling lights of the beer sign through the smile.

Mundo swung the pistol toward Jessard and fired. The mirror shattered and Jessard wasn't there.

"Illusions are often deadly, Mundo."

Jessard's hand gripped the wrist that held the gun, and Mundo felt his bones snap like twigs. As the gun fell, he heard himself scream, and then he saw Jessard's other arm coil behind the long, thin knife.

"This is death," Jessard said. "The real thing, Mundo, that for which the moral world must always deal. Witness Mr. Nemi here. Why, he has his throat cut i' the church." He laughed. "This is the richest moment of your life, Mundo, and, of course, the last." And then there was an explosion of sound, and Jessard jerked backwards with a look of astonishment. Mundo saw the black hole in Jessard's chest as Jessard fell onto a table. The table tilted and crashed to the floor on top of the body. One of the legs kicked spasmodically.

Hoey stood behind the bar, the rifle still aimed at the spot where Jessard had been. He walked around the end of the bar, the rifle held in front of him. When he reached Mundo, he looked at the arm that hung limply at Mundo's side, then he looked down at Jessard Deal, who had become still.

Mundo knelt and, with his good hand, felt Jessard's wrist. He stood up again and regarded Hoey. "How did you know he wasn't behind the bar?"

"I looked," Hoey responded.

"He would have killed me," Mundo said in a voice full of wonder.

Hoey kicked a chair out from one of the tables and sat down, the rifle across his lap. "He would have killed everybody," he replied.

Forty-nine

Cole McCurtain walked the river. Out of the corners of his vision he saw swift shadows, little scurrying knots of darkness that rushed away. Bats pulsed in the brittle air, and the stream made ripples of sound. He probed the trees and brush on either side and tried to penetrate the leaping darkness, but he could see almost nothing.

He had been sitting at home, waiting for his father. The house had rattled with a chill the furnace couldn't efface, and he'd sat at the kitchen table running an oiled patch through the barrel of Attis's thirty-thirty. When the rifle was ripe with gun oil, inside and out, he returned it to the bedroom. Then he pulled on his boots and the fatigue jacket, and, leaving the rifle against the table, he left the house and went to the river.

Standing on the bank and looking out over the sand and brush, he shivered. He felt something pulling him toward the heart of the river, and he moved in that direction, descending into the dry riverbed and making his way to the little stream that was all that was left of the aboveground river. Then he walked beside the stream, moving at a steady pace toward the north.

After an hour he broke through a tangle of brush into a small clearing, and he knew he was there. In the middle of the clearing four small oaks had grown up together, their twisted trunks close and their branches woven into a single mass. Attis's body lay cupped in the branches ten feet off the ground.

He knew what it was, and he began at once to climb the trees, bracing himself between the thin trunks and stemming upward until he could balance on the strong branches that held his brother like an outstretched hand. With his feet on parallel branches and his fingers gripping other branches, he worked his way out to the body.

Attis lay as if he had been placed there with loving precision. The thick mat of branches had kept him secure. The force of the river had stripped the body of clothing, and what was left was mostly bone.

Cole squatted on the branches and looked at his brother, holding his breath against the smell. After a minute had passed, he took off Attis's jacket and stretched it open. Then he began to place his brother's bones upon the coat. As the body separated, he fought back his fear and nausea. When he was finished, he folded the jacket as tightly as he could and knotted the sleeves to hold it shut. With enormous care, he brought the package down the oak trunks to the ground.

A cold wind picked up and began to race down the river, cutting through his flannel shirt. He shivered and clutched the bundle, walking quickly upriver toward home. Once again, he knew he was followed, though when he jerked his head around, all he saw were the tangled shadows and stars framed in the branches of tall trees. An intense cold was focused on his back, and he hunched his shoulders and hurried.

Fifty

"It's him, isn't it, your brother?"

Lee Scott stepped out from the shadow of the big pine behind the house, blocking the path to the back door.

"I knew you'd find him. I was counting on it. It had to

be you instead of that deputy sheriff."

Cole stood holding the bundle before him with both arms, the way a father might hold an infant.

"Pretty goddamned ironic, isn't it?" Lee Scott said as he continued to block the path. "Back from Nam all this time, and there he is wrapped in his field jacket like a body bag." He folded his arms and shifted so that his stance seemed more secure. "Not much left, huh? Nothing new there. Plenty came home like that, still are. Not even much smell left, huh?"

"Get out of my way," Cole said at last.

The agent stepped aside, saying as he did so, "You're thinking about taking him back there, aren't you? Where your Indian relatives are. For some kind of primitive burial? I did some research on you Choctaws. Thought it might come in handy."

Cole carried his brother's bones onto the porch and into the house, not stopping until he laid the bundle on one of the beds in the room they had shared. When he looked up, Lee Scott stood in the doorway.

"I want it," Scott said. "I'll take it with me and nobody will ever have to worry about it."

"What are you talking about?"

"The bones—the body. The government wants it."

"You're crazy. Get out of here."

"Any of these local yokels find out about this, they're going to take those remains away from you anyway, you know. They'll want forensic evidence. They'll need his rotted bones to find out who killed him. Then maybe they'll put him in a museum with all the other Indian remains. You'll never be able to do what you have in mind."

"Get the hell out of here," Cole said, raising his eyes gradually to the level of the FBI agent's face.

"I'm on your side," Scott said. "I won't tell anybody. You see, I know that it doesn't matter who killed your brother. I saw a lot of men in bags like that, and it never mattered who did it. It was just done. Part of a very big pas de deux that's being danced out everywhere. We learned the steps more precisely over there, but we were dancing before we went and the ball goes on. I used to dream about it, over there, about dancing the big one all through the jungle in the dark. You could never see your partner, just feel yourself swinging and spinning. And it's like that now. Know why I'm here? They sent me to make sure that your brother never surfaced again. They want him controlled and invisible. He's too fucking embarrassing to them. You see, they were afraid he was loose and was going to dance the ghost dance some more and remind people. Now they want those bones so they can be sure."

Cole opened the closet door and pulled out a lever-action thirty-thirty. "This was my brother's gun," he said. He worked the lever. "It's loaded. I have some things to do, so you'd better leave. If you don't leave, I may not kill you, but I'll have to turn my brother's remains over to Mundo then. And Mundo won't let things rest."

Scott nodded, "Okay, McCurtain. I read about that, too—what you have to do. That's primitive, but as long as no one else knows anything we won't interfere."

He stepped back from the doorway and started to leave, but after two steps he turned back. "It wasn't Dan Nemi, by the way. I thought you might want to know that."

Cole listened until he heard the back door close and the agent's car start up. When the sound of the automobile had died away, he leaned the rifle against the bed and unknotted the sleeves of the jacket. From the closet he took two blue sheets, which he partially opened on either side of the jacket. Then he began to clean his brother's bones.

Fifty-one

"It could not have been prevented," Luther said, "but they're coming home now." He leaned back upon the couch in Onatima's trailer, watching the old woman pour coffee from a shiny percolator.

"How is the shadow?" Onatima asked as she settled into the chair, drawing her legs under her.

"I think it's resting, waiting for them to arrive so it can go. Now that I sent the *koi* away, it rests better."

He accepted a cup of coffee from her and smiled his thanks. "It will be good to have Hoey here again. I wonder why I didn't send for him a long time ago."

"He wasn't ready," Onatima said simply. "Neither were you."

Luther nodded, looking into his coffee. "I been thinking about that river some more. They made that dam, and now couldn't nobody break it even if he wanted to. There's so much stuff behind it now, it would just about tear the whole world apart if it broke." He looked up from his cup. "But you know, old lady, that dam just can't last forever. Them fish know what they're doing. It's got to bust some day."

Fifty-two

Lee Scott drove directly to the Tiptoe Inn. Seeing the El Camino beside Mundo Morales's patrol car, and Jessard Deal's pickup next to Diana Nemi's, he eased his car around the side of the building and parked out of sight. He moved silently around the tavern to the front door, hugging the wall of the building with his gun held upright next to his cheek.

Peering through the crack in the open door, he saw silhouettes in the gray light and smelled the acrid aroma of gunfire. He kicked the door open and leaped into the room, landing with his legs spread and the pistol aimed with two hands before him. "Drop your weapons!" he shouted.

Hoey McCurtain fell to the floor behind the pool table. Mundo held up his unbroken arm and yelled, "Don't shoot!"

The FBI agent fired twice and Mundo dropped to the floor beside Hoey. The first shot plowed a furrow across the felt of the pool table and embedded itself in Dan Nemi's leg. The second shot ricocheted off a reinforced corner pocket, angled off the steel frame of the beer-box door, and struck the wall an inch from the man in the canoe. The beer sign began to flash, the ripples of sky-blue water seeming to pick up centripetal speed toward a radiant whirlpool in the center of the picture. The sign pulsed four times and went dark.

"Put down that gun or I'll blow your head off!" Hoey yelled.

"Don't shoot!" Lee Scott shouted back, throwing his gun on the floor. "I'm a federal agent."

Seeing the gun fall, Hoey stood up with the Krag aimed at Lee Scott's middle. "We know who you are," Hoey said.

Mundo rose to his feet. "What the fuck were you doing, Scott?" he yelled. "You goddamn near killed me."

"I smelled gunfire. I thought you were killers."

"We are," Mundo answered. "Turn the lights on. The switch is by the door."

Scott flipped the switch and Dan Nemi's body was flooded in yellow light from the globe above the pool table. In the strange light, the body seemed to float above the deep green felt. The agent approached the table slowly, his face growing pale through its tan.

"Jesus Christ," he said softly. "You cut his throat." His voice was hollow with wonder.

"No. Jessard cut his throat. Hoey shot Jessard." Mundo pointed with his thumb toward the body on the floor.

Lee Scott edged around the pool table and stared down at Jessard Deal. Blood had streamed from the big man's chest and flowed in a river beneath the pool table, around several chairs and tables, to run into the dam of the hardwood bar. There the blood had thickened in a shallow pool.

The agent backed away from Jessard's body, backing carefully around the pool table all the way to the tavern door. He stepped through the door, and they could hear him throwing up. A moment later he came back into the bar, wiping his mouth with a white handkerchief.

Mundo was on the phone, explaining the purely formal need for an ambulance and medical authorities to a dispatcher at the county sheriff's office. Behind the bar, Hoey was pouring a draft beer. As Lee Scott walked back to the pool table, Hoey watched him.

Scott studied Dan Nemi's face for a moment. Then he walked to the other end of the table and picked up Nemi's pistol, slipping it inside his coat. As Hoey watched him, the agent left the tavern.

"Where's Scott?" Mundo said when he hung up the phone and turned around.

Hoey lowered the beer and nodded toward the doorway as a car started and pulled away from the tavern. Mundo

257

stuck his head out the door and watched the car come from behind the Tiptoe Inn and disappear in the direction of the river. Already, the sirens of an ambulance were wailing in the distance.

"They're on their way from the hospital," Mundo said as he glanced toward the bodies. He walked quickly to the pool table. "Sonofabitch!" He pivoted toward Hoey. "Did you take the gun from this table?"

Hoey shook his head and drank the beer slowly. "The fed took it."

"What the hell?" Mundo said. "He's tampering with evidence. Why didn't you tell me?"

Hoey shrugged. "It don't make no difference."

"Without Nemi's gun, we can't prove anything even if we find the body."

"That don't matter no more," Hoey said, setting the empty glass on the bar. "These two here just canceled everything out. It's all over, Mundo, for now."

The ambulance skidded in the loose gravel in front of the bar, the siren dying with a final pulse. Then the paramedics rushed through the door, brushing past Mundo and Hoey to hover over the bodies.

Hoey poured another beer and pushed it toward Mundo, who absentmindedly picked the glass up with his good hand. They sat side by side on the barstools drinking and watching the white-coated men. "You'd better start making up your story, Mundo. You're going to be telling it from here to Christmas."

"What do you mean, 'making up my story'?" Mundo replied. "There isn't any story, just the facts, just what happened."

Hoey reached to touch Mundo's broken arm near the shoulder. "It just depends on how you put things together. Now we just got to figure out how we're going to put this one together."

"We'll just tell the truth, and Diana and Helen Nemi will tell their parts, too," Mundo said.

Hoey nodded. "Suppose I tell mine and you tell yours and Diana tells hers and Helen tells hers. And that fed tells his. And them two laying over there is already telling more'n anybody wants to hear. Who you think is going to put all these parts together?"

In the distance another siren was blaring through the bitter night. One of the medics stood beside Mundo, looking curiously at the limp arm.

"That looks broken," the medic said, reaching as he spoke to gently lift the wrist.

"Feels that way, too," Mundo said.

"You'd better go up to the hospital and have somebody look at that," the young man said.

Mundo looked around the room.

"Come on, I'll drive you," Hoey said. "These guys won't let nobody mess with things, and they can tell Carlton where to find you." He finished the second beer. "Maybe you should come say goodbye to your best friend."

Fifty-three

The spring lengthened and warmed, and the river began to disappear, slipping into the white sand to leave little, stagnant pools in shadowed curves and beneath hidden cutbanks. Fish followed the shrinking waters to the dark pools, and soon the pools boiled with life biding its time. At the edges, black clouds of inch-long catfish nosed the shallows, the more delicate spawn, such as trout and other cold-water fish, having long since perished. From the tangled river brush, fat raccoons appeared toward evening of the long days, stepping daintily into the shadowed crescents where the last pools hid. Foxes emerged from the higher canyons, and coyotes drifted down from the coastal mountains to wander the river by night. In the tangled shadows around each pool, herons stood like sentries.

Between late afternoon and evening, as the sun settled into the pines of the coast range, coveys of quail scuttled out of thickets to drink hastily. Casual flocks of doves rose from the alfalfa and grain fields and descended toward the larger pools, floating toward darkness on extended wings. A fog of mosquitoes lifted from the pools, and bats blinked across the stars to greet the rising insects.

In the hot summer, the Salinas was an underground river once again, a current of such purity and beauty that it could not be seen or touched.

Fifty-four

Diana sat back against a sandbank and watched the beautiful fish. Midway down the absolute clarity of water, four rainbow-colored steelhead held motionless in an invisible current. The sun cast shadows deeply into the pool and struck bright colors near the shallow edges. Up and down the river, the sycamores and cottonwoods were in leaf, with a green that seemed shockingly new. All around the sandpit, the river was dry, the white lace of dried moss lying where the stream and the little, leftover pools had held out longest. A big truck rumbled across the bridge upstream with a load of green alfalfa hay, and she turned halfway around to watch the truck out of sight.

She thought about her mother, imagining Helen Nemi in the house beneath the heavy oaks and the immense swell of the hills. In a month she'd leave for Berkeley, and her mother would be alone with the river and the town. Before she left there would be time to kill.

She watched the beautiful fish, envying the clean lines of their movements in the clear pool. To be surrounded by the isolate, invisible water was a dream. To find a holding place of such perfect clarity, and to hang, suspended on the facing current like a kite on a strong wind, effortless and alone. If one could live that way.

On a low sycamore branch near the opposite side of the pool, a crow leaned toward her and cocked its head. Suddenly it flapped from the tree and out over the river, rocking the clear day with its laughter.

Fifty-five

Mundo Morales bounced his daughter on his knee, listening to the chatter of the old women and watching Gloria bopping alone to the radio.

"Dance, hi'to, the dead do not mind." The viejo sat on the arm of the couch, more shrunken than ever, and waved a hand toward Gloria.

Holding his daughter in the crook of his good arm, Mundo got up and went to his wife. Gloria put one hand on his shoulder and laid the other very carefully on the cast that covered his free arm. The three of them began to do a delicate two-step in the middle of the small room. And as he danced slowly around the room, Mundo thought about water. How deeply did it run, and what did it look like down there in the dark? In the winter and spring, did it rise up to merge with the brown flood, or did it remain down below so that the two rivers ran one above the other, divided by the gleaming sand? How had it laid Attis McCurtain so gently in the branches of trees, as Cole had said it had?

There were so many things no one would ever know. When he'd seen Dan Nemi's gun on the pool table, his first thought had been to find the body and match a bullet to the rancher's pistol. But there was no body, only a cedar box full of bones cushioned by a fatigue jacket with words on it. Bones picked clean as the summer sand in the river. And now there was no gun. The gun had disappeared with the federal agent, and no one was interested in its disappearance. The official story was the obvious one. Jessard Deal had raped a girl. When the girl's father raged into the tavern, Jessard killed him. When Jessard tried to kill a deputy sheriff, Hoey McCurtain saved the deputy's life. It was a simple story. A half-breed missing from a mental hospital failed to complicate the story significantly. Two women in a ranch house near the river were a denouement.

He'd helped them put their things in the back of the pickup, and he'd accepted Attis's thirty-thirty, Attis's dog, and, incredibly, the '57 Chevy. "Vaya con Dios," he'd said as they drove away.

"My grandson has become more comfortable with the dead," the old man said to the Mondragon sisters, who stood at the end of the couch watching the dancers and smiling. "He knows at last who he is."

Fifty-six

It was spring when they left Amarga and crossed the river at dawn. They drove through the oat hills to the east, watching the moving shadows that became deer on the brightening hillsides. They camped on the Colorado River the first night and drove out of Needles before daylight and rattled the Dodge up into the piñon and juniper mountains of Arizona. From Flagstaff, they made their way across the high desert home of the Hopi and Navajo and Pueblo peoples. In a cafe in Holbrook, an ancient Navajo man watched them closely while they ate. When they stood up to leave, he smiled and raised a hand in greeting. The next night, they slept in an arroyo outside of Albuquerque and then pushed on into Texas and Oklahoma, where they drove past towns named Choctaw and Shawnee. In four days they were at the river, where an old man and old woman were waiting to take them home.